SAVING EMMA

SAVING EMMA

ALLEN ESKENS

MULHOLLAND BOOKS

Little, Brown and Company

New York Boston London

Mulholland Books / Little, Brown and Company
Hachette Book Group
1290 Avenue of the Americas, New York, NY 10104
mulhollandbooks.com

First Edition: September 2023

Mulholland Books is an imprint of Little, Brown and Company, a division of Hachette Book Group, Inc. The Mulholland Books name and logo are trademarks of Hachette Book Group, Inc.

The publisher is not responsible for websites (or their content) that are not owned by the publisher.

The Hachette Speakers Bureau provides a wide range of authors for speaking events. To find out more, go to hachettespeakersbureau.com or email hachettespeakers@hbgusa.com.

Little, Brown and Company books may be purchased in bulk for business, educational, or promotional use. For information, please contact your local bookseller or the Hachette Book Group Special Markets Department at special.markets@hbgusa.com.

ISBN 9780316566353
Library of Congress Control Number: 2023938990

Printing 1, 2023

LSC-C

Printed in the United States of America

I dedicate this novel to:
Alden (Pat) Patten
Donna Oliva and Barry Oliva (in loving memory)
You raised her well

SAVING EMMA

CHAPTER 1

I hold no faith in distant memories. To me they are as trustworthy as the boards of an aging footbridge, the planks heavy with decay. Time can corrupt a memory, spoil its shape, its color, its truth, wear it down to the point that it's barely recognizable.

For example, for many years I treasured a memory of my father. He died when I was still quite young, but I could picture the back of his head, his strong hands, when he'd carried me on his broad shoulders. It took me years to admit that image was stolen from a photo of us I'd found in my mother's closet, that my memory was only a fantasy born of my need to feel his presence.

When I went to college, and later law school, I allowed logic to blow out the last remaining flicker of that candle, my ersatz memories traded for reason. Truth wasn't truth unless I could hold it in my hand or usher it safely through a gauntlet of logical debate. And although I sometimes mourned the loss of that part of me that could believe just for the sake of believing, I eagerly put it aside.

And so, I feel somewhat duplicitous writing down this account of those ten strange days, which, even with all the reason and logic and training I can muster, I still can't explain. Where does one turn when logic fails? And I worry that years from now this memory, too, might bear little resemblance to the truth. Will I come to embrace what has happened, or will I deny it? All I know is that I cannot trust time to bring clarity, yet I feel too close to it all right now to make sense of it.

For that reason, I've decided to put pen to paper, to capture my most accurate version of the truth before it fades from my mind, and hope there comes a day where I can look back with some new perspective on the ordeal of those ten days, an ordeal that began when I met Ruth Matthews.

I was in my office at the law school, grading Criminal Procedure exams—my least favorite part about being a professor—when she showed up at my door. My first glimpse of Ruth was like taking notice of a moth—she appeared quietly, her clothing and demeanor faded, like dust on a wing. A slightly plump woman with hair the color of fireplace ash, she wore a gray sweater buttoned to the throat despite the warm June day, and a brown skirt that brushed the tops of her shoes as she walked.

The one thing that stood out was the metal crucifix that hung on a leather cord around her neck. Thick and heavy, it looked more like a yoke than an adornment. As big as my hand, it had been made of two steel bars crudely welded together. Ruth brushed her fingers across it as she stood timidly in my office doorway.

"Professor Sanden?" she asked in a voice so soft that it barely carried the short distance to my desk.

"Yes?"

"I'm Miss Matthews…I have an appointment."

I had forgotten about the appointment but stood and smiled as if I had been waiting. "Please, call me Boady." I waved her to the visitor's chair and tried to recall our brief phone call. She had a husband…no, a brother who had been convicted of murder and she was looking for help from the Innocence Project.

I had once been the director of the Innocence Project, but handed the baton off when it became a full-time job. Now I handled cases only as a volunteer attorney. Because I was just finishing my spring semester and I had no classes to teach that summer, I'd decided to take a look at her case.

Ruth came in and sat, clutching the heavy steel cross against her chest.

"That's a…striking necklace you have there."

"I made it myself," she said, beaming. "I sell jewelry to help support my brother's ministry. Would you like one?"

"I'm not a jewelry person," I said, brushing the stack of essays to the side. "So, this is about…your brother?"

"Elijah, yes. He was convicted of a murder, but he's innocent."

They all are, I thought. "When was the conviction?"

"Four years ago."

"Do you know if there was an appeal?"

"I think so, yes."

I swiveled to face my computer. "His last name?"

"Matthews…like mine."

I typed *State of Minnesota v. Elijah Matthews* into a database of appellate cases. If it was a jury trial for murder, it had likely been appealed. I could get the basic facts of the case from the Court of Appeals decision. The case popped up.

The first paragraph gave the procedural posture, a description of the trial, and how the case came to be at the Court of Appeals. I was only a couple sentences in when I read the name of the attorney who took Elijah's case to trial: Ben Pruitt. The name reached up from the page to wrap its cold dead fingers around my throat. Looking at the date, I realized that Elijah's case had probably been Ben's last before his world collapsed and he took a bullet to the chest.

I turned back to Ruth, ready to tell her that I couldn't take the case. Four years and it was still too soon. She held my gaze as she rubbed her thumb up the center of her crucifix. It was then that I noticed a single word etched into the metal: *FAITH.*

Had she had faith in Ben Pruitt when he took Elijah's case to trial? She would have been better off putting her faith in the toss of a coin.

I turned back to my computer and began reading again. Her

brother had been accused of killing a pastor at a megachurch, a man named Jalen Bale. I read further and saw that Elijah had prevailed in his insanity defense after claiming to be a prophet doing God's work.

I swiveled to face Ruth. "He was found not guilty by reason of insanity."

"And yet he's locked up," she said coldly.

"At the Security Hospital in St. Peter. It's not a prison."

"Why is he locked up if he was found not guilty?"

"Not guilty by reason of insanity," I said. "He had what's called a bifurcated trial. In the first phase, the jury determines if the State proved beyond a reasonable doubt that he committed the act—the murder. After that, there is a second phase to decide if he was so impaired by some mental deficit that he shouldn't be held accountable for the crime."

"But he didn't do it."

I put on my mask of empathy, which I'd often worn when I spent my days in the courtroom advocating for people like Ruth's brother. "According to this case, your brother believes he's a prophet—as in the Prophet Elijah...from the Bible."

"My brother is a prophet. He speaks for God."

I held a flat expression, resisting the urge to roll my eyes. "Do you understand what it means that your brother was found to be not guilty by reason of insanity?"

"My brother's not insane, Mr. Sanden. I assure you of that."

"The judge in his case would beg to differ."

"And I am bound by my faith to forgive that judge, for he knew not what he was doing."

This time I closed my eyes to hide my expression, took in a slow breath, then looked at Ruth again. "Your brother was determined to be so affected by a mental illness that he didn't know what he was doing. He didn't know that killing that man was a crime. The psychiatric experts who testified at his trial don't take that kind of determination lightly."

"Of course they're going to find him insane," Ruth said. "If someone in the tenth century had tried to explain gravity, they'd have been locked up too. People are like beetles crawling on the floor of a symphony hall, unable to comprehend the greatness of the music around them. You can't fault them for not realizing. They don't know any better."

I had ungraded exams on my desk, and here I was discussing bugs and symphonies with a woman who believed her brother to be a prophet. "Miss Matthews, do you know how the Innocence Project works?"

She looked at me with unwavering eyes and said, "Mr. Sanden, contrary to what you may think, I am not an idiot."

The moth had some steel in her spine. "I never said you were, but, Miss Matthews, we have a limited budget." I turned back to my computer to peruse the case again. "We normally need substantial new evidence of innocence, like DNA. We have to find something strong enough to reopen Elijah's case. I need more than just a belief that your brother is innocent."

"It's not a belief, Mr. Sanden, it's the truth."

"According to the facts..." I pointed at my computer screen, which she couldn't see. "The victim was killed with a rock that had your brother's DNA on it."

"His DNA was on that rock because he had handled it. He'd brought it as a gift! He didn't use it as a weapon."

"As he lay dying, the victim wrote your brother's name in his blood. That's a bit on the nose."

"Every problem looks like a nail if all you have is a hammer."

"I don't even know what you mean by that," I said.

"They wanted to convict Elijah, so they interpreted all the evidence to reach that conclusion."

"I'm sorry," I said. "But I can't devote resources to a case unless I have something to show that the jury got it wrong. You don't happen to have anything like that, do you?"

Ruth Matthews gave a light nod and opened her purse. "I have this," she said, handing me two pieces of paper.

I unfolded them and saw one was a newspaper article about a magician scheduled to visit the Hennepin County Library. The article had a picture of a man in his forties standing before a herd of kids. The man had a clownish top hat and a cape, and he held a string of colorful handkerchiefs tied together—performing the end of a trick.

The second piece of paper was an email, which read:

> *My dear sister,*
> *I have done what has been asked of me. What happens now*
> *is God's will.*
> *Elijah*

I turned the paper over, expecting more but finding nothing. "What am I looking at?"

"The date of the email."

I compared the date on the email to the date of Pastor Bale's murder. They matched. "Okay," I said. "The email was purportedly sent the same day as the murder."

"Not just the same day but the same time."

"Emails can be programmed to be sent on a given date and time, so…"

"He sent the email from a computer at the downtown library. Elijah was at that library when Pastor Bale was killed."

"It's a Gmail account. It could have been sent from anywhere."

"It could have, but it wasn't. Look at the picture." She pointed at the newspaper article.

The magician appeared to be in a meeting room at the library. Seeing nothing else of interest, I shrugged.

"Not that one." Ruth leaned across my desk, plucked the article from my hand, and slapped it down. "Look!" She pointed at a smaller picture at the bottom of the page showing the magician next to a small "Events" sign at the reference desk.

I shook my head. "Okay…and?"

"The man sitting at that table in the background—that's Elijah."

I looked closer and saw a thin man with white hair, possibly balding but too far in the background to make out any specifics. The man sat hunched forward as though reading.

As I studied the photo, Ruth pulled another picture from her purse and slid it into my line of sight. It was a photo of a smallish man with white hair. "This is my brother, Elijah," she said. "And that's him in the library."

I studied the two pictures, but there was no way to say for certain that they were one and the same. "This really doesn't prove anything," I said at last.

"It proves that Elijah couldn't have killed Pastor Bale. He had an alibi."

"The jury found him guilty, so I have to assume they didn't believe his alibi."

"The jury didn't hear about the alibi."

I eased back into my chair and crossed one leg over the other, a move that gave me a moment to process this curveball. Could Ben really have missed something as important as an alibi? I didn't want to believe it, but then again, I didn't want to believe much of what I had learned about Ben that year.

"Ben didn't—I mean, your brother's attorney didn't present the alibi to the jury?"

"No."

Ben, did you really fuck this up that badly? "Did the attorney ask your brother if he had an alibi?"

"I don't know. I wasn't there."

"But...you had this email. You could have said something?"

"If Elijah wanted my assistance, he would have asked for it. I don't interfere with his ministry without his guidance."

"Interfere? If this alibi is valid, you could have put a stop to everything."

"What happened to my brother was God's will."

"No. It was the judge's will. It was a court order that committed your brother, not God."

Ruth shook her head as if I didn't understand anything. "Mr. Sanden, my brother went to that hospital because God sent him there."

"If God sent him there...then why come to me?"

"Because God has spoken to Elijah. The time is coming for him to continue his mission elsewhere."

"If that's the case..." I heard the sentence form in my head before I said it, but I felt powerless to stop myself. "Why not just have God knock the walls down, like he did in Jericho? You don't need me for this."

Ruth didn't seem insulted, although she had the right. Instead, she gave a subtle shake of her head, a gesture that came across as pity. "It's like trying to explain a symphony to a beetle."

Then she stood, placed her fingertips against the heavy cross around her neck, and closed her eyes. Her lips moved softly as she murmured something. When she opened her eyes again, she smiled at me and said, "I know you'll help Elijah. I can feel the Spirit moving in you already."

On that score, she could not have been more wrong.

Then she made her way out of my office, pausing at the door to say, "Have a blessed day."

After she left, I went back to grading exams, but I couldn't concentrate. I felt angry, and I wasn't sure why. I leaned back in my chair and stared up at the plaster ceiling. The man thought he was a prophet. I pictured him wandering the streets, lost in delusion, shouting incoherent ramblings at people who rushed past not making eye contact. I couldn't help but think that Elijah Matthews should stay in the Security Hospital. Surely that was the safest place for a man who followed the commands of a voice in his head?

But I was also thinking about my own days in Catholic school, where the nuns would preach God's love on Monday and then slap us in class on Tuesday. Was I letting my own baggage interfere with my judgment? How many times had I told my students that passions and prejudices had no place in the law? Facts, and statutes, and legal precedents, those were the stones we used to build our fortresses.

For my own peace of mind, I would look into this case, do my due diligence before writing Elijah Matthews off.

I picked up the picture from the library. I needed to nail down Pastor Bale's time of death and verify whether or not this man was Elijah Matthews. It shouldn't take long to punch a hole in Elijah's supposed alibi. Although I had no official quitting time, I felt restless and decided to work on the case at home. A few hours of research in my quiet study, I thought, and I could put Ruth and Elijah Matthews behind me.

If only it had been that easy.

CHAPTER 2

Our home on Summit Avenue wasn't a mansion, but it held its own. Not far down the street from the governor's residence and other esteemed houses that carried the names of men who constructed mills and railroads at the turn of the century, ours was a Victorian built in 1891 by a man who had made his fortune selling hats. It had a large stone porch, windowed turrets, and intricately carved gables. It was a house you might walk by and think, *A man must have his life together to live in a place like that.* The first time I'd seen it, I had certainly thought that. Glance our way as you passed by, maybe catch us in silhouette through a window, and you might assume us to be the epitome of an American family: father, mother, and daughter, every thread of this fine tapestry carefully woven. But these days I knew: One step closer and you'd see that we more accurately resembled a poorly stitched quilt.

You would see that my wife, Dee, and I are of different races, she Black and me white, which isn't as big of a deal now as it was back when we first got together. You would see the gray that peppered my brown beard and the silver that twined through my wife's black hair, and think that we looked too old to have that fourteen-year-old child. And then you would notice that Emma holds no resemblance to either of us at all. Her hair shines with a hint of red and her features are fine. But it all would make sense once you understood that Emma was not our flesh-and-blood daughter; she had been our ward for the past four years.

When I pulled into our driveway, Dee and Emma were nestled on the front porch, sitting close together in our Adirondack chairs, heads tipped, eyes focused on something on Dee's lap. Emma was small for fourteen and looked even smaller curled up next to Dee. She had a smile on her face until she saw me pull in, at which point she retreated blankly back to whatever they were looking at. I tried to pretend that I didn't notice, but this was a reaction I had been seeing more of in Emma lately.

I parked beside the house, the warm summer evening nice enough that I left my car outside of the garage. Entering the house through the side door, I grabbed a glass of water from the tap and three oatmeal cookies from the cookie jar, a peace offering for a conflict I didn't understand, and headed out to the porch.

"Hey, ladies," I said in my cheeriest voice. "Who wants a cookie?"

Dee greeted me with her big smile and an outstretched hand for the cookie, but Emma didn't even look up. Over their shoulders I could see that Dee held Emma's sketchbook in her lap, open to a picture of our dog, Rufus, a black Lab, beautifully drawn. I looked at the sketch and then at Rufus, who lay on his rug on the other end of the porch. The sketch was spot-on.

"Remarkable," I said, setting Emma's cookie on the side table. "I love how you captured the light shining on his coat."

Emma stiffened in her chair but said nothing. It was as if the mere sound of my voice clawed at her skin. Dee noticed it too, but she covered her disappointment with quick support. "Hasn't she drawn it perfectly?" She slid a hand onto Emma's stiff shoulders, and with Dee's gentle compliment Emma relaxed a bit.

There had been a time, even just earlier this year, when Emma would spend her evenings in my study with me, sitting in one of my Queen Anne chairs with her legs crossed and her homework on her lap. I had offered to bring in a desk for her, but she always said she preferred the chair. But in the past few weeks, something had shifted.

Last week, as she'd finished her last year of middle school, she studied for her exams up in her room.

And that wasn't the only change. She'd started searching for reasons not to eat with us at the dinner table, and when I forced her to take her seat, she acted like she was a hostage, her head slumped down, hair covering her face. At first, I'd brushed it off; Emma was a teenager, after all. They were supposed to be sullen. But I was beginning to worry this was more than normal teenage angst.

So I'd been trying to hold out an olive branch. A week ago, I had offered to take her to Como Park again so she could sketch—she'd had fun there last November, drawing a bonsai tree in the arboretum. But when I asked, she said no thanks and locked herself in her room. Two days ago, I asked her what type of pie she wanted me to get at the grocery store, a question that used to put a smile on her face. But all she said was "It doesn't matter."

As I looked at her perfect rendering of Rufus, I tried again. "Maybe we should send you to art school in the fall. Or maybe private classes? You really are talented."

"No thanks," she said, standing and taking her sketch pad back from Dee, who let it go somewhat reluctantly. "I wouldn't want to be a burden."

Emma walked past me and into the house, Rufus jumping to his feet to follow her. I watched through the window as they climbed the stairs. "She's going to her room again," I said. "I don't get it—what'd I do wrong?"

Dee and I had had this conversation each of the last few nights, so she merely shook her head and took a tepid nibble from her cookie.

"Does she say anything to you...about me?"

"No," Dee said with a sigh. "I try and get her to open up, but..."

"She was smiling when I drove in. Then she saw me."

I knew Dee didn't want to hurt me, but even she couldn't deny that was true. Instead, she crouched to pick up a scrunched piece of thick white paper from under her chair. A page from the sketch pad. She unfolded it to reveal a drawing of the three of us, a re-creation of a photo we took last summer at a colleague's barbecue. We were seated at a picnic table eating corn on the cob, pausing only to smile for the shot. Emma's sketch was an excellent likeness. I looked at the drawing, then at Dee.

"She said she didn't like this one," Dee said. "Tore it from the book."

"Why?"

"She didn't say, and I didn't push it. You know how she dodges things."

I looked away. It had been a wet spring and the lawn was a vibrant green. Two squirrels chased each other from one tree to another and birds flitted about. Soon, evening would fall and the yard would become dotted with fireflies. It was picture perfect, but none of that tranquility could erase the heaviness in my chest.

"When you were her age," I asked, "were you...I mean...is this normal teenage stuff?"

"No," Dee whispered. "And I can't help but think it goes back to that last visitation with Anna. It seems to me, that's when the attitude started."

Visitation. Just the thought of that word made me want to spit. It had been a little over a month since Emma spent a week with her Aunt Anna, and it was true: Ever since that visit, Emma hadn't been the same.

"You don't think that Anna told her about...Ben...and everything?" I asked.

I was stepping into territory that Dee and I had grown to avoid. Emma knew bits and pieces of the truth; she knew that her mother had been murdered and that her father, Ben Pruitt, once my best friend and law partner, had gone on trial for that murder. She knew that her father died before the trial resolved, shot by a police detective.

But what she didn't know—what we had so far kept from her—was that Ben had been shot while in my study, after happily laying out in detail how he had killed Emma's mother. Most of those details remained buried in police reports, filed away after Ben died, the shooting deemed justified by an investigator from the Attorney General's office. Dee and I had always planned on telling Emma the full story, but Emma had been through so much. And how do you drag a ten-year-old girl through such horrors? There are no self-help books out there for that.

Because I was Emma's godfather, and had been granted temporary custody while Ben was on trial for murder, I fought to keep Emma with us, a fight that pitted us against her Aunt Anna. It was a slog, but in the end, we won and Emma became our ward. Despite our victory, Dee and I found ourselves second-guessing every decision, none more than the decision to grant Aunt Anna visitation.

I had been the one to convince Dee to give Anna three visits a year, and now I regretted it. We had agreed to a weeklong visit around Christmas and a week over what had been Emma's mother's birthday—that was the visit that happened a month ago. The third visit lasted a single day and was scheduled around Emma's birthday so that Anna could take her shopping.

Emma had turned fourteen just three days ago, so the shopping spree with her Aunt Anna was scheduled for tomorrow.

"It's got to be Anna," Dee said. "She's poisoning Em against us."

Dee had warned me about just such a thing. Dee and I were well-off, but Anna was downright rich. "It'll be a constant competition," Dee had said. "Anna will try to outdo us—bribe her. We take Em skiing at a local hill and Anna will fly her to Switzerland. I'm not going to buy her love, but you can damned sure bet that Anna will try to."

My strongest counterargument was that Emma would someday turn eighteen. "She'll have the right to make her own choices," I'd said. "We might as well ease into that cold water while we still have some control over the situation. As long as we're her guardians, we have the law on our side. We can set the rules."

Dee had acquiesced. Now Anna's poison seemed to be taking effect.

I walked to the front of the porch, hoping that the cool evening air might help me calm down, give me an idea of how to patch these holes in my family's quilt. The breeze brought no answers. I couldn't help thinking that if I could just get Emma to open up, I could fix everything, change her back to the loving, sweet child she had been just a few months ago. Maybe the time had come to tell her about her father? But if I was going down that path, I would first have to come to terms with my role in Ben's death.

CHAPTER 3

Emma was up, breakfast eaten and backpack loaded, by the time I came downstairs. I glimpsed her sitting on the porch, Rufus on her lap. He was too big to be a lapdog, yet he looked the picture of contentment wrapped in the arms of his favorite human. Dee, who was in the kitchen making coffee, nodded toward the front door, urging me to the porch. I stepped outside, trying to think of something nice to say while keeping my distance, moving toward Emma as I might approach a scared rabbit.

"It's going to be a beautiful day," I tried, then winced at how lame I sounded.

She only tipped her head down to give Rufus a kiss on the snout.

Her silent treatment was killing me. I wanted to ask her what I had done, but knew she was looking forward to the shopping spree with her aunt today. Calling her out might do nothing more than spoil her day. I decided that I would sit her down when she came home, clear the air then. For now, I quietly went back inside, pretending that nothing was wrong.

At eight a.m. sharp, Anna pulled into the driveway in her Mercedes-Benz. Emma helped Rufus off her lap and bent down to give him one last hug. Then she picked up her backpack and headed down the steps. I was surprised that she still looked sad, not at all the image of a teenager about to go shopping with a limitless credit card. Dee had come to the door behind me and called out to Emma, "We'll see you at five."

Emma waved a hand over her head without turning around.

I followed Dee back inside, poured myself a cup of coffee, and went to my study, hoping to get my mind off Emma. I pulled out the pages that Ruth Matthews had given me yesterday, thinking that Elijah's case might be the distraction I needed, but it was just the opposite.

I couldn't help but glance to the corner of my study, to where Ben had been standing when he was shot. The loss still hurt. He had been more than my law partner. He had been my protégé and my best friend. He was ten years younger than me, but we got along like brothers. Together we had built the finest little criminal defense firm in St. Paul. We made the office fun by giving each other challenges: push-ups for losing a motion, sit-ups if a client's check bounced. I once bet him a 5K run that I could win a particularly difficult jury trial. He ran the thing drinking Colt 45 beer.

Emma's birth came at a time when our friendship burned its brightest, a solar flare of good fortune. We were having one of our best years at the firm, which called for new cars all around. We had been featured in a trade rag for winning a high-profile murder case, and to top it all off, Ben's wife, Jennavieve, was bringing a child into the world.

Ben and I had been prepping a case when he got the call from Jennavieve. I could tell by the mix of elation and worry that lit his eyes that the time for Emma's birth had arrived. At the hospital, Dee and I waited in a room with comfortable chairs and dim lighting until he came and announced that Emma, his jewel, had been born.

He took us to the birthing suite and introduced us to her: tiny, and pink, and beautiful. Ben was so happy he could barely speak. Jennavieve, exhausted after all her hard work, slept on the opposite side of a curtain as we whispered and fawned over this marvelous new life, something plucked from heaven itself.

Ben had known a little bit about the heartache that Dee and I had gone through, although I had kept the details private. People who have never faced that kind of grief can't understand the depth of loss that follows a miscarriage. Maybe that was why he tripped over his words a bit as he asked me to be Emma's godfather. I was honored but felt unworthy of the task. On the drive home, I asked Dee what being a godfather would entail.

"You make her feel special," Dee had said. "Give her gifts at Christmas and on her birthday. Let her know that she would be loved and cared for if she were your own."

Three years later, one of my clients died in prison, a man who was innocent of the crime for which he had been convicted. I had failed him, and his death sent me to a dark place. It was Dee who convinced me to give up my practice and become a professor, and in doing so, had probably saved my life.

I'd handed my practice to Ben, and right away I saw us drifting apart. We tried to make time for lunches or an occasional drink at the Saint Paul Club, but in time, family vacations together became postcards. Golf Wednesdays melded into an empty promise to catch a round someday. By the time he showed up at my door, frantic, with ten-year-old Emma in tow, Ben and I were barely acquaintances. Emma and I were strangers.

Even then, she'd been thin and quiet, a refugee adrift on an ocean of sadness. I had no toys in my house, so I gave her a sketch pad and some pencils, a distraction to keep her busy while Ben and I discussed the fix he was in. I had closed the doors to my study, leaving Emma alone as we worked through the details of his alibi. I was certain he was innocent; Ben was a good man—he was my friend.

But I had been a fool.

I would like to think that I acted appropriately that day, when I plopped Emma down in my parlor with that sketch pad, but Dee later pointed out my error.

"Why didn't you call me?" she had asked, furious.

"I...um..."

"That poor girl just lost her mother. She's in a strange house, and you just let her sit there? For how long?"

I shaved an hour off the actual time, but it didn't matter. Dee was right. I was Emma's godfather. I was supposed to make her feel safe.

"Sometimes you need to shut off that lawyer brain of yours," Dee had said. "You need to think like a human being."

"But I *am* a lawyer. That's why Ben came to me."

"Emma came to you too. She was falling down a hole that had no bottom. It's your job to take care of her when Ben can't."

Three months later, Ben too would be dead.

Now, at my desk, I looked at the news article that Ruth Matthews had given me, the one with the magician's name on it: Bob the Brilliant. I searched online and found an old post that referenced the event at the downtown library. The performance had begun at six p.m. I found myself hoping that Elijah's victim had been killed at any time other than six p.m. If the times didn't match, there would be no alibi—no case for me to worry about.

I searched again for Bob the Brilliant and found a phone number. I dialed it.

The man on the other end answered with a sleepy "Hello?"

"Is this…Bob the Brilliant?"

"Not anymore," he said. "Who's this?"

"My name is Boady Sanden. I'm with the Minnesota Innocence Project."

"Okay."

"This is going to sound strange, but I'm looking into a murder that happened four years ago. The guy who was convicted is now saying he was at the downtown library in Minneapolis when the murder occurred. I believe you were there doing a show."

"I can't say that I remember. I did quite a few libraries back in the day."

"I saw some pictures from your performance in the local paper, and there's one shot where the guy might be sitting in the background. I was hoping you might be able to confirm the date and time of the performance? Also, if you have any pictures…"

"My wife—ex-wife—took the pictures. If I have anything, it would be on my old laptop."

"Could you look?"

I heard him sigh before saying, "I guess."

I gave him the date of the performance and my email address, thanking him in advance.

Next, I needed to lock down the time of death. It would be in Ben's file, and I knew just where to find it. Because I had once been Ben Pruitt's partner, the court had appointed me to wrap up his practice after he died. I had stored all his old files in a storage unit.

I grabbed some cold pizza and a banana for lunch, kissed Dee goodbye, and got in my car. With any luck, I could find the hole in Elijah's alibi and be done with this wild-goose chase by noon.

CHAPTER 4

It was a little after nine a.m. when I pulled into the storage complex, the lonesome crunch of gravel announcing my presence as I rolled to the unit where I had stored Ben Pruitt's old files along with some of his personal stuff: his marriage certificate, framed diplomas, family photo albums. I hadn't been to the unit since the day I closed Ben's practice, locking the door with a combination lock, the code being Emma's birthday. I hadn't planned on returning until seven years had passed, the time that the Ethics Board recommended files be kept before destroying them.

The door creaked as I rolled it open, stirring dust motes that twinkled in the air like glitter in a snow globe. Ben had been buried in Lakewood Cemetery in Minneapolis, his funeral attended by only three of us, Emma, Dee, and me. The service had been so pat and hollow, we could have been burying an empty box. But in the storage unit, Ben's memory came soaring back—this was a crypt built of his life's work: a failed law practice, a dead wife, an orphaned daughter. The sadness of it all almost made me pity him.

Ben's office had been a mess when I'd arrived to close it down, files stacked in piles, papers stuffed in drawers with no rhyme or reason. The hallmarks of an attorney at the end of his rope. After months of sorting and cleaning, I had reduced the mess to a phalanx of twenty-eight banker's boxes, which now lined the walls of the storage unit. On top of one of the boxes was a blue binder with the names of all of Ben's clients, the date that each case had been closed, and the box number where the file was now stored. Elijah Matthews's file was one of the last.

I had handed Ben a thriving business but he squandered it, his client base dwindling to the point that he needed to take on a public defender contract to keep his doors open. That's how he had come to represent Elijah. I knew about the public defender contract because the chief public defender had called me for a reference. I had heard the rumors about Ben's practice sliding—missed hearings, unhappy clients, motions filed late—yet despite the rumors, I recommended Ben for that contract. I shouldn't have, but he was my friend.

Ben had always driven a nice car, kept his membership at the Saint Paul Club, traveled and dined well, but behind it all I'd discovered he was broke, even though his wife, Jennavieve, was wealthy. It wasn't until Ben came to me, accused of her murder, that I learned that he had been on an allowance, making her money an obvious motive for him to commit the crime. I had turned a blind eye to it all. Ben would never kill Jennavieve for money. He loved her. He wasn't that kind of man.

At least that's what I had thought.

I pulled a box off a low shelf to sit on as I read Elijah's file. It was thin for a murder file. As a public defender, Ben hadn't handled the appeal, the handoff to the appellate division something that you did as a matter of course, regardless of how airtight the conviction seemed. The appellate attorneys had sent Ben a copy of the trial transcript, which he had tossed into the file. Somewhere in there I would find the time of death. If the picture from the library didn't match, there was no alibi. I could discard this quixotic quest in short order.

I ran a finger down the table of contents, found the testimony of Detective Griffin MacDonald, the lead investigator. Skimming the questions, I came to a discussion of the time of death. A now-retired cop by the name of Ray Gideon had gone to Pastor Bale's office at the church at six that evening and found Bale lying on the floor behind his desk, his head bashed with a bloody stone. Because Bale had been making outbound calls on his phone up until 5:30, the death had been within that half-hour window.

I found a booking photo of Elijah Matthews and compared it to the picture from the news article. In the booking photo, Elijah wore a calm smile as though he were pleased about something, the kind of expression one might wear to a niece's wedding. The photo from the library was grainy and distant. It might be Elijah Matthews, but it might not.

I found Ben's notes and turned to his first interview with Elijah. There were only three lines written:

> First interview:
> Babble. Won't give a straight answer.
> This guy is a walking insanity defense.

Below that was a doodle of a man smashing a rock into another man's head. Ben was a good enough artist for me to see that the man doing the smashing was Elijah Matthews. I looked for more notes but found none. I dug through the file, hoping to see a jot or scribble about a potential alibi. Nothing. He had never asked. He hadn't prepared any strategy beyond the insanity defense.

In my many years of being a lawyer, I had seen shoddy work. Once, a lawyer showed up for a murder trial unable to correctly pronounce his client's name. Another time, I watched as a bailiff forced a colleague to take a breathalyzer during an omnibus hearing, and when the lawyer blew a .16, he got carted to jail for contempt. But to have it come from a man I had trained—a man I recommended—it just about made me sick.

My phone buzzed in my pocket and showed an email from a B. Daniels. Not recognizing the name, I almost didn't open it, but did and found a message from Bob the Brilliant. It read: *The show started at 6:00 p.m. As for pictures these were all I could find.* Attached to the email were four images. I opened them.

The first showed Bob standing with a librarian, posing at the front desk. In the background I could see the man who looked like Elijah. I flicked my fingers across the screen of my phone to enlarge the picture, hoping to get a better view, but the man remained out of focus. I was about to move on to the next photo when I saw the clock on the wall. I zoomed a bit more to see the hands. It looked like the time was about 5:45.

I did a quick check on my Maps app to see that the fastest route from the library to the church was eighteen minutes. If the murder happened between 5:30 and 6…the man in the library could not have gotten there in time. I am not proud that my next thought was a hope that the man in the background wasn't Elijah Matthews.

The next two pictures were taken as Bob the Brilliant performed a trick with large silver rings. I found nothing in those pictures that helped my case. But the fourth had been taken from behind Bob the Brilliant, a shot of the audience, maybe thirty or forty children in all. They sat on the floor, their eyes locked on the magician, their mouths open in awe, and in the back of the crowd, standing with his hands in his pockets, was a man slightly out of focus, smiling with mild enjoyment. My jaw dropped.

I held the booking photo next to my phone. It sure looked like Elijah. If it wasn't him, it was a damned close likeness.

Leaning against the shelf behind me, I played the devil's advocate. Maybe the clock in the library was off by a few minutes? Or maybe this was an elaborate scheme to create double jeopardy and Bob the Brilliant was in on it? There had to be an explanation that could account for Elijah being in both places.

But nothing came to me other than Occam's razor, the notion that the simplest answer is usually correct. The simplest answer here was that Elijah had an alibi for the night Jalen Bale was murdered and Ben had missed it.

Disheartened, I picked up the transcript and opened it to the table of contents to see what kind of case Ben had put on, who he had called as witnesses in Elijah's defense. I found that Ben had called only one witness: Elijah Matthews. I opened the trial transcript and read Elijah's testimony.

CHAPTER 5

<u>**Testimony of Elijah Matthews.**</u>

COURT: We're back on the record. The jury is
          out. Mr. Pruitt, I understand that you
          wanted to put something on the record
          before we bring the jury in.

PRUITT: Yes, Your Honor.

COURT: Go ahead.

PRUITT: I have explained to my client that he
          has the right to remain silent and he
          has the right to testify on his own
          behalf. With that said, it has been my
          advice to him that he not testify. But
          it is his wish to do so. I just wanted
          to make the record clear that I have so
          advised him.

COURT: Okay, Mr. Matthews, you heard your
            attorney. You've been informed of your
            right to testify. Your attorney can't
            make you testify or not testify. It's
            your decision, you understand that?

MATTHEWS: I understand that, yes.

COURT: And if you testify, Ms. Addams, the
            prosecutor, will be able to ask you
            questions—and you will be required to
            answer her questions. You understand
            that?

MATTHEWS: I do.

COURT: And your attorney is here to give you
            his best advice on the matter. You
            understand that?

MATTHEWS: Yes.

COURT: Mr. Pruitt has a great deal of
            experience in matters like this. He's
            an experienced attorney.

MATTHEWS: He is.

COURT: And he has advised you that it might
            not be in your best interest to
            testify.

MATTHEWS: He has.

COURT: So, with that in mind, is it still your
           desire to testify on your own behalf?

MATTHEWS: Yes.

COURT: You are hereby waiving your
           constitutionally protected right to
           remain silent?

MATTHEWS: I am.

COURT: Okay, we'll call the jury back in.

(Jury is brought into court.)

COURT: The State has rested. Defense counsel,
           are you prepared to call your first
           witness?

PRUITT: Defense calls Elijah Matthews to the
           stand.

Direct examination of Elijah Matthews by Mr.
Pruitt.

(Witness **Elijah Matthews** is sworn in.)

PRUITT: Mr. Matthews, you have been accused of
           killing Pastor Jalen Bale by striking
           him with a stone, causing his death.

Let me just get to the heart of the
matter. Did you kill Pastor Bale?

MATTHEWS: What happened to Pastor Bale was in
God's hands.

PRUITT: Okay, but you understand that Pastor
Bale's death was the result of someone
hitting him in the head with a stone.

MATTHEWS: I am aware of that.

PRUITT: So, my question to you is did you
strike Jalen Bale in the head with a
stone?

MATTHEWS: I follow God's commandments.

PRUITT: And one of those commandments is "Thou
shalt not kill."

MATTHEWS: It is number six on the list.

PRUITT: When it comes to Pastor Bale, did you
follow that commandment?

MATTHEWS: I always obey my God.

PRUITT: Um…I guess I have no further questions.

COURT: Ms. Addams, you may cross-examine.

Cross-examination of Elijah Matthews by Ms. Addams.

ADDAMS: Thank you, Your Honor. Mr. Matthews, are you a prophet?

MATTHEWS: God chose me to be a prophet before I was born.

ADDAMS: God speaks to you?

MATTHEWS: God does and has appointed me his watchman.

ADDAMS: Does God tell you when someone is being a false prophet?

MATTHEWS: Yes.

ADDAMS: You saw the videotape that I played in court, the one where you were judging Pastor Bale to be a false prophet?

MATTHEWS: I do not have any such power. I do not judge. God judges.

ADDAMS: But in that tape...that was you on stage calling Pastor Bale a false prophet? That was your voice?

MATTHEWS: I am an instrument of the Lord. Those were His words, but yes, it was my voice.

ADDAMS: And when you do what God tells you to
           do, you are doing God's will?

MATTHEWS: It is God who directs the lives of His
           creatures. When God directs me to act,
           by definition, I am doing His will. I am
           merely a vessel.

ADDAMS: You would agree that in the Bible, God
           puts to death those who presume to
           speak falsely in God's name.

MATTHEWS: Deuteronomy 18:20.

ADDAMS: If a false prophet is put to death,
           that is also doing God's will.

MATTHEWS: God destroys such people.

ADDAMS: So, if a false prophet can be put to
           death, it's not a violation of God's
           commandment of Thou Shalt Not Kill.
           It's God's will, isn't it?

MATTHEWS: As Job said, my words sound guilty, and
           everything I say seems to condemn me.

ADDAMS: I don't disagree.

PRUITT: Objection.

COURT: Sustained.

ADDAMS: Mr. Matthews, in the Bible—in First Kings—when a prophet unmasked four hundred and fifty false prophets, what happens to them?

PRUITT: Objection. Irrelevant and lack of foundation.

ADDAMS: Your Honor, it's relevant to understand the importance of the Defendant's claim that Bale was a false prophet. That accusation has context and that context is relevant.

COURT: The witness may answer if he knows.

ADDAMS: Mr. Matthews, what happened to the four hundred and fifty false prophets?

MATTHEWS: God put them to death.

ADDAMS: God put them to death? Or did a prophet put them to death?

MATTHEWS: The prophet was doing God's will.

ADDAMS: And what was the name of that prophet who put to death the false prophets?

MATTHEWS: Elijah.

PRUITT: Objection.

ADDAMS: I withdraw the question.

COURT: Ladies and gentlemen of the jury, you
           will disregard that last question and
           answer.

ADDAMS: I have no further questions, Your
           Honor.

CHAPTER 6

As I sat in that storage unit, reading over Elijah's file, I thought about the law of transferred intent. If a man aims a gun at his enemy, fires, and accidentally hits an innocent bystander, the law transfers the intent of that action from the intended victim to the bystander. Why wouldn't such a notion apply to the incompetence I had unleashed upon Elijah Matthews? I had not been the attorney who screwed up the case, but I had been the one who recommended Ben for that public defender contract. I couldn't help but feel that I was, at some level, culpable for Elijah's plight.

If Elijah had an explanation as to why he didn't tell Ben about his alibi, it might get me off the hook and ease my conscience. I needed to talk to Elijah.

I had cold pizza in the car. I could eat lunch on the drive. I packed Elijah's file in my briefcase, locked the storage unit door, and hit the road.

The Minnesota Security Hospital is in St. Peter, an hour and a half south of the Twin Cities. I called as I drove, and after getting transferred a couple of times, managed to track down a Dr. Rebecca Cohen, who was a member of Elijah's treatment team.

"The Innocence Project?" she said. "So you're coming here because you think Elijah might be innocent?"

"I'm just reviewing the case. I was hoping to meet with Mr. Matthews, maybe ask him a few questions—if that's okay."

"That would be fine. Do you have any evidence that calls his case into question?"

"We're still in the investigation stage," I said.

"When you get here, I'll have a pass ready. Pick it up in the guard shack as you drive in. I'll also leave directions to the unit where Elijah is residing."

"I appreciate that."

"Could I ask a favor though?" she said. "After you meet with Elijah, could you stop by my office? I would like to have a chat if you don't mind."

"Happy to," I said, although that was a lie.

The Security Hospital, Minnesota's first mental asylum, had been built in 1866 on land donated by the City of St. Peter. A facility that embraced the therapeutic value of hard work, it had held every level of patient from the criminally insane—as they called them back then—to housewives locked away under the abusive pretext of nervous break-downs. Over the years it had grown to become a self-contained city within a city, with forty-three buildings sprawling across 360 acres of rolling hills.

When I arrived at the hospital, a pass awaited me at the guard shack, just as Dr. Cohen had promised. I made my way to a two-story building that had the look of a high school but with fewer doors. A burly man at the visitors' entrance—a security counselor because hospitals don't have "guards"—searched my briefcase and ushered me through the metal detector. I placed my car keys in a locker but was allowed to keep my wallet, phone, and briefcase.

The man escorted me to a conference room where I would be alone with Elijah. The security counselor would remain in the hall-way, watching through a window to give us privacy. I was a little uneasy about it all because the thing about mentally unstable people is that they are…well, unstable.

I had once represented a young woman accused of stabbing her teacher in the neck with a pencil. My client was clearly mentally ill, and when I asked the judge for an evaluation of her mental competency, she attacked me. Because she had been shackled and cuffed, there was little she could do beyond hip-checking me into the counsel table and knocking me to the floor. She threw herself on top of me and tried to bite me, but the bailiff pulled her off. I walked away with only scratches, thankful that I had kept my pens locked away in my briefcase.

I had seen Elijah's picture, so I knew him to be smallish, but the man they brought in looked like the back end of a hunger strike. His hair, as white as desert bones, crowned his head like the laurel on a Roman conqueror. His shoulders were rounded, giving him the posture of an old man, but I knew him to be younger than me, late forties if I recalled. He wore khaki pants and a white long-sleeved shirt buttoned to the neck and to the wrists. No belt, of course.

When he saw me, he smiled as though I were an old friend. He wore no cuffs or shackles, and when I took his hand to shake, he looked into my eyes as if searching for something buried. Then he gave a curious nod and took a seat.

I pulled Elijah's file from my case, found the picture of him in the library, and placed it facedown on the table between us. "My name is Boady Sanden," I said. "I'm an attorney with a program called the Innocence Project. Have you heard of it?"

"You have been sent to free me of my bondage," he said.

I'd done my time in Catholic high school, and in college I'd dabbled in the early days of the church as part of my history major, discovering gospels that hadn't made it into the Bible, and books like Enoch and Jubilees that had once been canonical but had fallen out of favor. I'd delved into everything that the priests had left out of their Sunday sermons, reading the Bible from cover to cover like a novel. By the time I graduated, I had become a full-fledged agnostic. And while I was in no way still fluent in chapter and verse, I recognized Elijah's answer as coming from Exodus.

"No one sent me," I said. "I drove down from St. Paul because I have a couple of simple questions to ask you."

"Ask and you shall receive. Seek and you shall find. Knock and the door will be opened to you."

This was going to be a difficult interview. I turned the picture over. "Is that you?

He barely glanced at the picture before returning his attention to me. "Some said 'He is the one,' but others said, 'No, he isn't, he just looks like him.' So the man himself said, 'I am the man.'"

"Okay, I'm going to stop you right there," I said. "If all you're going to do is regurgitate tired old quotes, then you're wasting my time."

Elijah smiled. "I certainly don't want to waste your time, Mr. Sanden."

It caught me a little off-guard that he had remembered my name. I didn't think that he was paying attention. "So you can converse without all that gibberish?"

"God gave Adam free rein to eat of any tree in the garden. Eating from the tree of knowledge was a choice."

I pointed at the picture. "I would like you to answer with a simple yes or no. Is that you there in the library?"

"It is I."

"And was this picture taken the day that Pastor Jalen Bale was murdered?"

"It was the allotted day and the allotted time."

"That's a yes?"

"Yes."

"You were at this library on the day and at the time that Pastor Bale was killed."

"You seem surprised at this."

Was this man so obtuse that he didn't see what we were talking about? "You had a potential alibi."

"Potential?" he asked.

"No court's going to let you out just because I have a picture."

"I don't rely upon courts or judges for my salvation. God is my protector; He saves those who obey Him."

"Stay with me, Elijah." Talking to this man was exhausting. "Did you tell your trial attorney about this picture—about being at the library?"

"Who so keepeth his mouth and tongue keepeth his soul from troubles."

"Is that a yes or a no?"

Elijah remained quiet for a moment, like a teacher waiting for an unruly student to settle down. Then he said, "Mr. Pruitt never asked."

"He never..." A hint of anger seeped into my tone. "You had a duty to tell your lawyer if you had an alibi. He needed to know. An alibi is an affirmative defense. It has to be disclosed to the prosecutor. If you don't tell anyone, you waive it. That means you don't get to use it."

"I am not childish in my understanding. I took the path that God laid out for me."

"You kept your alibi a secret."

"Mr. Sanden, I was meant to come here." Elijah waved his arm around the conference room like a game show host. "And now God has sent you. If I hadn't come here, we would never have met."

I lifted my hand to my face and rubbed my eyes, massaging the headache that was building up behind the bridge of my nose. He really was insane. But being mentally ill by itself isn't enough to get you locked up at the Security Hospital; you also had to be dangerous. If Elijah hadn't killed Pastor Bale, he didn't belong here.

"I'm going to look into your case," I said. "I don't know what—if anything—will come of it, but I'll do what I can to get you out of here."

"God will save me from my troubles."

I wanted to tell Elijah that if God was going to do all the work—and undoubtedly get the credit—he didn't need me. But I bit my tongue, reminding myself that this man was deeply disturbed.

I bade Elijah goodbye and made my way back through the thick steel doors and to my meeting with Dr. Cohen.

CHAPTER 7

Dr. Cohen met me in the concourse of Summit Hall, a newer building attached to Elijah's unit. I hadn't expected it to be as nice and airy as it was: lots of natural light, with a café as well as a gift shop that sold crafts made by the patients. I bought a cup of coffee and sat at a table to wait.

A woman in her early forties, with a face cut from granite, picked me out of the small crowd and came over. "Mr. Sanden?"

"Dr. Cohen?" We shook hands. "I appreciate you getting me in to see Elijah so quickly."

"When you said that you were from the Innocence Project, I figured I should pull a few strings."

I sat back down at the table and waited for her to join me, but she remained on her feet. She said, "You are the people who look into wrongful convictions?"

"That's us."

"And you think that Elijah might be one of those wrongful convictions?"

I felt odd looking up at her from my chair, like a student looking up at a stern teacher, so I stood again. "I'm still in the preliminary stages. First, we investigate to see if there's any evidence of innocence. Usually, we're talking about DNA and the like, but we try to cover all the bases."

She seemed interested. "Has your investigation uncovered anything important—or is that confidential?"

"It's very preliminary."

"Would you be up for a walk?"

"Why not," I said.

We headed out of the building into the sun, our pace a gentle stroll. "I'm curious," Dr. Cohen said. "What were your first impressions of Elijah?"

"He's polite. Religious—likes to throw Bible quotes around. I'm no expert, but I suspect that a lot of mentally ill people believe that they talk to God. I mean, if I heard voices in my head, that's what I would think."

"Yes, schizophrenics often have religious delusions. Anywhere from twenty-five to fifty percent of them."

"So you're telling me Elijah is par for the course?"

"No, that's not what I'm saying at all." Dr. Cohen looked at her watch. "Do you know what Elijah is doing right now?"

I shook my head.

"He spends his recreation time in the library, often reading his Bible alone. But lately, he's been sitting with another patient—I'll call him John. John is here because he killed his best friend. He became convinced that his friend had been molesting children. John felt that he couldn't tell the police because…well, John's been in and out of hospitals all his life. Why should anyone believe him? He decided that the only way to save the children would be to kill his friend.

"They shared an apartment, and one night, as his friend lay sleeping, John went into his room and hit the man with a hammer. Once we got John back on his meds, he tried to blind himself by driving the cap of a pen into his eyes. He succeeded in his left eye, but not his right."

I don't know if Dr. Cohen was trying to impress me or shock me, but she had done neither. When I taught about the insanity defense in my criminal law classes, I used cases with outrageous facts to keep my students awake too.

Dr. Cohen continued: "More recently, he managed to get his hands on a flashlight battery. He rubbed the battery acid in his right eye and lost most of the vision in it as well. In the eight years that John's been here, we've tried everything—neuroleptics, behavioral therapy—but his symptoms remain severe and resistant."

Dr. Cohen stopped at a building with no fences, opening and beckoning me through the unlocked front door. Inside a nurse sat at a station. Beyond her, patients wandered a wide, well-lit hallway with the freedom of hotel guests.

"Where is Martha?" Dr. Cohen asked the nurse.

The woman pointed down the hall. "Common room," she said. Dr. Cohen started walking again, talking as we made our way.

"A month ago, I had a session with John, one of hundreds that we've had, but this one was different. Midway through, he began to cry. This is a man who had called me every foul name he could think of. He had threatened to kill me and everyone else in the hospital. But that day he cried like a child. He was inconsolable over that fact that he had killed his best friend. Mr. Sanden, I can't tell you what a breakthrough that was. To be honest, I cried that day too. He was showing true remorse."

She looked at me as if she wanted to gauge my reaction. "I wish I could say that it was modern medicine that brought about his change, but it wasn't. It was Elijah. They had been spending time together... talking. I don't know what Elijah said to him, but it brought John out of his darkness."

We turned a corner and entered the common room, a cheery space filled with tables and comfortable chairs. A row of windows looked out over an open lawn. Dr. Cohen pointed to a woman, midthirties, with pleasant features, sitting near a window, a ball of yarn on her lap, knitting needles in her hands.

"You let them have knitting needles?"

"This is the last stop before they leave us. She's waiting for her review hearing, and absent any surprises, she will be transferred to an apartment up in Anoka. Social Services will be involved, but she will—for all intents and purposes—be free."

"What brought her here?"

"She killed her child, a daughter, only a year old."

The woman looked like a cross between Doris Day and Donna Reed. The thought of her killing her baby made my stomach flutter.

"It's part of the court record, so I can tell you that when she came to us, she was suffering from postpartum psychosis and hadn't spoken a word since the day of the tragedy. She wouldn't eat or even acknowledge anyone in the room. Full-on catatonic. She was with us for what…two years before Elijah started talking to her. At first, we had concerns. We kept a close eye on them, but as long as he didn't get too close, we allowed it."

"Let me guess," I said. "Elijah got her to talk."

"I can hear your skepticism, Mr. Sanden, and it's not unfounded. Skepticism is good in my profession. Psychiatry is far from exact. We try one thing and if it doesn't produce results, we try another. If it works…well, even if it's a placebo, it's a good thing. And yes, after a few months, she had a breakthrough."

"Do you know what he said to her?"

"She told me that…" Dr. Cohen paused and looked at me as though weary of my incredulity. "She told me that Elijah spoke to her about her daughter. He told her that her daughter was with God and that she was forgiven. She wouldn't reveal everything Elijah had said to her, but the turnaround was…well, *miraculous* is a good word for it."

"Wait…Doc…you don't think that Elijah really talks to God?"

"I'm just telling you that Elijah helped that poor woman, and he's helping John. How it's happening is beyond my power to diagnose." Dr. Cohen nodded toward the exit. "Walk me back to my office."

"You have a fondness for him," I said, opening the door for her.

"I do," she said. "There's something about him…"

We stepped back into the sunshine and Dr. Cohen stopped walking. She paused, fidgeted, looked away from me and then back. When she didn't resume speaking right away, I prodded. "And…?"

"One day, Elijah and I had just finished a session. I was getting ready to leave when he leaned over and said, 'You're going to make a great mother.' I nearly choked on my tongue."

"Were you…pregnant?"

"That's the thing. I was. I had just found out that week. I wasn't showing yet. I hadn't told anyone except my husband. I was thirty-nine. Pregnancy at that age can have complications, so I was keeping it a secret. But he knew."

"I'm sure there's a reasonable explanation. I've seen magicians and mentalists conjure up facts that seemingly can't be explained—until they are. Elijah spouts gibberish. Maybe within all that nonsense he said one thing that hit home."

"Maybe," she said. "But it got to me. I think it has affected how I look at him—how I treat him."

"In what way?" I asked.

She started walking, the sun above us beating down hot and muggy. "Do you know what a Jarvis hearing is?" she asked.

The name rang a distant bell in the gloom of my memory. "It's a hearing for…people who aren't responding to meds. You need a court order to go up to the next level, right?"

"It's kind of a catch-22. Say the treatment team needs to try some serious medication—a neuroleptic—something that has a long-term side effect. First, we ask the patient and if they agree, we deem them competent enough to make that consent. But if they refuse, we deem the patient incompetent and get a court order."

"And what's this got to do with Elijah?"

Back at Summit Hall, Dr. Cohen stopped in the shade of the portico and turned to me. "He's scheduled for a Jarvis hearing in ten days."

"Okay."

"Mr. Sanden, Elijah has been diagnosed as bipolar and schizo-phrenic. We've been giving him an ever-increasing panel of medi-cations, but it's having no effect. He's still convinced that he talks to God. My team has recommended that he undergo electroconvulsive therapy. Are you familiar with ECT, Mr. Sanden?"

I was. I had learned the term in law school, but not as part of any class. I had learned it from a friend. It had not ended well.

On a hill in the distance the grounds crew mowed the lawn. A pickup truck with the logo of a vending machine company drove along the street behind us. People passed back and forth on the side-walk. If a person didn't know better, they might think they were walk-ing through any small town in America. But this wasn't Mayberry; it was a place where hope dangled at the end of a long frayed rope.

"Are you opposing the ECT?" I asked.

"Yes, but I'm being pushed off Elijah's team."

"Because you won't go along with it?"

"We've tried everything to bring Elijah out of his delusion. Med-ication isn't doing the trick. ECT might be the only treatment left to pull him back to reality. As a clinician I have no medical reason to oppose the ECT. At the same time, though, I can't bring myself to go along with it. ECT is a significant procedure. He could lose years of memory. It will change him in ways that..."

There was a bench in the portico. Dr. Cohen gestured toward it, and we sat.

"Can I ask you a personal question, Mr. Sanden?"

I nodded, wary.

"Are you a man of faith?"

"I was once a Catholic, but not anymore."

"So you have some background in the Old Testament?"

"I'm no scholar, but you might call me a hobbyist."

"I'm Jewish," she said. "When I studied the Nevi'im, I was told about the prophets. My entire religion was formed by men who talked to God thousands of years ago. I believe in my heart that God spoke to those men."

I smiled politely. "And you think Elijah talks to God? Works miracles?"

"I'm not saying that." She looked as though she was struggling with a thought, unable to hold eye contact, her stony façade crumbling. "It's just...God spoke to Ezekiel and told him to lie on his left side for three hundred and ninety days. God told him to eat bread baked over cow dung and Ezekiel did it. Isaiah walked the earth naked for three years because God told him to. If Ezekiel or Isaiah were alive today...don't you think that they'd be in a place like this?"

As far as I was concerned, Dr. Cohen's argument didn't exonerate Elijah so much as it indicted Ezekiel and Isaiah.

"The problem is," she said, "I don't have a medical basis for opposing the ECT. At the same time, I don't want to see Elijah undergo that trauma. He has ten days. The hearing has been set. Once it happens, the team will begin treatments immediately."

"Maybe he needs the treatment. I mean...he thinks he's a prophet."

"If Elijah killed that man, then...yes, it's incumbent upon us to make it so he's no longer a danger to the world. But if he's innocent... Being a prophet is at the very core of who he is, Mr. Sanden. If he's innocent of the murder, it would be a crime to take that away from him. It doesn't matter if he's mentally ill—we don't have that right."

"So all I have to do is prove his innocence in ten days." I had said it sarcastically, but Dr. Cohen didn't flinch.

"We all have our burdens," she said. "I can't stop it from my end; I've tried. That's why they're taking me off the team. You're his only hope."

Ten days wasn't enough time to do anything. I wanted to tell her that her hope was naïve and misplaced. Instead, I stood and said, "I'll do my best."

My words rang hollow in my ears.

CHAPTER 8

Back in my car, I checked my phone. No new messages from either Dee or Emma. So as I drove to St. Paul, my thoughts instead drifted back thirty years to my only experience with electroconvulsive therapy.

His name was Richard Gullivay, and we had met the first week of law school. I had watched a movie called *The Paper Chase* and believed that getting into a good study group was imperative. With that in mind, I'd paid careful attention to my fellow students, whittling names off my list as they stumbled to keep up in class. Richard, however, stood out.

On first blush, he came across as insecure, a man completely devoid of social skills who, like me, spent every spare minute in the library studying. I think people shied away from him because of that awkwardness, but I noticed what others didn't: He was absolutely brilliant.

I've never been sure why he agreed to study with me, as I brought very little to the table. I was a hick from Missouri who had barely made it into college. My grade point average was lower than what most law schools allow. Had I not kicked ass on the LSAT, I would not have made it in at all. I knew nothing about the legal world beyond what I picked up from watching shows like *L.A. Law* on TV.

Richard, on the other hand, came from a family of attorneys. His mother and uncle both practiced in the Twin Cities, and he had an older brother who had just graduated summa cum laude from Pepperdine. I've been in the legal realm for nearly three decades now, and can still say with confidence that I have never met anyone who could spot the issue in a case as easily as Richard could.

But Richard had demons, too. Exam week brought out a side of him that unnerved me. When I arrived at his apartment to study, he refused to answer my knock. At first I thought that he had forgotten our appointment, but as I was leaving the building, I noticed that his windows were all open. It was five degrees outside. I went back up and knocked—pounded—on the door until he opened it. He stared at me blankly as I walked in, dark rings etching his eyes.

Looking around, I saw that the Torts outline we had drafted together was strewn around the carpet. His refrigerator was open and empty. He had pulled his bedding into a pile in his closet, where he had been sleeping. He couldn't tell me what day it was or whether it was morning or afternoon. Freaked out, I called his mother.

Richard didn't take his Torts final that winter, or any other exam. I didn't see him again until the fall, when I was starting my second year and he arrived to repeat his first. When I saw him, I wanted to embrace him, but he looked at me like he didn't remember me. I said my name and he only smiled and shook my hand.

Over the next few weeks, I joined him at his table whenever I saw him in the student union. Eventually the frost between us melted away and he confided that he had had a mental breakdown, something I admitted that I already knew. He made a joke about it and we shared an uncomfortable laugh.

We started making time for each other again, lunches, the occasional game of racquetball. One beautiful fall afternoon we were sitting on the lawn in front of the school, the trees around us full of red and yellow leaves; I was reading Constitutional Law and he was working on his Criminal Law outline. It caught me off-guard when he threw his book to the ground and cursed through gritted teeth.

"I should know this stuff already," he said. "This is the second time I've taken this class. It's so fucking frustrating!"

"You had a year off," I said, trying to be helpful. "You can't expect to retain everything."

"That's not it." He lay back in the grass, his forearm across his eyes to block the sun. "It's not time. I can't remember because...I had my brain shocked."

"What?"

"Electroconvulsive therapy."

"You're kidding, right?"

"That's how they cured my depression. They sent these small doses of electricity through my brain."

"Damn."

"I know. But now I can't remember shit. That first day of class...I couldn't remember your name."

"I did wonder," I said slowly.

"I remember taking the classes last fall, but I can't remember half the stuff I learned."

"Wow, that's...that's...I don't know."

"There are days when I wear clothes from my closet and it's like I'm wearing them for the first time. One morning, I looked at my driver's license and didn't recognize my own picture. I just don't feel like me sometimes. Does that make sense?"

It didn't, but I nodded as if I understood.

That fall, as finals approached, I kept an eye on Richard, sitting with him in the library, driving past his new apartment on my way home. The first sign of trouble came the day before his Criminal Law exam. I found him studying in the library, wearing his winter coat. I took a seat across from him.

"Ain't you hot?" I asked.

He acted as if the question confused him. Then he stood and took off his coat.

51

"You okay?"

He looked at me with dead eyes. "There are five major affirmative defenses to a crime."

"That's right."

"I can only remember four."

A year earlier, he'd known all five like I know my middle name. "Which ones do you have?"

He answered with great deliberation. "Duress, necessity, self-defense, entrapment, and..."

"And insanity," I said.

The corners of his mouth bent down like he wanted to cry. "Thanks," he said. "How could I forget?"

That night, I drove past his apartment and saw one of his windows opened to the cold autumn air. I pulled hard to the curb, ran up three flights of stairs, and pounded on the door, but he didn't answer. I remembered the firm where his mother worked, so I used a neighbor's phone and called her again.

In the twenty minutes that I waited for her, I continued to knock and coax him to open his door, but when he didn't answer, I think I already knew what we would find inside.

His mother arrived, frantic and out of breath, the key to his apartment in her trembling fingers. Unable to work the key into the lock, she handed it to me. I slid the key in and turned the knob.

Richard hung from an electrical cord that he had tied to a ceiling fan, his feet dangling, his neck stretched, his head twisted to the side, eyes open and red. There were claw marks on his neck as though he had fought to free himself after he kicked the chair away. Pages of a class outline lay scattered around the apartment, torn and crumpled by a frustrated hand.

I ran to Richard and wrapped my arms around his waist to lift him up. His flesh was cold beneath his shirt, the muscles of his torso stiff against my cheek. Richard's wailing mother picked up the chair he had kicked to the floor and climbed up to his side. I lifted as she pulled the cord from around his neck.

What I laid on the linoleum floor wasn't my friend Richard. He had been intelligent and funny, his wit so sharp that you often didn't feel the slice of the blade until it was too late. He had been warm and generous with his affection, too, far more forgiving of the frailty of others than of his own flaws.

What lay on the floor was a hollow vessel, a vase emptied of its flowers.

I can no longer think of Richard without seeing the image of him hanging from that ceiling fan like a fish on a stringer. As I drove back to St. Paul, I thought about Richard—and Elijah. Soon, he would no longer hear the voice of God. He would no longer believe himself to be a prophet.

The chime of my phone pulled me from my memory. It was Dee. I answered, "Hey, honey."

"They're late," she said. "She was supposed to have Emma back here by five sharp. It's almost twenty after."

"Call Emma and see what the holdup is."

"I tried. It rang once and went to voice mail."

I focused on what Dee was saying. One ring and then to voice mail. A dead battery? "Maybe she forgot to charge her phone," I said carefully.

"Have you ever known Emma to let her phone go dead?"

Dee had a point, but Anna was notorious for pushing the boundaries. "Maybe they went to a movie or something where she had to turn her phone off."

"I tried to text her, too."

"And?"

"Doesn't show that the text got delivered."

"Okay?"

"If her phone was turned off, the text would still go through."

Was that true? "I'm sure Emma's all right," I said. "I'll be home in...ten minutes. If she's not home by then, I'll call Anna."

I took a breath to let a wave of anxiety pass. Just thinking of Anna caused my blood pressure to rise. She had yet to bring Emma home from a visit on time. And presents—we had made a simple request that gifts be limited to three hundred bucks, yet every birthday and every Christmas, the packages poured in—thousands of dollars' worth of clothing and jewelry. The woman had a talent for turning everything into a fight.

"Something's not right," Dee said. "I can feel it."

"If Anna's screwing with us, we'll cut her off," I said. "The law's on our side. But I'm sure it's nothing to worry about."

By the time I ended the call, I knew that I hadn't convinced Dee that things were all right, but there was no sense getting worked up until we knew it was more than just a faulty phone.

Still, I pictured Emma leaving that morning, heading toward Anna's car wearing her backpack—stuffed full. Why would Emma take a full backpack on a one-day shopping spree? The more I thought about it, the more I came to agree with Dee. Something was not right.

CHAPTER 9

I called Emma as soon as I got home. Dee and I stood in our kitchen, my phone on speaker. The call went straight to voice mail. I sent a text and it never left my phone.

"It's almost as if she's blocked us," Dee said, clutching the edge of the counter for support.

"That can't be the case," I said. "I'll call Anna." I pulled up Anna's number and held my thumb over the send button. *No good deed goes unpunished*, I thought to myself, thinking of how Anna fought for custody back when we filed to be Emma's guardians. She had been Anna Adler-King then, a woman with money, clout, a husband—and a lover on the side. With no help from us, her husband found out about the lover, and by the time we went to court, Anna was neck-deep in that fight. She had dropped the ball on Emma's case, and although it was a battle, we had walked out of court as Emma's guardians.

I finally hit send, but my call went straight to voice mail: *You've reached Anna Adler. Leave a message.*

"Anna, it's Boady..." Dee was staring at me anxiously.

What to say? "Stop screwing with us"? "Why the hell can't we get ahold of Emma?" "You're half an hour late"?

"We've been trying to reach Emma," I said. "I assume you're on your way and are running late. You need to call and let us know." My message was inartful at best.

We'd granted Anna's visitations with Emma only after she'd

shown up at our door. Emma had been at school and Dee at work. In her late forties, Anna was tall and slender and carried herself like a woman who had never wrestled with insecurity.

When I answered the door that day, I had looked around for her attorney, as I rarely saw Anna without some other line of defense. Seeing no one, I asked, "Can I help you?"

"Can we talk?"

I neither moved nor answered her. After a few uncomfortable seconds, she continued. "I have no right to ask…" She dropped her eyes, tucked her shoulders, and twisted her fingers. Was she nervous? Her demeanor came across as unnatural, something studied and practiced.

"You know that I love Emma," she said.

I knew no such thing. Anna Adler struck me as a woman incapable of love, at least nothing more than how one might "love" a good glass of wine or a high-end purse.

"She's all the family I have left. She reminds me of Jennavieve… when we were children."

I could not picture Anna as a child: romping though a pile of dead leaves, playing in mud, or climbing a tree.

"I was hoping you might let me see her, like…visitation. Just a few days a year."

I credit Anna for having the decency not to summon fake tears; she had to know that I would never buy it. After fighting us for guardianship the way she had, Anna now came across like a thief seeking a loan from the bank she had just tried to rob. I almost laughed, but instead said, "I'll talk to Dee."

When I told Dee about Anna's request, she put into words what I had been thinking. "She'll try to poison Em against us."

"I agree," I had said. "We have no reason to grant her visitation whatsoever. But…"

"You're not actually considering this," Dee said.

I had put on my lawyer hat by then, rational, dispassionate. "If we deny visitation, Anna might go back and ask for a court order. If she did, we would be at the mercy of a judge's ruling."

"I don't trust her."

"Neither do I," I said. "But she's Emma's aunt—her only blood relative."

"And you think blood is better than what she has with us?"

"I didn't say that." I had somehow become saddled with a position that wasn't mine to defend. "What if we had lost and Anna had been granted guardianship? Wouldn't you want visitation?"

"But she didn't win."

I gave up. "If you don't want to…I'm fine with that."

I knew where we were going to end up. I think Dee did as well, but she needed time to find her own way there. She walked out of the kitchen—out of the house—and took a seat on the porch to ponder. I stayed behind to give her space.

The kitchen had a ten-foot ceiling framed by crown molding that could have been nailed there by men who had served in the Civil War. When we first moved in, we had painted the walls a cheery butterscotch to catch the light and radiate warmth, but I felt none of that comfort as I waited for Dee to return.

I peeled a banana and turned on some music—oldies rock to take me back. Van Morrison's "Tupelo Honey" came on and I got all squishy inside. That was the song for my first slow dance with Dee.

Of all the precious memories I guard, few compare with that first dance. She was Diana back then. We'd sat next to each other in our ninth-grade history class, me staring at the walls and her reading her textbook. We never spoke, but I knew who she was—everyone knew. As the only Black student in my school, she stood out like a drop of paint on a white canvas.

Our first dance happened in the little town of Dry Creek, Missouri, at a parish picnic on the Fourth of July. My friend Thomas and I had gone with no plans other than to win a couple six-packs of

Coca-Cola at the ring toss and maybe take in the fireworks. Those picnics always ended with a dance held in a local gymnasium, a sweaty affair that to me seemed a waste of two dollars. But Thomas had met a girl and twisted my arm until I agreed to go.

I had never danced before, and I didn't like the idea of shelling out money to watch others do it. The girl Thomas had his eye on happened to be Diana's cousin up from Memphis. It didn't take more than a song or two before Thomas and the cousin were on the dance floor, leaving Diana and me sitting on the bleachers—together, but alone.

The thing is, I wanted to dance with her, and she hinted that she wanted to dance with me, but I was scared of looking like a klutz. I sat there staring at my feet, the rivulets of sweat trickling down my forehead. It wasn't until Diana insinuated that I didn't want to dance with her because I was white and she was black that I finally got up the nerve to ask her.

To this day, we disagree on what that first song—a fast song—was, but the second song was "Tupelo Honey," a song as slow and smooth as its title. I had never held a girl in my arms before, and I was ill-prepared for the rush of emotion that hit me. And when Van Morrison sang, *"She's as sweet as Tupelo honey,"* I was sure he was talking about Diana. I was clumsy and sweaty; I nearly choked on my thick tongue when I tried to talk, but I walked off that dance floor holding Diana's hand in mine, and somehow knew that I never wanted that to change.

We were going steady by Christmas. She was smart, and funny, and strong. Being a mixed-race couple in Missouri in those days had its problems, but Diana walked through it all with immeasurable grace. I remember one day as we were walking downtown, this jacked-up truck drove past and some yahoo wearing an oversize Stetson stuck his head out the window and yelled, "Salt and pepper!" I was about to flip the asshole off when Diana gently lowered my arm.

"I wonder why they think that's an insult?" she said. "Think about it. You like salt and pepper on your eggs, right?"

"Yeah."

"But if you put just salt on your eggs or just pepper, it wouldn't taste as good, would it?"

"Not really."

"You need them both to make it taste just right. One without the other...well, it'd be missing something."

I had never thought about it that way. We were salt and pepper, flavorful, complementary, a perfect coupling. She had turned an insult into a compliment. Nothing deflated those with small minds more than to have their insults go unappreciated.

Diana had always been the smart one. Being with her made me want to be smart too. She was the reason that I started doing homework in school, moving from a C-minus to a B-plus average. It was Diana who shifted my life's ambitions from hanging Sheetrock for my neighbor's drywall company to getting a college degree. She was kind, and gentle, and funny. She would have made a wonderful mother.

Somewhere around the time we graduated from college, I had taken to calling her Dee. She didn't seem to mind. And when Emma came to live with us for good, she called her Mama Dee. The first time it happened, Dee nearly cried with happiness.

As a lawyer, I couldn't help seeing Emma through the maze of rules and statutes that made up guardianship law. It gave structure to my role in Emma's life. But for Dee, the court order was nothing more than a piece of paper. It didn't relate to how she held Emma when she cried, or helped her with her homework. Dee never sought guidance from the law when she worried about Emma making friends or held her when Emma woke crying from a bad dream. As far as Dee was concerned, Emma was our daughter.

That day, Dee had stayed on the porch for most of half an hour, contemplating Anna's request for visitation. When she finally came back in, she said, "Limited visitation—a week or two a year. But I'm telling you right now, Anna's going to be poison for Em."

I had no idea, back then, just how prescient Dee's words would be. We now saw that poison working its way through the veins of our little family. I looked at Dee, leaning against the counter, her hair grayer than ever.

"I'll drive out to Anna's and get Emma," I said. "If they show up here, call me."

CHAPTER 10

Anna Adler's wealth stretched into the tens of millions of dollars, an inheritance divided between her and her sister, Jennavieve, when their father passed away. After Jennavieve's death—and then Ben's—Jennavieve's share went to Emma, which we put into a trust. On paper, Emma was a wealthy young woman, but Dee and I never touched that trust, even though by law we could do so for normal living expenses. We wanted Emma to grow up doing chores for her allowance like we had. We didn't want her defining herself by money.

Anna, on the other hand, had no problem flaunting her wealth. I had never been beyond her driveway, which circled in front of a house that looked like a French château, but knew the place had five bedrooms, seven baths, and commanded a spot on Lake Minnetonka that overlooked the Minnetonka Yacht Club. Eleven thousand square feet—or so Zillow said—all for one woman and her butler.

I rang the bell and waited a few seconds as Adler's butler, George, answered the door.

"I'm here to pick up Emma," I said.

George was a squat man, fortyish, with enormous arms, who probably lived off a steady diet of raw eggs and lamb's blood. He nodded to me and said, "Ms. Adler is expecting you." He stepped back and waved me in.

She sure as hell should be expecting me.

The front door opened to a two-story foyer with a curved staircase and marble floors. It had been painted a light pastel yellow, which surprised me. I had expected the house to be as dark as the heart of its owner.

George led me to an office in the back of the house. Glass shelves on white walls held antique clocks and delicate vases, the kind of relics that seemed an addiction of the rich. The wall behind Adler's desk was all windows, curved to overlook a lush backyard. And beyond that, the blue waters of Lake Minnetonka. There were two chairs on the visitor's side of the desk, and George put his hand on the back of one, a sign for me to sit there. I did, but George didn't leave the room. Instead, he took up a position just inside the closed door, standing with his back to it, his feet spread slightly, and his hands clasped behind him like a soldier at ease.

"I promise I won't steal anything," I said.

George didn't respond.

I crossed one leg over the other and settled into the chair to wait—and wait. After several minutes, I wanted to walk out and find Emma myself, but with George there, I chose to remain in my seat, repeating the mantra that I had the law on my side.

"Is your boss coming?" I asked.

"She'll be here shortly."

"Bringing Emma."

George didn't answer.

When one of the clocks on the shelf showed that fifteen minutes had passed, I stood and faced George. It would be a felony for him to stop me from leaving the room. "I'm tired of waiting," I said. "I'll get the police and come back if she's not here in the next—"

George stepped aside as if to let me pass, but the knob of the door turned and in walked Anna, dressed in a black suit, her patent-leather heels lifting her an inch taller than I as she walked past. She wore a subtle smile that unnerved me.

"Where's Emma?"

She didn't answer, but took a seat behind her desk.

"I need you to go get her." I kept my tone polite but assertive.

"I don't think so."

"Your failure to return her puts you in jeopardy of a criminal charge. I don't want to go there, but if you force me…"

"Why have you never told Emma about how her father died?" Anna asked, looking at me the way a cat might look at a wounded mouse.

I remained standing but put a hand on the back of the chair beside me. "How I choose to raise Emma is none of your business."

"Oh, but it is my business. She's my niece, the last of our family. We have a bond that goes far beyond anything a judge might order."

"That's not how the law sees it."

Slowly, Anna leaned back in her chair. "Ben died in your house, in your study, and you never mentioned that to her."

"There's a time and place for that discussion, and I'll be the one to choose them."

"You blocked your internet so that she couldn't read about what happened. It seems you feel a need to hide what you did. Are you ashamed? Or…maybe you feel responsible."

It was becoming clear that whatever this was, it had been orchestrated, carefully arranged like leaves scattered across the wire of a snare.

"You need to bring Emma to me," I said. "I'm giving you a mulligan here, but I'm losing my patience."

The corners of her mouth inched up ever so slightly. She looked at George and nodded.

George opened the door and an older man wearing a loose-fitting gray suit entered carrying a manila envelope. He gave the envelope to George, who then handed it to me. It was thick with papers and sealed with tape. The man in the gray suit said, "Mr. Boady Sanden, you've been served."

The man was all business, but Anna smiled like a woman holding a royal flush. I found the lip of the envelope, tore it open, slid the stack of papers out, and dropped the envelope to the floor, somehow aware that what I held was explosive.

The first document was a petition to change Emma's guardianship to Anna Adler. The document went out of focus for a moment and came back. *What?* This had to be a joke. I turned the page and saw the term *emotional harm.*

Anna said, "If you skip to the last page, you'll find a temporary order stating that Emma will stay with me until the matter is heard in court."

I looked hard at her. "What are you doing? I will not let this stand, you fucking bitch!"

Anna's smile broadened. "Why, Mr. Sanden, are you threatening me?"

The man in the gray suit spoke. "Ms. Adler is represented by counsel in this matter—me. Communicating with her directly is an ethical breach—as is a threat of violence."

"I didn't threaten—" I stopped. They were probably recording the conversation. I turned to the man in gray. "Tell your client that she has filed a frivolous action and I will see her in court."

I turned and left the office, George following me as I stormed out the front door and to my car.

I drove a few miles away before pulling into an empty parking lot, my hands shaking too hard to trust myself behind the wheel. I couldn't seem to catch my breath. I wanted to call Dee, but this wasn't a conversation to have over the phone. And before I tried to explain it to her, I needed to understand it myself.

I picked up the papers and began reading.

CHAPTER 11

Dee had always wanted children. I knew that from our senior year of high school, after a vague first conversation about it filled with what-ifs. She had been offered a scholarship to the University of Minnesota, two states away from our home in Missouri, where I had been accepted as well. We were already tying our futures together, so why not cast ahead and talk about a family? We were so young, but somehow it seemed a natural next step.

We married after college and the what-ifs took on the weight of stones. She stopped taking her birth control pills and sex went from a game of tag to a relay race, every step intentional, synchronized. I had just started law school and she was on the bottom rung of a career as a commercial loan officer with Wells Fargo. A child at that time would have upended our world, but none of that seemed to matter to Dee. I never told her about my quiet hopes that the baby would wait, and she never voiced her disappointment as the months became years with no baby to hold.

On the night I graduated from law school, she took me to dinner to celebrate. A toddler sitting near us caught her eye. She winked and waved at him with the tips of her fingers, her smile a very thin mask that broke my heart. I had the distractions of a new career on my horizon, but she could no more ignore her yearning for a child than she could her need for food, or water, or oxygen.

Then, on my twenty-eighth birthday, she gave me a small box

wrapped in gold paper. Inside was a pair of baby shoes. It took all of two seconds to connect the dots. I looked at Dee and asked, "Are you?"

She nodded, her eyes full of tears, which caused me to cry as well. I was going to be a father. At last, it felt right. We spent the night in each other's arms, trying out names and reveling in the excitement of what was about to happen, knowing that a baby would change our lives forever. By the time we went to bed, we had agreed that if it was a girl, we would name her Evelyn, after Dee's mother, but if it was a boy, we would name him Thomas, after my friend who nudged us together for that first slow dance.

After that, every conversation we had seemed to circle around to the baby. What kind of diapers were best? Would he or she be musical like Dee or a reader like me? We had dreamt of Christmas stockings and Halloween costumes. It was a time of immeasurable hope and joy—and it lasted a mere three weeks.

The doctor delivered the news with a practiced sorrow that felt like an insult. We had lost the baby, but *baby* wasn't the word she used. She said that we had lost the *pregnancy,* as though our son or daughter hadn't really existed. I was furious, my anger the single expression of grief available to me in that moment. I wanted to scream my child's name at her, but I didn't. The doctor was just doing her job.

I held Dee there in the examination room as she cried. I held her in our bedroom that night and for many nights to follow. The wound seemed one that might never heal.

When she got pregnant the second time, we avoided any discussion of names, as though the mere mention of something so presumptuous would invite tragedy. We went about our lives as though nothing spectacular loomed ahead. The one change, however, was that Dee insisted we start going to church again. We had grown up Catholic, but other than on Christmas and Easter, I had stopped going to mass after I left home. Dee, on the other hand, still attended on occasion. She said that the rhythm of the liturgy and the familiarity of the hymns brought her comfort. With that second pregnancy we were in church every Sunday.

Our second baby—our second pregnancy—lasted five weeks longer than the first. Pulling Dee out of that spin took the better part of a year.

She was thirty-two when she found out that she was pregnant for the third time. That same day she quit her job, and I took over all cooking and cleaning, doing everything I could to eliminate stress. When we passed the twelfth week, we let some of those old dreams leak into our conversations, wading in slowly as though stepping into a very cold lake.

When we hit the twentieth week, we became bold, buying a baby stroller and crib. We chose a room for the nursery, a bedroom we had been using for storage, and I slowly began transforming it as Dee napped.

By week twenty-three, I had painted the room a pleasant green and installed a changing table filled with diapers and Desitin. We bought enough onesies to outfit an army of babies. We had summer clothes and winter clothes, hats, mittens, and tiny knitted socks. We had books, and toys, and hope.

She was a girl, but the name Evelyn was off the list. We had already lost a child by that name. We went back and forth with ideas until we settled on Julia, a name that carried no connection to a relative or friend, but a name that spoke to us—sang to us—as we sat in the quiet of her nursery.

In week twenty-four we learned about placental abruption. We learned that losing a child in the twenty-fourth week was no longer a miscarriage, but a stillbirth. We learned that our earlier grief held no comparison to the gut-wrenching agony of losing a child with a face, and hair, and fingernails. We learned that beyond the depth of our previous sorrow there existed a cavernous tomb below which no greater heartache could survive.

We buried Julia beneath a marker that bore her name and a single date.

I never told Dee this, but after taking the crib and baby clothes to Goodwill, I carried Julia's ultrasound pictures and a few other keepsakes up into the attic, a dusty room with a plywood floor and more than its share of cobwebs, the one space in the house that Dee refused to go. While there I found my old pocketknife, one that had belonged to my father, and used it to carve Julia's name into the rafters. Impressed with my work, I decided to give names to the two miscarriages and carve *Thomas* and *Evelyn* into the wood as well. I don't know why I did it other than to try to keep their memories present in that old house.

Dee never went back to Wells Fargo. My practice had taken off, so we didn't need the money. But she also stopped having lunch with her friends and going to movies. She had made one last trip to church, to meet privately with the priest, and when she came home, she was near catatonic in her grief.

It took time and patience, but when I finally got her to talk about what had happened, she told me that the priest said that our baby's soul was in Limbo, a place on the outskirts of hell where unbaptized infants go for eternity. I knew that Limbo had been a compromise between factions of the early church, an easing up of Saint Augustine's stance that unbaptized babies all went to hell, but I couldn't believe that's all he'd offered Dee. How could anyone, priest or otherwise, look a grieving mother in the eye and speak such cruelty? I had never held animosity toward the church, but when Dee told me what happened, I wanted to punch that priest. I wanted to tell the whole lot of them to go straight to hell—had I still believed in such a place.

We lost Julia twenty-three years ago. After that there were no more pregnancies, no more hopes or crushing disappointments. In time, Dee got her realtor's license and pursued a career she hadn't expected. We found a new normal, just the two of us, but there were still times when I saw that grief pass behind my wife's beautiful brown eyes. While walking through a zoo or attending a performance of *The Nutcracker,* or just having a quiet meal in a restaurant, a nearby child would catch her eye and she would smile a lilting smile, and I would know that she was thinking about Julia, or Evelyn, or Thomas.

Then came Emma.

Last year had been our happiest, a zenith for our little family. In the spring, we took Emma zip-lining to celebrate her thirteenth birthday. On the drive home, we stopped at Minnesota's largest candy store, a bright yellow warehouse on the side of the highway, and bought her enough candy to last until Halloween. Afterward, we took her to a fine restaurant for dinner and birthday cake. When we arrived at home, her present awaited her, a black Labrador puppy. She squealed with excitement and named him Rufus.

That had been a good day, one of our best. And when we tucked her into bed that night, the dog on a rug beside her, she gave Dee a big hug and said, "Good night, Mama Dee." Then she held her arms open for me and I leaned in so that she could give me a hug as well. Until that day, she had no nickname for me, simply calling me Boady, but that night, as she hugged me, she said, "Goodnight, Poppy."

I didn't know what to say. Emma had opened a door that I had never expected to walk through. I wanted to tell her that she was brave for taking that step. I wanted to let her know how it tugged at my heart to hear her call me Poppy. But in the end, I simply said, "Goodnight, sweetie," which fell far short of what I meant.

My feeble reply followed me to bed that night and remained with me in the morning. I wanted to sit her down and tell her what it meant to me, but when she came down for breakfast, she was in a hurry to play with Rufus. I didn't want to step on her excitement and I let the moment pass. Looking back now, I wish with all of my heart that I hadn't.

By last weekend, her fourteenth birthday, I was back to being just Boady. Dee and I had taken her out to eat, but she had seemed distracted. Reading the documents that Anna had served me, I now understood why. She had to have known what her aunt was up to. The packet contained reports by both a psychologist and a guardian ad litem that Emma had apparently met with on her visit to Anna's for Christmas.

But one document in the packet, more than any other, slipped a blade between my ribs. Emma had signed an affidavit begging to be taken out of our home and delivered to Anna. At the heart of her request was a statement that turned my blood cold: *Boady Sanden was responsible for my father's death.*

By the time I pulled into my driveway, I had gone through denial and anger. I sat in my driveway and stared at the closed garage door in front of me, my fingers latched to the steering wheel, unwilling to let me leave the car.

Inside, Dee waited for me to bring Emma home. Instead, I brought a packet of papers that would upend her world. Emma didn't want us—she didn't want me. I had once been her Poppy, but now she thought so little of me that it broke my heart. I closed my eyes and thought about Dee. This was going to destroy her.

CHAPTER 12

Dee waited for me at the kitchen island, the fabric of her spirit worn threadbare. "Where's Emma?"

I shook my head.

"What happened?"

I would have given all the money I had not to see that look of fear in her eyes as I held out the stack of papers. "We need to sit down."

"What happened?" Her tone grew urgent as she took a seat at the dining room table.

"Anna launched an attack," I said.

"But…we have a court order. You said…"

I had said that we were safe from Anna. I had said that no one could take Emma away from us. I had told Dee to trust me.

"She got an ex parte order," I said, digging through the pages to find it.

"Ex parte?"

"She took her case to a judge on an emergency basis. He signed the order. Anna's accusing us of causing emotional harm to Emma… because Ben died here. She's been planning this at least since her visit last Christmas." I slid the report across the table. "She arranged to have Emma meet with a guardian ad litem and a psychologist over those last two visits."

Dee started reading.

"Hired guns," I said. "They claim that having Emma live in a house where her father was shot is akin to emotional torture. It's bull-shit, but—"

Dee held up her finger to stop me from talking. Her eyes darted along the sentences as she read. "Emma thinks that you...helped to kill her father?"

"Anna's manipulating her." I slid Emma's affidavit to Dee and waited as she read Emma's words.

When Dee got to the heart of the attack, she began reading aloud. "'I've been living with Mr. Sanden for four years and he treats me like a visitor. I feel no bond...'"

I had read that in the car, rejecting it at first, but I had circled back to it as I drove home. Had I really treated her like that?

Dee spoke in a whisper, all that her body could muster in the moment. "She felt like a visitor here in her own home."

I could tell when she came to the part about Ben's death, because she stopped breathing for a moment, her fingers taking on a slight tremble. Then in a weak voice, she read aloud. "'The Sandens hid the truth about how my father died. They blocked internet sites that covered the story. I believe...'" Dee stopped and looked up at me before reading on. "'I believe Mr. Sanden lured my father to his death. I believe his involvement is why they have worked so hard to keep the truth from me.'"

"She thinks I murdered her father," I said. "Anna's got her all twisted up."

Dee laid the affidavit on the table and closed her eyes, squeezing the tablecloth between her fingers.

"She won't win," I said. "I'm still a damned good lawyer. I'm going to go through the statute with a fine-tooth comb. I'll read every case on the matter. I'll haul Anna in for a deposition—find out exactly how she manipulated Emma. I'll—"

"For Christ's sake, Boady!" Dee shoved the papers off the table. "Do you hear yourself?" She kept her face turned down, unable to look at me as she spoke. "Our daughter was taken from us and you're talking about depositions and discovery."

"There's going to be a hearing. I have to—"

"Stop thinking like a lawyer!"

"But...it's how I—"

"Your daughter has been kidnapped. They did it with a court order, but it's still a kidnapping—and you...you analyze it like you're filing taxes. Where's your anger? Why aren't you breaking things? Emma doesn't need a lawyer. She needs a father."

"But we're not her parents, we're her guardians. The way we get her back is through the law."

Dee looked at me as if I had just punched her in the gut. She shook her head in disbelief. It was only then that I realized what I had said.

"I'm sorry," I said. "I didn't mean it the way—"

She held up her hand to stop me. "Yes, you did. You've always seen Emma as your ward. You fed her, clothed her...put a roof over her head. But she needs more from you than what the law requires. She needs you not just to pay bills but to be a father. You're the only one who can do that. She has no one else."

Rufus waddled into the kitchen and nuzzled into the side of my leg. I reached a hand down and patted. I could think of nothing to say in my defense.

Dee must have sensed my wound because she took my free hand into hers and said, "I know we see this differently—Emma being with us. But you have to understand that she loves you, no matter what she wrote in that stupid affidavit. She still needs you."

"She said she has no bond with me." Those words were hard for me to say aloud.

"When a teenage girl tells you what she wants—listen to her. She said she feels like a guest in our house, so she's telling you that she wants more from you. When she says she doesn't feel a bond..." Dee lifted my hand to her heart. "I promise you, that's exactly what she wants. She wants a father, not a guardian, don't you see that? She wants a family. And if she can't get that here, she'll go to Anna."

I had never imagined I was denying Emma that way. I couldn't see it. "I'll get her back," I whispered. "I promise."

Yet even as I spoke, I looked down at the mess of papers on the floor. I wanted to believe that I could keep my promise to Dee, but a tiny voice whispered that it was already too late.

That night, as Dee lay on Emma's empty bed, I sat at my desk in the study, staring at the corner where Ben Pruitt had been standing when he was shot. I couldn't help thinking about his lies. He had lied about not killing Jennavieve. He had lied about being a good father and loving his daughter. How could he think he was a good man when the rest of the world would see him as a monster for what he had done? I thought of Elijah, who believed himself to be a prophet when everyone else saw him as insane. And then there was me. How could I have been so blind to how I treated Emma? Was Emma's affidavit how the rest of the world saw me?

Rubbing my hands over my eyes, I woke up my computer and found the phone number for Professor David Fitzgerald, a colleague who taught guardianship law. Fitzgerald had guided me through the maze of rules and statutes when we first filed to become Emma's guardians. I was about to hit send when I remembered that Fitzgerald had taken the spring semester off to be with his dying mother. For a second, I considered searching for his mother's obituary—to see if he might now be available to help me. I quickly rejected that ghoulish thought.

Instead, I went to the school website and found the name of his replacement, an adjunct professor named Erica Dennis. No picture, but it said that she was a partner at a firm called Gibson and Price. I called the firm. It was past five o'clock, so I got an automated receptionist telling me that if I wanted to reach Erica Dennis, I should hit 5.

I hit 5, intending to leave a message, but a woman answered.

"This is Erica Dennis." She sounded impatient.

"Um...I wasn't expecting you to be there," I said.

"And yet here I am."

"My name is Boady Sanden. I'm a professor at—"

"Professor Sanden?" The edge in her voice melted away. "I was a student of yours back...six years ago, but I'm sure you don't remember me."

I didn't. Six years? I hadn't realized that she was so young. "You're working late," I said.

"Catching up. Taking over Professor Fitzgerald's classes kind of put me behind."

"I have a question...a situation, really. But I don't want to bother you if..."

"No. I could use the break. What's your...situation?"

"I'm the guardian of a girl and...there's a wrinkle in the case—more than a wrinkle, really...Truth is, it's a complicated mess and I could use some advice. I thought about calling David—um, Professor Fitzgerald, but he's, you know..."

"Would you like to come in?"

"If I could...just to run it by you."

"That's fine." She paused and then said, "How does...say, ten in the morning sound?"

"I don't want to put you out. If you're too busy..."

"It's fine. I'd be happy to help."

"You sure?"

"I'm sure."

"Ten tomorrow, then. Thanks."

I hung up the phone and immediately regretted the call. She was busy, and young, and less experienced than I had expected. I should have asked for a referral.

I decided that I would keep my appointment with Ms. Dennis, but after that, I would call David Fitzgerald and get a referral for someone with a decade or better under their belt, someone with a little gray in their hair. I needed an attorney who could wield the law like a sword, someone who could wreak legal devastation on Anna Adler for what she had done.

I needed someone who would help me get Emma back and fix the mess I had created.

CHAPTER 13

The next morning, I sat alone at my desk watching the clock slowly tick toward my appointment with Erica Dennis. Dee had a day full of showings and had left after breakfast. I leaned back in my chair, put my feet on my desk, and pondered the conversation that I was about to have with Ms. Dennis, the history I would need to dredge up—even though my study was the last place I should have been having such thoughts, because if I looked closely, I could still see where the bullet hole lay hidden behind new plaster and paint. The blood had been cleaned up, but there were times when I swear that I could still smell it. In the quiet of that morning, I felt him there.

Four years ago, Dee and I sat in the back pew at Jennavieve's funeral, the only place in a church where I felt the least bit comfortable, and looked upon Ben and Emma sitting alone in the front. When the service ended, the other mourners gathered in small pockets but kept their distance from Ben. Emma stood at his side, looking lost and numb.

I had gone to Ben, and when I embraced him, he whispered, "You're the only friend I have left. My life is in your hands."

In a matter of days, he would be arrested for Jennavieve's murder. A few months later, he would be dead. But back when he whispered those words to me, I had believed in his innocence with all my heart and soul. I had been willing to wage war to keep him out of prison.

That had all changed when I discovered—mid-trial—that Ben's

alibi had been a lie. I was hurt, but more than that, I was pissed. He had used me, leveraging our friendship to blind me to who he really was. I'd wanted nothing more than to put him in prison where he belonged, keeping him far away from Emma.

As his attorney, though, I had a duty to fight for my client and keep his secrets. And if I was successful in keeping him out of prison, Emma would grow up in the home of a sociopathic murderer. I'd been tormented by the decision I had to make, until I found an archaic ethics rule that charged me with the duty of preventing fraud upon the court. The rule was gray at best and fraught with potential downsides, but I decided to use it to tell the court that Ben had lied on the stand, presented an alibi that wasn't true. My plan would either work or cost me my license and my reputation, but it didn't matter. I was willing to lose everything to make things right.

However, Ben found an entirely different way out. He chose a bullet to the chest so that he would not have to live in a world where Emma knew the evil he had done. I had backed him into a corner, and although I hadn't pulled the trigger, I had been his executioner.

Dee and I had kept these details a secret from Emma at my insistence. I was sure that if we told her the truth, she would hate me. Although I'd never wanted Ben dead, I had done everything I could to make sure he would be out of her life. I had done it for Emma, but how do you explain that to a grieving child?

Movement in the corner of the study pulled at my attention. I expected to see Rufus circling the floor looking for a place to lie down. Instead, I was startled to see a man rising up to stand before me, blood dripping down his shirt. *Ben.* His eyes hollow, his cheeks gaunt. He touched the hole in his chest and whispered, "My life was in your hands...and you did this?"

I woke with a start, my feet still propped up on my desk, my heart thumping in my chest. The room was empty. How long had

I been asleep? Panicked that I might be late for my appointment with Ms. Dennis, I looked at my watch. Only fifteen minutes had passed.

I still had time to kill before my meeting, but I decided to spend that time driving around with the windows down. I couldn't stay in this study a second longer. I packed the guardianship documents into my briefcase, next to my file on Elijah Matthews, and left.

Gibson and Price, attorneys-at-law, occupied a corner space on the thirtieth floor of the IDS Center, a skyscraper of glass and light. I was met by a receptionist who offered me coffee or water. I declined both and took a seat to wait.

A couple minutes later a young woman came to the reception area and held out her hand. "Professor Sanden, it's good to see you again."

I tried to remember her from my class, but nothing clicked. She was tall with the strong build of a powerlifter beneath a black business suit. She wore her long brown hair pulled back in a ponytail, and very little makeup. I replied with a simple "Hello."

She led me down a short hallway lined with doors, bronze name-plates listing the attorneys and staff as we passed. In her office she waved me to a chair and circled around to the business side of her desk.

"So, you have a guardianship you need help with," she said.

"I just need someone to take a look at it," I said, pulling the papers from my briefcase. "Maybe steer me in the right direction. I handled the initial guardianship myself, but Professor Fitzgerald walked me through it."

Erica started reading.

"Her name is Emma," I said. "She's been with my wife and me for just under four years now. Her father transferred temporary custody to us when he was being investigated for the death of Emma's mother.

It was an unusual circumstance to say the least. A few months later, when he died, we filed for guardianship. The order was signed—"

Erica held up a hand to quiet me and kept reading. Then she looked up. "They are accusing you of being complicit in the death of Emma's father. Let's start there."

During my drive, I had rehearsed a nutshell version of my history with Ben. It flowed out of my mouth with ease—until I came to the hard part.

"Emma's mother was found dead in an alley...stabbed. Ben was at a conference in Chicago when it happened—or so it seemed. We were on the cusp of winning the case when I discovered that his alibi was a lie. When he knew that I knew, he came to my home—to my study. He brought a gun."

"This is the same house where you now live...where you were raising Emma?"

"Yes."

She nodded. "Go on."

"Ben wanted to keep me quiet about what I knew. It was...bizarre, to tell you the truth. We sat together like old friends, calm as can be, as he threatened to kill me. What Ben didn't know was that my law clerk had been outside my house when he arrived. She saw that he had a gun and she called a friend of mine, a cop."

"So at this point it was just you and Ben in your house?"

"Yes, my wife was out of town."

"Okay."

"Well, I faced the door and saw my friend, the cop, sneak in. When I think back...if I had said something...maybe I could have convinced Ben to surrender. All I had to do was keep my head; but I didn't. Ben took a bullet to the chest. He shot at the cop from point-blank range, but he missed on purpose. I think he wanted to die rather than go to prison."

"And you never told Emma about this?"

"No."

"Why not?"

I had prepared an answer to that question, but in the moment, I couldn't find it. Finally, I said, "Every time I think about what happened that night...I can't help but feel responsible for Ben's death. I think, deep down, there's a part of me that wanted Ben to die—or at least felt that he deserved it. I could have stopped it from happening but didn't."

Erica put the petition down, leaned back in her chair, and steepled her index fingers to her lips. She studied me for a bit before saying, "He had a gun, right?"

"He did."

"Had he threatened you with that gun?"

"He wanted to work out a deal to keep me quiet."

"That sounds like a threat to me."

"Yes, but...I don't think that he would ever have pulled that trigger. A simple word from me might have saved his life."

"Ben killed his wife. Did you know Ben well enough to see that coming?"

"I guess not."

"You were under threat. It sounds to me like you are blameless in what happened to Ben."

"I appreciate that, but I don't feel absolved."

"The bigger problem is the house. You're raising Emma in a house where her father was killed. They can't attack your guardianship without proof of emotional, psychological, or physical harm. Raising her in that house...You see how this is going to play out, right?"

I knew exactly what Erica was saying, but my home on Summit Avenue was more than just a house. I had been raised in a shack in the hills of Missouri by a widowed mother who could barely keep food on the table. Now I lived on the same street as the governor. I counted the city's finest among my neighbors. My house had become a trophy, my reward for years of struggle.

But more than that, many of my best and worst memories were in that house. The heartbreak of our miscarriages balanced against the joy of having Emma in our lives. I knew there were problems with staying there, but somehow, deep down, I felt that leaving the house would mean leaving those memories—good and bad.

In my silence, Erica continued, "The house is going to be a concern."

"What about the case?" I asked. "If you were in my shoes, how would you proceed?"

"I can't formulate a plan until I've read all of the documents."

"You have the gist. I just need a little guidance. I can do the legwork."

"I'm sorry, Professor, but I think we need to get something clear. I don't guide people. If I take a case, it's my case. I call the shots. That's non-negotiable." She held up the papers. "This is going to be a hand-to-hand combat, and if you want me with you, you'll have to trust me. I get the reins or I don't take the case."

My first thought, fair or not, was that Erica was far too young. I wanted gray hair and tweed. I wanted a grizzled general, not a fresh-faced lieutenant. She had been a student of mine a mere six years ago. How much could she know?

My second thought was that she was tough. She held my eyes as she told me that she wouldn't allow me—a law professor—to interfere with her strategy. I had given that same speech more times than I cared to remember back when I had a private practice. It was a speech born of confidence.

I slowly rose from my chair and extended my hand. "Ms. Dennis, the case is yours if you're willing to take it."

She shook my hand. "I'll do a good job for you, Professor Sanden."

"Please, call me Boady."

"If you call me Erica."

I sat back down and I asked, "So, what's next?"

She stacked the papers together as she spoke. "You have the right to challenge the ex parte order. They've set a hearing date for Monday to give you your due process review. I'd like to look this over before I say what our strategy might be for that hearing."

"There's something you should know about Anna Adler," I said. "She's got money—lots of it. She's going to throw everything she has at you, so be ready."

"This won't be the first time I've battled Goliath," she said.

"What should Dee and I be doing?"

Erica thought for a second and said, "We'll need a psychologist to review their expert's report."

"Dr. Mochol," I said. "Dee and I consulted with her when we first became Emma's guardians. She can be brought up to speed in no time."

"That's a start," Erica said. "Let's meet again tomorrow. I need time to go over these documents to get a full picture. Can you come back tomorrow morning?"

"That works."

"What about for your wife?"

"I hadn't planned on bringing her," I said. "The law's kind of my arena."

"Bring your wife," Erica said. "This is all hands on deck. She needs to know what we're up against."

There was a part of me that wanted to spare Dee from the battle I saw coming. But there was another part of me that was afraid she too would blame me by the end. What if Dee saw that I was at the center of all our problems? The thought of not measuring up in my wife's eyes was hard to face.

In the end, I am a man of many faults, but pride has never been one of them. I would give Erica control of the case, allow her to dig up the good alongside the bad, and let the chips fall where they may. If I was truly at fault, Dee had a right to know.

"She'll be here," I said.

CHAPTER 14

I gave thought to calling Dee and telling her about my meeting with Erica, but what was there to tell? Instead, I texted her a short message:

> Met with attorney. She needs to read the paperwork
> and get up to speed. I'll fill you in when you get home

But once back in the halls of our house, I felt restless. I remembered I had a few Criminal Procedure exams yet to grade, so I settled into my study once again. Like Scrooge dismissing his first spectral visitor, I reassured myself that I was alone. No Ben. No smell of blood. I finished the exams in a little over an hour.

Next, I spread Elijah's file out across my desk. I ran an internet search for Pastor Jalen Bale and found pictures of his church in Minnetonka, a huge building with no steeples or stained-glass windows, and an auditorium with a large stage instead of a sanctuary. The place looked more like a conference center than a church.

As for Pastor Bale, he had been a handsome man, midforties, tall, dark hair, Clark Kent chin, and a smile that seemed to emanate its own light. I found a video of him preaching from that stage, his eyes dancing over the audience, his voice resonating like low-rolling thunder. A toll-free phone number flashed along the bottom of the screen, asking for donations. Tiny beads of sweat trickling down his temple accentuated his fervor as his speech climbed toward a crescendo.

"That's not me talking—that's God! God is the one telling you that you can have abundance. You can have health and prosperity. But God's blessing doesn't come without sacrifice. You must do the work to prove yourself. The Gospel of Mark tells us that anyone who leaves home for Jesus will receive much more in return; that's God's promise to you. How much more? Mark answers that too. God will return to you one hundred times more than what you give."

He stopped and looked directly at the camera, his face glowing with rapture. "One hundred times what you give...that is what God has promised to you. And he will deliver—just as sure as I'm standing here today. But it has to start with you. You have to prove to God that you are willing to give of yourself. You have to give—"

I clicked off the video and scrolled online until I found another picture of Bale, a much younger version: blue jeans and a collared shirt, his hair poorly trimmed, standing with four other people, all holding shovels. Two men in suits stood to his left, and to his right a woman and a young man. The caption beneath read: *GROUND BREAKING FOR NEW CHURCH.*

The article explained that Jalen Bale, a pastor who operated a homeless shelter in South St. Paul, was expanding his shelter to add on a new chapel. The article identified the two men in suits as being members of the South St. Paul Council. The young man to Bale's right was Lucas Mammon, a former resident of the homeless shelter who was now studying to become a minister himself. The woman, similar in age to Pastor Bale, was identified as Lilith Cain, a philanthropist who had purchased the land for the church. Something about that name sounded familiar, but I couldn't place it. A second picture further down in the article showed Lilith Cain talking to the council members, holding an infant in her arms.

Then I remembered that Mammon and Cain had both been witnesses at Elijah's trial. I clicked back and forth between the two pictures of Jalen Bale, one from the homeless shelter and one from the megachurch. They were the same man, yet they weren't.

Next, I played a CD from the file. According to the investigator's report, that CD contained a video providing Elijah's motive for Bale's murder. It began with Pastor Bale preaching a similar sermon. In this video Bale looked far less shiny. His clothing hung loose on his frame, his shirt was wrinkled, and he was pale, with subtle rings under his eyes, as if he hadn't been sleeping well. He struggled to stay on message.

"You have to know that the Lord will...He will give you abundance, just as Malachi said, but you have to do your part. You have to...It's all about tithes...That's where it all comes from. Malachi...he said...he said, 'Bring the full amount of your tithes to the temple.' He said...'Put me to the test...I will open the windows of Heaven and pour out on you in abundance all kinds of good things.'"

Bale paused to lick his lips and wipe sweat from his forehead. When he spoke again, his words were rote, like a child saying a nightly prayer that he didn't understand. "Just put God to the test. But you have to...It's all about your tithes. You can't expect God to do his part if you don't..."

That's when the camera shifted to stage left. Elijah Matthews, dressed in coveralls like a janitor, climbed up from the audience and pointed his finger at Pastor Bale. "Have you not heard the cry of your God?" he said, his voice far louder and more powerful than I would have expected from such a small man. "He has sent you a prophet. I have come to warn you to give up your evil ways and do what is right."

Bale stared at Elijah, suddenly speechless, like a man who had just come face-to-face with his executioner.

"You are forcing God to bring upon you the destruction he has promised."

Bale's stance went slack. A stagehand wearing a headset entered from the wing and grabbed Elijah by the shoulders. Elijah yelled, "You know how to make it right, Jalen Bale. You know what must be done."

A second stagehand came out of the shadows and took ahold of Elijah's arm, and the two men pulled him backward. But Elijah never took his eyes off Bale, yelling, "You are a false prophet. You have displeased the Lord."

Bale remained on stage for several seconds, his eyes glistening with tears, spittle webbing his lips. Another stagehand walked over, put an arm around Pastor Bale, and escorted him to the wing. The video ended.

I tucked the CD back into its case and pulled out a stack of police reports.

The first report I read came from the Hennepin County crime lab, analyzing the DNA profiles found on the murder weapon. Pastor Jalen Bale had been struck twice in the head with a stone, rectangular like a brick, only a bit larger. The stone had been taken from the debris of the old homeless shelter that Bale had operated in his younger days. Elijah had brought the stone to Bale at his new church, a strange sort of calling card, and used the connection to get a job on the maintenance staff. Witnesses said that Bale kept the stone on his credenza as a souvenir of those old days. The lab had pulled three DNA profiles from the stone, all epithelial—skin cells. One matched Jalen Bale, one was Elijah's, and the third had never been identified.

Ben had scribbled a couple notes in the margin: **Alternative killer** and **Reasonable doubt?**

"At least you weren't completely phoning it in," I said out loud.

I looked at the chair on the other side of my desk, the same chair where Ben had sat on the night he died. I pictured him watching me dig through his file, his gun resting on his lap, a sad smile on his face.

"You used to be a good attorney," I said to the chair, "a decent human being. What happened to you?" I couldn't stop myself from getting angry at him.

Next, I found a police report that mentioned that besides killing Bale, the murderer stole the preacher's laptop. Again, Ben Pruitt had scratched a small note in the margin: **A prophet in need of a computer?**

"Did you follow up?" I looked up to ask the empty chair. "Did you do an investigation? You didn't give a damn about Elijah Matthews. It was all about you."

I found another note written in an interview with a witness named Ray Gideon, a retired cop from North Dakota. He had been the one to find Bale dead. He told investigators that Bale had invited him to his office that night, but the lead detective found no evidence of any such appointment.

Ben's note read: **Do you have a motive, Mr. Gideon?**

"Did he?" I asked.

Ben didn't answer my question.

"You really fucked this up," I said. "Too busy planning Jennavieve's murder to put any time into it, I guess. Did you come to me for help because we were friends? Or because I would believe your bullshit story? And you brought Emma into it, leverage to keep me on your side. You used me."

The next report I read was from the blood spatter expert. This was powerful evidence for the State. Bale had written Elijah's name in blood as he lay dying. Had I been on the jury, I'm not sure if Elijah's potential alibi would have mattered.

In the margin, Ben had drawn two stick figures, one on his hands and knees, his melon head gushing droplets, the second standing behind the first, arms raised high to wield the stone.

The crude sketch made me even angrier. This was where Ben had put his limited energy—drawing? "Did you know that Emma could draw too?" I asked the imaginary Ben. "Did you know that she worshipped the ground you walked on? You could have divorced Jennavieve—walked away broke, sure, but with Emma. How could I not see your greed—your selfishness—all along?"

If Ben was in the room with me, he had no answers to my questions.

"I might be a lousy guardian, but you...you were a lousy father... and a lousy friend." I raised the blood spatter report in my hand. "And you were an absolute shit of a lawyer."

My voice echoed into silence. I was alone.

CHAPTER 15

<u>**Direct examination of Ralph Forsyth by
Ms. Addams, cont.**</u>

Addams: Mr. Forsyth, as an expert in blood
spatter evidence, were you able to
determine—to a reasonable degree of
scientific certainty—where the killer
would have been standing in relation
to the victim when the first blow was
struck?

Forsyth: Yes.

Addams: And could you explain that to the jury?

Forsyth: The cast-off blood from the murder
weapon left a line on the ceiling. This
would have been caused by the killer
raising the stone for that second blow.
The line is directly behind Pastor

Bale's desk, consistent with him sitting in the chair.

Addams: Anything else?

Forsyth: Yes. I found cast-off blood spatter on the desk, on the floor, and on the credenza behind the desk. When those droplets are mapped out, there are two places within that radius where there are none. There were none on the seat of the victim's chair, which indicate that he was sitting in that chair at the time of the attack. And there was no cast-off on the credenza directly behind the chair. That would be explained by the killer standing directly behind the victim at the time of the attack. The killer's body would have blocked spatter from landing on that section of the credenza.

Addams: So it's your testimony that the killer stood directly behind Mr. Bale when the blows were struck?

Forsyth: That's what the pattern of the spatter indicates.

Addams: Let's talk about the blood on the floor. Pastor Bale was found facedown behind his desk, his head in a pool of blood, is that right?

Forsyth: Yes.

Addams: But he had managed to write the name of his attacker—

Pruitt: Objection. Calls for a conclusion beyond the foundation of this witness.

Court: Sustained.

Addams: Okay, Mr. Forsyth, when you examined the body at the scene, was there anything unusual about the pattern of the blood around him?

Forsyth: Yes. The name Elijah had been written on the floor in the victim's blood.

Addams: Where in relation to the body?

Forsyth: Right next to the body.

Addams: Within an arm's length?

Forsyth: Easily.

Addams: Anything else?

Forsyth: There were drag marks, smears of

blood that suggest that the victim had attempted to pull himself up. The short length of those drag marks indicate that he had pulled himself only a few inches before either quitting or becoming unable to move any farther.

Addams: What did you conclude from that?

Forsyth: That it was likely that Mr. Bale was alive for a short period of time after he fell to the floor.

Addams: Let's talk about the name Elijah being written in the victim's blood. Did you uncover any evidence to indicate who wrote that name?

Forsyth: It appeared to have been written by the victim himself using his right index finger.

Addams: And how did you come to that conclusion?

Forsyth: The victim had cast-off on the back of his hands—looks kind of like tiny freckles—but his right index finger was completely covered in blood. Think of dipping a quill into an inkwell. It's consistent with the victim using his right index finger to write that name.

Addams: Were the victim's fingerprints found in
           the smear of letters in that name?

Forsyth: We were able to match fingerprints
           on the letters E, I, A, and H to the
           victim's right index finger.

Addams: And when, in relation to the attack,
           would the name Elijah have been written
           in the victim's blood?

Forsyth: Immediately after the attack.

Addams: And how can you tell that?

Forsyth: The blow to the head sent small
           droplets of blood spatter to the floor.
           Those thin droplets dry rather quickly,
           especially around the edges. Had the
           name been written more than a couple
           minutes after the initial attack, we
           would have found evidence of dried
           edges beneath the lettering of the
           name. We found none, which indicated
           that the blood spatter was still fresh
           and wet when the name was written.

Addams: Did you see any indication that someone
           other than the victim wrote that name
           Elijah in blood on the floor?

Forsyth: We looked for evidence that the

attacker used Mr. Bale's hand to write the name, but found none. As I said, the blows to the head caused a freckling of spatter on the back of the victim's hands. If an attacker held the victim's hand to write that name, we would expect those droplets to be smeared. We found no such smears on the back of the hand or around the index finger itself.

Addams: So to sum up, the evidence is consistent with Mr. Bale writing the name Elijah on the floor and inconsistent with the attacker using Mr. Bale's finger to write that name.

Forsyth: That is correct.

Addams: Thank you. I have no further questions.

Cross-examination of Ralph Forsyth by Mr. Pruitt.

Pruitt: Mr. Forsyth, is it *possible* that the attacker wrote that name but had been careful not to put a blood smear on the back of Mr. Bale's hand?

Forsyth: There was a lot of blood.

Pruitt: Please listen to my question, Mr.

Forsyth. Is it *possible* that a careful attacker could have written that name without leaving blood smears on Mr. Bale's hand or finger?

Forsyth: It would be nearly impossible.

Pruitt: Nearly impossible is not the same as impossible.

Forsyth: I suppose you could say that.

Pruitt: So you cannot rule out that his attacker wrote that name to throw off investigators.

Forsyth: Not completely, but it's highly—

Pruitt: And it's your testimony that Pastor Bale was struck on the back of his head while sitting at his desk?

Forsyth: That's what the evidence supports.

Pruitt: Mr. Forsyth, if you were in your office, sitting at your desk, and a man who had threatened to kill you walked in, would you remain sitting at your desk and allow that man to walk behind you where he could—

Addams: Objection. Argumentative.

Court: I'll sustain that objection.

Pruitt: I have no further questions, Your
            Honor.

Addams: Redirect, Your Honor?

Court: Go ahead.

Redirect examination of Ralph Forsyth by Ms. Addams.

Addams: Mr. Forsyth, if I were to toss a nickel
            in the air—just one toss—and let it
            fall to the floor, would you agree that
            it is theoretically possible for that
            nickel to land on its edge?

Forsyth: Theoretically possible...I guess so,
            but in reality, it would be nearly
            impossible for that to happen.

Addams: And the suggestion by Mr. Pruitt,
            that the killer used the victim's
            finger to write that name in blood
            without smearing any of those blood
            freckles, would that also be "nearly
            impossible"?

Forsyth: Yes, it would be nearly impossible.

Addams: No further questions.

CHAPTER 16

After lunch, I drove out to Jalen Bale's megachurch.

My understanding of what a church should look like is drawn from my Catholic school days, where statues of Jesus and the Virgin Mary stared down at me as I fought to stay awake, where stained-glass windows cast prismatic light upon the altar, pulpit, and the ornately carved wooden confessionals. It had impressed upon my young mind an air of majesty and awe. But even as a child, I'd struggled to reconcile the extravagant beauty with the message about a carpenter who wore rags and sandals.

Jalen Bale's megachurch, however, was a whole new level of brash. Above the entrance, eight-foot-tall golden letters on a wall of royal blue invited me into the Church of the New Hope. Granite steps with gold handrails led up to four sets of enormous double doors. As with the churches of my youth, standing before them I felt small—David standing before Goliath, desperately digging in my pocket for a sling.

I climbed the steps, opened one of the doors, and stepped inside what looked like a convention center. A hallway twenty feet wide stretched out in front of me, lined on one side with booths advertising merchandise: DVDs, Bibles, clothing, books, and something called Healing Spirits. At the end were a set of restrooms and an elevator.

On the other side, a wall of doors curved along what had to be the back side of the auditorium. Signs above the doors announced section numbers along with short messages like *Serve God* and *Give to Be Blessed*.

Life-size pictures of the new pastor, Lucas Mammon, hung in the spaces between the doors. I wouldn't have recognized him as the young man holding a shovel in the photo of the ground-breaking ceremony had his name not accompanied the posters. He was older, sure, but it was more than that. This Pastor Mammon had a smaller nose, a bolder chin, and capped teeth.

I hadn't called ahead. I didn't want to explain my visit or give anyone time to prepare for my questions. I wanted to see facial expressions when I announced that I was reopening the murder investigation.

The building was eerily quiet except for the distant whir of an electric motor coming from the auditorium. I peeked inside. Four thousand seats fanned out in a semicircle around an extravagant, multilayered stage, a circular section in the center jutting out so that the preacher could walk out high above his flock. Blue carpeting covered the stage and a bright purple proscenium arch framed it. On either side of the stage, large TV screens offered a zoomed-in view for those in the cheap seats.

In the aisle ahead of me, an older man ran a vacuum cleaner. I caught his attention, and he turned it off, giving his back a stretch. He said nothing as I made my way toward him.

"Excuse me." My voice sounded small in the emptiness of the auditorium. "I was hoping to see Pastor Mammon. I don't suppose you could point me in the right direction?"

"Ain't my job," the man said.

"Well, it's kind of important that I see him."

"You and everyone else. Sorry, I can't help you."

"If I take the elevator, would that—"

"No one's allowed upstairs unless they was invited. You want to see the pastor, you'll have to give him a call."

My plan to catch Mammon off guard was losing steam. I grasped at a straw. "Did you work with Elijah Matthews?"

The man's features sharpened as he appraised me anew. "Who wants to know?"

"My name's Boady Sanden. I'm with the Innocence Project. I'm looking into the death of Pastor Bale."

"Innocence Project?" He put his vacuum aside and stepped closer. "You think…maybe Elijah didn't kill Pastor Bale?"

"Tell me about Elijah?"

The man looked around as though there was a chance someone might be listening. "He was a good guy. A little screwy in the head, but that don't make him bad, just different—special, you know?"

"Special how?"

The man stared at me for a long time before asking, "Are you really here to help Elijah?"

"If I can."

He leaned in. "What if I was to tell you that Elijah could see things…like the future and stuff."

I didn't allow a single facial muscle to twitch. The slightest show of incredulity might send the rabbit running. "What did he see?" I asked.

"One day, we was cleaning tile in the men's room and he says to me, he says, 'Lawrence'—that's me, I'm Lawrence. He says, 'If you seek your happiness in the Lord, He will give you your heart's desire.' Just out of the blue like that. That's from the Bible—Psalms—did you know that?"

"No, I didn't."

"Neither did I, until Elijah told me it was."

"And?"

"I'll be honest with you: When Elijah first came here, I couldn't understand why Pastor Bale took him on. I mean, he was an okay worker, but he was always quoting the Bible and stuff. Couldn't hold a conversation with the guy because nothing he said made sense. I'd say, 'Did you clean up that mess in the men's room?' and he would say, 'I have sprinkled clean water upon it and cleansed it of all its filthiness.' I mean, who talks like that? But when he said that thing to me about finding my heart's desire..."

Something held Lawrence back from saying more. He studied me, maybe hoping to glean from my demeanor whether he should finish his story. Apparently I passed his test.

"Do you believe in miracles, Mister?"

I knew that our conversation would end if I answered truthfully, so I lied. "I do."

Lawrence nodded as if to seal our bond. "That night, I was walking to a bar, and along the way I passed a small church...just a beat-up old thing. Must have passed it a thousand times before. It had this flower box that was falling off the front, and I decided that night to stop and tack it back on. You know, make it halfway presentable. When I finished, I heard a woman inside singing a hymn. It was the prettiest thing I'd ever heard. I couldn't help myself. I went in and took a seat in the back. The place was empty except for that woman sitting at the piano up front. When she saw me, she invited me to come sit with her."

A sheepish grin lifted Lawrence's face and his eyes glistened like he was a child opening a present. "That woman," he said, "she's my wife now."

"And you think Elijah did that?"

"I don't know. Maybe. I mean, how do you explain it? I'm fifty-two years old. I've been alone all my life. Then Elijah says what he says... that I'm going to find my heart's desire and such, and bam! So...yeah, I think there was something at work there. I don't know how, but he said it would happen and it did. No one in the world has to believe it but me...but I do believe it. That's all that matters."

"Do you think that Elijah killed Pastor Bale?"

Lawrence shook his head slowly. "Elijah's a kind man, as peaceful as any man walking this earth. He wouldn't harm a hair on your head. No, I don't think he killed Pastor Bale."

"Well, I'm here to try and prove that. I would really love to have a chat with Pastor Mammon, but..."

"You think talking to Pastor Mammon might help Elijah?"

"I have to start somewhere. Can you help me?"

I could almost see the debate taking place behind Lawrence's eyes. Once he made up his mind, he said, "I can point you in the right direction, but after that, you're on your own."

"I'll take that," I said.

He led me out of the auditorium and to the elevator. When the door opened, he waved me inside. "Pastor Mammon's office is to the right when you get off the elevator. Do me a favor and don't tell him we talked. I can get in trouble."

"No problem."

"I hope you can help him," Lawrence said. "Elijah, I mean."

"I hope so too."

As the doors shut, I saw Lawrence close his eyes, his lips moving as if in silent prayer.

CHAPTER 17

The elevator opened to a small sitting area—a leather sofa, a smattering of chairs, and a coffee table. To my left a hallway ran the length of the building with office doors staggered along both sides. To my right were a set of glass doors with *Pastor Lucas Mammon* stenciled on them. Beyond the glass I could see an empty receptionist desk and the door to Mammon's inner office. The receptionist's desk looked more like a display model than an actual workstation: no computer screen, no pens, no papers.

I walked through the outer office and knocked on Mammon's door. First came silence, then an invitation that sounded like a question: "Come in?"

The office was like no pastor's office I had ever seen—or imagined. Enormous, nearly the size of half a tennis court, it had wood-coffered ceilings and an Oriental rug that probably cost as much as my car. Windows looked out over a courtyard full of summer flowers, and a packed mahogany bookshelf ran the length of the room. Mammon sat behind a desk big enough to hold a queen-size mattress, its wood shining with polish. Behind him a credenza held pictures of him posing with politicians and actors.

"Can I help you?" he asked.

"I apologize for coming unannounced, but I happened to be in the neighborhood. I'm Boady Sanden." I approached and held out my hand. He neither stood nor extended his hand to shake, so I withdrew the offer. "I'm on the board of the Innocence Project. I was hoping we could chat."

"The Innocence Project? That group that undoes criminal convictions?"

"*Wrongful* criminal convictions," I corrected.

"How did you get up here? We're closed."

"The door to the church was open. I was wandering around until I found the elevator. I figured I might have better luck up here."

Mammon picked up his phone and dialed. "Lawrence, did you know the entrance is unlocked?"

Pause.

"Tell them to take their deliveries around back."

Pause.

"I don't care. We can't be leaving the doors unlocked. Any bum off the street could walk in and rob us blind." He hung up the phone and narrowed his gaze on me. "If you're looking for a donation, I don't handle those things. You'll have to make an appointment with Mrs. Cain."

"I'm looking into the death of Pastor Bale. May I sit?" He didn't move, so I helped myself to one of the visitors' chairs.

"I don't understand," he said. "It's an open-and-shut case."

"Something came up."

Mammon leaned forward. I had his interest. "Something like what?"

He was like a fish considering a worm. I could use that curiosity. "I have a few questions." I reached into my pocket and pulled out the picture from the ground-breaking ceremony, laying it on the desk in front of him. "Could you tell me a little bit about Jalen Bale?"

When Mammon saw the old picture, his eyes went soft. He gently picked it up. "Where'd you get this?"

"Internet."

"We were so young...so clearheaded."

"Can you tell me about the Jalen Bale in that picture?"

"We were building an addition to the homeless shelter. We built a bigger kitchen and new showers. We added a chapel to get the tax breaks."

"Is that where you met Pastor Bale?"

"I met Jalen..." He settled back into his chair and stared at the picture in his hand. "I had been homeless, a dumb kid with issues: drugs, alcohol, gambling. I'd hocked my dad's golf clubs to pay off a debt, so he kicked me out. I didn't have anywhere to go. It was winter. I was cold and hungry." Mammon held the photo as though it were a sacred text. "Jalen took me in and we became friends."

"If you don't mind my asking, how does a homeless shelter in South St. Paul grow into this?" I motioned around me.

Mammon turned the picture around and pointed at the woman standing next to him. "That's Lilith Cain. She put up a lot of the money, and what she didn't have, she found. She's a hell of a fundraiser. After we added that chapel, Jalen started preaching instead of just feeding people. He could really fill the seats. Lilith saw his potential and pushed him to get bigger and better. Five years later, we broke ground here. This is her show."

"She sounds driven."

"The most dangerous place in the world is between Lilith Cain and what she wants. You've heard of her, right? Her husband, Ed, went to prison for defrauding folks in a Ponzi scheme."

Ah yes. Not only did the name ring a bell, but he had been a footnote in a lecture I taught about restitution. Ed Cain had cheated people out of tens of millions of dollars selling stocks in a fund that he artificially inflated. He robbed Peter to pay Paul, but kept most of the money for himself. The feds tried to grab back as much as they could after he was convicted, but they recovered less than half.

"His wife built this place?"

"We all built it," he said, with a touch of irritation. "But she was the driving force. She can raise money like nobody I know. I guess she wanted to make things right, after what her husband did."

"So, what did you bring to the table?"

Mammon shifted uncomfortably in his seat. "I'm just here to do God's work."

A plaque on the wall behind Mammon read that he had received a Certificate of Theology from Liberty University, probably an online course. I recalled reading somewhere in the file that Jalen Bale had a master's degree in divinity from Rutgers.

"You took over after Jalen died?"

"I did."

"That must have been quite a step up for you."

"Jalen was my friend."

"I'm just trying to understand the dynamics."

"The dynamics? Jalen was killed by a mentally deranged man named Elijah Matthews. Those are the dynamics."

"Tell me about Elijah."

Mammon's tone turned sharp. "Did you know that Elijah brought the murder weapon here? A stone from the homeless shelter. He used Jalen's memory of the old days to soften him up. That's the only reason Jalen gave him the job. Then Elijah killed him with that very brick."

"According to the reports, the killer stood behind Bale and struck the fatal blow. But there's a video showing Elijah calling Bale a false prophet. Does it make sense to you that Bale would let Elijah into his office if there was tension between them?"

"I never understood the connection between them. Jalen used to sit here with Elijah for hours, talking, debating back and forth. After Elijah jumped up on stage and threatened Jalen, I told Jalen we should fire him, but Jalen seemed to…I don't know…It was almost as if Jalen felt he needed Elijah. It was like Elijah was Jalen's personal Rasputin."

"In the video—from that day Elijah jumped up on stage—Bale seemed a little…out of sorts."

"Out of sorts doesn't come close. The more time he spent with Elijah, the more depressed he got. Jalen used to love preaching, but toward the end there he didn't have the heart for it. He was saying the words, but...if you don't put your heart and soul into it, they're just words."

"And you think Elijah caused that?"

"What else? If Jalen had listened to me and fired that nutjob, none of this would have happened."

"Do you know what they talked about?"

"Jalen never said...but..."

"But?"

"A week before Elijah killed him, Jalen asked me to dig up an old file full of promotional stuff that me and Lilith had put together back at the shelter. We'd made this video to take to organizations like the United Way—show them the kind of work we were doing."

"Did he say why he wanted it?"

"He said that he was doing Elijah's work. That's why I remember it. I mean, a pastor doing the work of a janitor."

"Would you mind if I took a look at that file?"

"Don't think it still exists. I cleaned out the desk when I moved in. I mean...there was no point in keeping Jalen's stuff here. I gave it to the maintenance staff. They probably tossed it."

"Would you mind checking?"

Mammon glared at me and I held his gaze. Then he picked up his phone and dialed. "Lawrence, could you come up here?"

Pause.

"Thanks."

As we waited for Lawrence, I stood and walked to the wall of books and ran a finger along some of the spines: *Hermeneutics on Old and New Testament, Greek Translation of the Gospels, Exegesis of the Letters of Paul.* Every book had a thin layer of dust on top. They were books for show, not reading was my guess.

"It's quite a collection," I said.

"Thank you." He sounded tired of my presence.

"I read the apocryphal gospels some years back. I found the Gospel of Thomas particularly interesting. I don't suppose you could recommend a good treatise on the subject?"

"None come to mind."

I pulled a book off the shelf—the title *The New Testament Apocrypha*. "You have one right here," I said.

He looked at me like I had just spit in his punch bowl, his lip curled up, his nose wrinkled. "Those are Jalen's books—and no, I haven't read them. I don't have the big brain that Jalen had, but I'm a damned good preacher. If you watch my videos you'd see."

"I didn't mean anything—"

A knock at the door and Lawrence entered.

Mammon said, "Lawrence, remember when we cleaned out Pastor Bale's things?"

"Yes," Lawrence answered.

"That stuff got thrown away, didn't it?"

"Um...no, sir. I put it in storage."

Mammon paused, took a breath, and appeared to swallow a knot of irritation. He forced a smile onto his face. "When you have time, I'd like you to find a file, one of those accordion ones. It has the word *Promotions* written on the front. Could you dig that out for Mr....I'm sorry, what was your name?"

"Sanden," I said.

"Mr. Sanden would like to take a look at it."

"Sure thing."

"Get to it when you can."

Lawrence backed out of the office like a peasant exiting the court of a king.

"I'm sure there's nothing of value in there, but I'll call you when he finds it."

"I appreciate that," I said.

"Just tell me one thing...Why are you opening up an old wound? Elijah Matthews threatened Jalen. Everybody saw it. Jalen wrote Elijah's name in his blood as he lay dying. That seems pretty cut-and-dried."

"And yet it's not."

"Based on what?"

"I'm afraid I can't discuss any new evidence."

"Jalen was my friend. If it wasn't for him, I wouldn't be where I am."

"You wouldn't be pastor...sitting at his desk, staring at his books?"

Mammon's cheeks flushed red. "I think we're done here."

"For now." I took the picture of the ground-breaking ceremony off the desk, turned my back on Lucas Mammon, and walked out of his palatial office.

Back on the ground floor, I found Lawrence waiting for me next to one of the merchandise kiosks.

"I get the feeling you're looking to kick a hornet's nest," he said.

"If it helps me find the truth, yes."

"You think that file I'm digging up might have something in it to help Elijah?"

"I don't know. It's something Pastor Bale was working on just before he got killed. It may mean nothing, but then again..."

"I'll get it for you," he said.

I dug an old business card from my wallet and handed it to him. "When you find it, maybe give me a call. I would hate to see that file accidentally get destroyed."

Lawrence looked at my card and nodded. "I'll do that," he said.

CHAPTER 18

Cross-examination of Lucas Mammon by Mr. Pruitt.

Pruitt: Mr. Mammon, can you account for your whereabouts on the night that Jalen Bale was killed?

Mammon: *Pastor* Mammon.

Pruitt: Excuse me?

Mammon: I'm Pastor Mammon, not Mr.

Pruitt: That's right. And you became pastor after Jalen Bale was murdered.

Mammon: Well...I wouldn't put it that way.

Pruitt: Had Pastor Bale not died, would you be the pastor at the Church of the New Hope?

Mammon: No, but—

Pruitt: Where were you on the night of the
           murder?

Mammon: I'm not...I came here to testify about
           the friction between Pastor Bale
           and Elijah. I didn't think I would
           be asked...I mean...how is that
           relevant?

Pruitt: Your Honor, would you instruct the
           witness to answer the question?

Court: The witness will answer counsel's
           question.

Mammon: I was home watching TV.

Pruitt: Alone?

Mammon: Yes, alone.

Pruitt: You have no witnesses to corroborate
           that.

Mammon: Why would I need to corroborate
           anything?

Pruitt: And do you still live at that house...
           the one where you were home alone,
           watching TV?

Mammon: I don't understand.

Pruitt: If you went home...to your house to watch TV after you testify here...would it be the same house?

Mammon: No.

Pruitt: Isn't it true that you moved into a new house just three months after Pastor Bale was murdered?

Mammon: Well...yeah, but—

Pruitt: A house four times larger than the one you had been living in?

Mammon: I don't see what that's got to do with—

Pruitt: Did you pay for that house?

Mammon: The church owns it.

Pruitt: Does the church own any other houses?

Mammon: It owns Mrs. Cain's house.

Pruitt: The church also owns your car, does it not?

Mammon: Yes.

Pruitt: And that watch?

Mammon: Yes. The church owns it all.

Pruitt: The Church of the New Hope pays for those things because you are the pastor there.

Mammon: And an elder.

Pruitt: But before Jalen Bale died, you were neither a pastor nor an elder, isn't that true?

Mammon: I was an associate pastor, but no, I wasn't an elder.

Pruitt: Prior to Pastor Bale's death, the only two elders were Pastor Bale and Lilith Cain.

Mammon: That's true.

Pruitt: After Pastor Bale died, you took Bale's place as an elder.

Mammon: I did.

Pruitt: So with the death of Pastor Bale came a promotion to pastor, a mansion, a Mercedes, a Rolex-

Mammon: You're making it sound like—

Pruitt: With his death, you gained millions, didn't you?

Mammon: Jalen was my friend.

Pruitt: Your Honor, would you instruct the witness to answer the question?

Court: The witness will answer the question asked.

Mammon: Yes…because of Jalen's death…I gained financially.

Pruitt: I have no further questions.

CHAPTER 19

I got home before Dee, and when she pulled into our driveway, she looked tired. We were the same age—fifty-five—but the years had been kinder to her than to me. Her hair flared out in long tight curls of silver that brought out the glow of her soft black skin. The only time her face held a wrinkle was when she smiled or when she worried—as she did now.

"I hired an attorney," I said instead of hello.

She sighed with relief and said, "A good one?"

"She's a partner in the firm, so she should know what she's doing."

"How long has she been a partner?"

"I didn't ask." Which was true.

"What do you know about her?"

"Um, she's a former student of mine."

"A former..." Dee's brow furrowed. "How old is she? What's her track record?"

"I don't know, exactly."

"Are you...?"

I made a beckoning gesture with my arms. "What?" I asked.

"You spent six months researching your car before you bought it. Your choices of running shoe had you downloading articles on the biomechanics of the foot. Yet when it comes to our daughter, you just pull a name out of a hat?"

"I didn't pull a name out of a hat," I said.

"Boady, this is our one chance to get her back. You understand that, right? If we don't win, she'll be out of our lives forever. No graduation party, no wedding, no grandchildren. Do you not see what's at stake here? We may never get to see her again."

"We don't know that she'll be out of our lives. Once she's eighteen, she can make her own decisions."

"She's made her decision." Dee raised her voice as if that was what was needed to get through to me. "She chose Anna over us because she wants a family. She wants to belong."

"We gave her everything she needed."

"How can you say that when you still call her your ward and not your daughter?"

"She's Ben's daughter; I can't change that. She's here because Ben wanted us to raise her, but in the eyes of the law—"

"For God's sake, Boady." Dee now spoke softly, but her words carried the power of a thunderclap. "Do you hear yourself? You still think this is about laws and documents. She's a child. Do you think she cares about the words on a piece of paper?"

"Of course I wish I didn't have to crawl to a judge to keep her here, but like it or not, the law is our only hope."

"Why fight to get her back if she's nothing but a ward?"

"Because Ben wanted us to raise her—"

"Ben's dead. Emma's alive. Stop making this about Ben."

"I'm not...I'm just saying that as a matter of law, she wouldn't be here if it weren't for Ben."

"As a matter of law..." Dee shook her head. "Don't you feel any of this?" She held her gaze on me until she could no longer stand to look at me. Then she turned and walked out of the room, her feet padding quietly up the steps.

I wanted to follow her; I ached to follow her, but I couldn't bear to see that look of disappointment on her face again. Rufus seemed similarly confused, standing at the bottom of the stairs. He waited for me to go after Dee, and when I didn't move, he crept up the steps alone.

The old house became still, the quiet so heavy that it hummed in my ears. In the silence, Dee's parting words echoed in my head. *Don't you feel any of this?* Did I? Had I always been this way or had I—somewhere along the way—surrendered my ability to feel emotion?

I remembered a day when Dee and I were juniors in college and had gone to a club to dance. Diana was a great dancer, lithe and fluid in her movements, and I had pieced together some go-to moves so that I didn't look foolish at her side. We were about to call it a night when a couple guys stopped by our table, beer bottles in hand, shit-eating grins on their faces, cocky in their size and number. One guy wore a bandanna like he was Axl Rose. He spoke to Diana as though I wasn't there.

"Hey honey, you want to dance with a real man?"

Diana put her hand on my forearm to keep me from standing up. She leaned in so that I could hear her above the dance music. "Ignore them," she said.

I looked at my drink as I gave her request due consideration.

"I seen you out there," the guy continued. "I bet you're a hellcat."

Diana's grip tightened on my arm.

The second guy, chubbier than the first, stood back a couple steps, his cheek twitching as though he couldn't choose an expression. Diana refused to make eye contact, but I lifted my face and looked at the man in the bandanna. He ignored me as he leaned on our table. "Come on, honey. It's just a dance—unless you want more."

I stood and the man turned to face me. He puffed his chest and started to speak, but I punched him in the mouth before he could get a word out, driving my fist into his face with everything I had. I followed it with a second blow that glanced off his ear. He fell backward to the floor.

His buddy seemed frozen at first, but then leapt forward to throw a punch into my ribs. I spun and went after him with blind rage, my fist catching him in the throat. He stumbled off-balance and I grabbed him by the shirt and shoved him onto the first guy, who was trying to get to his feet. The three of us landed on the floor, me on top as I punched at anything that moved.

Before I knew it, a bouncer had grabbed me around the waist, lifted me off the pile, and thrown me to the side. Diana and I were escorted out while the two goons were held back so that there would be no second act in the parking lot.

In my first-semester criminal law class, I found myself analyzing that fight to see what I might have been charged with. It's possible that I broke the guy's orbital bone when I threw that first punch. That would have been a third-degree assault—a felony. And although they had provoked it, provocation is not a defense. I had a duty to retreat. Instead, I lit into the guy.

It's hard to describe the satisfaction I had felt when that first punch landed hard on the mouth of a man who had insulted my girlfriend. I had acted out of emotion, not reason, and even though Diana had chastised me for the fight, she also joked that I had been her white knight. But that had been the last time I let myself act from the heart, with no fear, no paralyzing intellectual debate.

Don't you feel any of this?

Had I forgotten how to feel? Had I forgotten how to fight, not as a lawyer, but as a man?

I walked to the bottom of the steps, stared up at the emptiness of the hall, and wondered what she was thinking. I pictured Dee lying on our bed, facedown, crying into her pillow. I would not disturb her solitude, but I couldn't stand to be downstairs alone. I slipped out of my shoes, and in my stocking feet, climbed the stairs.

CHAPTER 20

At the top of the steps, I turned into Emma's room, still painted a warm green from back when we planned to bring home baby Julia. Rufus already lay on Emma's bed, and when he saw me, he slid off, knowing that I disapproved. He took his place on the rug, tail curled up behind his legs. When had I become a man who kicks dogs off furniture?

I eased myself to the floor next to him and rubbed his head. On a shelf in front of me lay Emma's treasures, small trinkets that spanned the divide between childhood and adolescence: a painted rock next to a curling iron, seashells beside a smart watch, a tube of lipgloss sitting atop a picture book about Greek myths. I remembered buying that book for her.

On warm evenings, I used to sit on the front porch and watch the world go by. One evening, Emma joined me. She looked so small sitting in that big Adirondack chair, her feet dangling above the porch floor. At first, she sat quietly watching cars, waving at neighbors, and listening to birds. But in time she got bored and wanted to talk.

That was when I started telling her stories.

Having been a history major in college, I began with stories about Thomas Edison creating the light bulb or Teddy Roosevelt on San Juan Hill. She seemed to enjoy them, and soon our little story time had become a ritual that lasted into the fall. But as the rain turned to snow, I had run low on history, so I moved on to Greek myths.

One day, when she asked me to go out onto the porch, I just wasn't in the mood. A cold breeze had descended on Minnesota, and even though we had enough blankets and coats to keep the wind at bay, I declined her invitation. The next day, I bought her the book of myths. In my own lunkheaded way, I thought I was solving a problem. She wanted stories. I wanted to stay warm. It was a win-win. But I don't believe she ever opened that book.

Had I really not realized it had never been about the stories?

On the floor beneath Emma's bed, I saw the corner of her sketch pad. I slid it out and paged through, finding sketches of Dee at the kitchen table, napping on the couch, sitting on the porch steps. I found drawings of Rufus lying on Emma's bed or out in the yard. I found drawings of shoes, and hats, and books...but I found no drawings of me, only the rough edges of pages she had torn out. She had made me invisible.

Rufus took a deep breath and let his body settle against my leg. I put my hand on his neck and stroked his soft fur. "I know you don't believe this," I said, "but I miss her too." He nuzzled his head against my hip, scratching an itch on his nose, oblivious to the depth of my failings.

Then I noticed something out of place. We had furnished Emma's room with items probably better suited for a little girl, a dresser and four-poster bed painted glossy white with lines of gold inlay. At the base of her dresser, the kickplate seemed to be tipped out of frame. I pictured her standing at her dresser, getting angry with me and driving her toe into the bottom of the dresser to release steam.

I scooched over to realign the board and it hinged upward like a loose tooth. As I lowered the board back into place, I saw a piece of paper sticking out from beneath the dresser. I tugged it and was surprised to feel it had weight. I pulled harder and a thick stack of papers came free. I was confused until I saw that the top page was a newspaper article, the headline: ST. PAUL ATTORNEY CHARGED.

It was an article about Ben getting arrested for Jennavieve's murder.

Beneath that were articles about Ben's trial and death, articles that came from websites that we had blocked on our computers. One of the articles was a discussion of domestic violence that included Ben's case. The article was only two weeks old. Of course she would find them. It was naïve to think that we could keep her in the dark.

Beneath the articles I found emails and other correspondence between me and Dr. Mochol, the psychiatrist we had hired. Had Emma dug through my computer files? Shaken, I scooted back beside Rufus, leaned against the bed, and began to read.

An hour later, I lightly knocked on the door and then entered our bed-room, where Dee lay on the bed. I held up the stack of papers. "I found something."

She sat up, looking confused. I handed her the stack of articles. "I found them underneath Emma's dresser. She'd been researching Ben's death."

"I can't believe..." Dee shuffled through the pages.

"It gets worse," I said, directing her to the bottom of the stack in her hands. "Emma's been going through my emails. Remember the night before she left, when I suggested she go to art school in the fall? She said that she didn't want to be a burden?"

"Yeah."

"It seemed a strange response, but...here's why she said that." I pointed at an email I had sent to Dr. Mochol.

Dee had brought up the idea of adopting Emma, but I had dragged my feet on the subject. Dr. Mochol had emailed to ask why, and I'd replied:

> Dr. Mochol,
>
> I guess I don't see the need for adoption. The court order grants us authority on par with that of an actual parent. Making her our daughter seems an unnecessary burden. And if truth be told, there's a part of me that feels

uncomfortable taking that route given my role in her father's death. I'm not sure I should be the one to take his place.

"Oh, my God. Emma read this?"

"I didn't mean it the way it sounds."

"How did you mean it?"

"I just…" My shoulder sank. "I don't know."

"You didn't want her."

"But I did."

"Not as a daughter. No wonder she's been acting the way she has. My God, she must have been devastated."

"But I don't feel that way now."

"Now? Don't you think that now is a bit too late?" Dee stood and walked out of the room without letting me respond, although I don't know what I would have said.

We ate our dinners separately. She had a bowl of cereal in the kitchen before going for a long walk. I ate a peanut butter and jelly sandwich in my study while I sent a copy of the email to Erica Dennis. She would need to know about my blunder, how I had paved the way for Anna to turn Emma against us—against me.

That night was the first time in our married lives that Dee and I slept in the same house but in different beds—she took Emma's room, while I tossed and turned alone. And in the morning, we barely spoke as we got ready for our meeting with Erica. Even Rufus seemed to understand that I had screwed up, walking away from me when I tried to pet him. The only light in that long tunnel was the possibility that Erica would have some hopeful news, maybe a strategy that we could take to court to get Emma back.

Unfortunately, that light at the end of the tunnel was about to blow out.

CHAPTER 21

Dee and I arrived on time for our appointment and Erica greeted us cordially, inviting us back to her office. Once we settled in, Erica brought Dee up to speed.

"Because the judge issued an emergency ex parte order, we have the right to a hearing within five business days. We are on the court's calendar for Monday at four thirty, the last hearing of the day. In my experience, the hearing will be a rubber stamp."

"We're going to lose?" Dee asked.

"We won't get the ex parte order overturned, but we can argue for visitation." Erica held up the email I had sent—the one that had crushed Dee the night before. "We have some work to do repairing things between Emma and..."

"And me," I said.

Dee didn't look at me.

Erica continued. "The bigger hurdle is that your house itself is part of the problem. They have a psychologist saying that returning Emma to that house will be harmful because...well, that's where her father was killed."

"Maybe we can get our own expert to refute that," I said.

"All that does is gives us dueling experts," Erica said. "If that's all we got, the judge will play it safe, keeping Emma out of that house."

"We'll sell the house," Dee said.

I turned to her. "We'll what?"

Dee laid her words out slowly but forcefully. "We will sell the house."

"That's not a bad idea," Erica said. "It'll show the judge how important Emma is to you." She nodded her approval.

"Wait..." I said, "just like that?"

"Yes," Dee said, "just like that."

I wanted to argue the point, but I was outnumbered, so I tucked it away for later when it would be just Dee and me. "What's our goal for Monday?"

Erica said, "We'll shoot for a return of custody, but we'll lose. The backup plan is to get visitation, maybe in a place that's neutral. It's imperative that we get as many visits as we can."

"Why is it imperative?" Dee asked. "I mean, I want to have every second I can with Emma, but the way you phrased it..."

Erica looked at me like a teacher waiting for an answer. When I didn't say anything, she said, "Because Emma's fourteen."

Now it was Dee who looked to me to explain what that meant, but I didn't know. I remembered reading something about that age in the statute, but the best I could pull from my memory was that it had something to do with receiving notice of the hearing.

Erica must have sensed my confusion. She folded her fingers together and leaned toward us, her voice low and soft to pull us in. "In the guardianship statute, there's a clause that says that if a person subject to a guardianship has reached the age of fourteen, they have a say in who their guardian will be."

I thought back to Emma's affidavit telling the judge that she wanted to be with Anna and not with us, her words now taking on weight. It was no coincidence that everything had come to a boil just days after Emma's birthday.

"In a case like this," Erica said, "it's probably going to come down to where Emma wants to be. If she doesn't want to return to you...say, because..." Erica looked at me and didn't finish her sentence. "Well, a judge would be hard-pressed to order her back into your custody."

"But if we can get the judge to order a visitation," Dee said, "can we try and get Emma to change her mind?"

"It's a fine line," Erica said. "We want her to change her mind, but we can't offer her any incentive. That would be witness tampering."

"But..." Dee seemed to be flailing for a lifeline. "If we can remind her how we're a family..."

"That's the goal," Erica said. "If I can get the judge to order visitations, we have a chance."

I reached over and put my hand on Dee's and gave a light squeeze. She didn't reciprocate.

"Other than selling the house," Dee asked, "is there anything else we can do?"

"I've called Dr. Mochol, and I think she'll be good for our side. We also need to get our own guardian ad litem. The woman Anna used is a hired gun. She's had some credibility issues in the past; a judge will see that she's on Anna's side because of the paycheck. I'm going to request a guardian I know who has an impeccable reputation for honesty and fairness. On the upside, the judge will give weight to his report. On the downside, he may see pros and cons on both sides of the argument. It's a risk, but I think this is the way to go."

"I like it," I said, wanting to feel like part of the team. "It sounds like a good plan."

Erica ignored me and continued. "When Emma lost her parents, she inherited, what...somewhere in the neighborhood of twenty-five million dollars?"

"It's in trust," I said. "We've never touched a dime of it."

"That's good. I've seen hundreds of cases where the guardian starts dipping into the trust to buy stuff for themselves."

"We don't want her money," Dee said. "We love her." She passed me a glance that made me nod in agreement.

I said, "We hired a conservator to handle her trust."

"I saw that," Erica said. "Gordy Baker. I know him. He's one of the best, as ethical as they come. You did everything right when it comes to Emma's money, but…"

"But what?" I asked.

"I've been thinking about this case…and what if this really isn't about Emma?"

"What do you mean?" Dee said.

"Emma's mother held fifty-one percent of the shares in Adler Industries—Anna Adler has forty-nine percent. That gives Emma the controlling interest. What if this is simply Anna's way of getting control of the company? If we could prove an ulterior motive, that might put us on even ground."

"We're not on even ground?" Dee asked.

"No, Mrs. Sanden, we're not. As it stands right now, one judge has already sided with Ms. Adler. If we don't do something to change things, we will lose."

Dee seemed to freeze in her chair.

"I'm sorry to be blunt," Erica said, "but I don't want any of us going into this fight with false hopes. I'll do my best to get you visitation. If that happens…" Erica looked at me when she spoke. "I don't know any other way to say this, but if Emma doesn't change her mind, she won't be coming home."

CHAPTER 22

Dee and I divided our tasks and split up after our meeting with Erica. I dropped her off at home, where she was to contact Dr. Mochol and give her what she needed for our report. And although she didn't say it, I suspected that Dee was going to begin the process of finding a new house for us.

For my part, I drove out to meet with Gordy Baker, the conservator we had hired to manage Emma's trust. If there were an ulterior motive behind Anna Adler's chess moves, he might know it.

Gordy worked out of an office building in Hopkins, a nondescript space that told the world that he was a man who gained clients through results, not adornments. I had been to his office only once before, on the day that I hired him. I didn't call ahead this time because I suspected that he might try to avoid me now that Anna was temporarily in charge of the conservatorship. My instincts were correct—sort of.

His receptionist took my name, punched a number into her phone, and informed Gordy that I was there. She nodded, looked at me, and then handed me the receiver.

"Gordy, I—"

"I'm sorry, Mr. Sanden," he said, "I can't meet with you."

"Can I make an appointment?"

"No…I mean, I can't meet with you at all. You're not the guardian. I have to answer to Ms. Adler now."

"I just need a minute or two—"

"That wouldn't be appropriate," he said. "I'm sorry."

The line went dead.

I handed the phone back to the receptionist and left the office, unsure of what I should do. I was at my car when my phone buzzed with a text. It was from Gordy, and it read, simply: Parking ramp. Ten minutes.

Gordy's office had a flat, open parking lot, but across the street I saw a ramp. I drove there, parked, and texted the number of my parking stall back to Gordy.

Soon, Gordy pulled into the stall beside me. He wore the same white shirt, khakis, and shabby blue jacket he had worn the last time I met with him. He took a seat in my car. "Sorry for the cloak-and-dagger," he said. "I thought it best we meet somewhere away from the office."

"Why? What's going on?"

"I can't say for certain, but I think one of my partners might be feeding information to Anna Adler. He started asking questions about Emma's account a few months back. I didn't think much of it until I received that court order appointing Anna as the temporary guardian. When her lawyer served me my copy, he warned me that if I talked to you, they would haul me in front of a judge with an ethics complaint."

"You're joking."

He looked at me, deadpan. "You know how this works. When you were the guardian, I answered to you. But according to the court order, you're no longer the guardian. I have to answer to Anna Adler. That's the law."

"So why are you here?"

"I felt like you deserved answers, even if I can't give you detailed information about the account."

"I'm just trying to figure out..." I thought about how to put it in a way that Gordy might be able to answer. "You've been handling Emma's trust for four years now. You have to know...Is Anna attempting to take control of Adler Enterprises?"

"Mr. Sanden, you're asking me a question you know I cannot answer."

"What if Anna fires you and gets some lackey to do her bidding? She can steal Emma's inheritance."

"That doesn't change the fact that I can't talk to you about Emma's conservatorship. I can't talk to you about Emma's trust even if I want to...desperately."

Desperately. The word caught my attention, as I believe it was meant to. Gordy was telling me something without telling me anything. "I'm just looking to get pointed in the right direction."

Gordy thought for a while and said, "Mr. Sanden, I've given you everything I can already. It's all there in black-and-white."

Black-and-white? Reports? From the beginning, Gordy had sent me extensive reports, notes, and tedium in abundance: minutes from the monthly corporate meetings, quarterly reports, annual revenue ledgers. "In black-and-white," I said, nodding my understanding.

He looked at his watch. "I should get back...just in case they're watching me."

"I'm sorry if I put you in a pinch," I said. "I want you to know that I appreciate all you've done for Emma. Maybe one day we'll be able to continue this chat in your office."

"I'd like that," he said as he stepped out of my car. Then he paused and leaned back in. "You know, Mr. Sanden, it's always amazed me how far some people will go to turn a no into a yes."

With that he shut my car door, got in his own car, and drove away.

Turn a no into a yes. Gordy had given me nothing, but at the same time I felt as though he had turned me toward the sun and shoved. I had the haystack—now to find the needle.

CHAPTER 23

As I stared at the piles of documents Gordy'd sent me over the years, I remembered why I'd sought a career in criminal law and not corporate. Give me blood and gore. Give me passion and violence. Give me a riddle about mortal wounds. But corporate accounting? I'd be asleep faster than if I'd taken a handful of Xanax. Still, alone in my study, I settled in to read.

I started with monthly reports detailing the battle of the shareholders: Anna Adler versus Gordy Baker, who was there as proxy for Emma Pruitt's trust. As the owner of fifty-one percent of the shares, Emma's trust had the final say on everything; Anna could do nothing without Gordy's approval, and according to the minutes, Gordy approved very little.

In that first meeting, he had approved one proposal and rejected three. I opened the minutes for the next month and read six more rejections—zero approvals. Were these rejections what Gordy was pointing me to? The sheer number of rejections made that a credible argument, but there had to be a smoking gun, some rejected project that had been the breaking point for Anna. The minutes didn't set out a description of the projects, just a name and the vote tally, so I had my work cut out for me.

I ran an internet search on the first rejection, the Millet Acquisition, and found Millet Industries, a company that had developed a yogurt-based shampoo. Gordy had been smart to reject the idea; the company declared bankruptcy a year later.

The next rejection was the Prodigal Project. Again I went to the internet, but the term *prodigal project* came back with over five million hits. After an hour of searching, I had found nothing that looked like an investment. I leaned back in my chair, pinched my dry eyes shut, and rubbed them with my fingers. Before me were hundreds of rejected proposals over the span of four years. I was beginning to think that my research was quixotic.

When I opened my eyes again, Dee stood in the doorway. "I want to show you some houses," she said.

She came around my desk and typed into my keyboard. With a click of the mouse, we were looking at a house in Lake Elmo, at least half an hour away. The rooms were white, bright white—blindingly white. My blood pressure ticked up just looking at the screen.

"I know it'll be a drive for you to get to classes," she said, "but it's got a huge yard and the school system is fantastic."

"Lake Elmo?"

"It's a hot area."

"How much?"

"Under a million. With the sale of our house, we could walk away with cash in hand."

"It's...bright."

"We can paint it. Like I said, we'll have cash left over for stuff like that."

"It's just...Isn't there anything closer?"

Dee clicked on another property, this one listing for $1.2 million. "It's on Crocus Hill. It's more expensive, but it's beautiful."

It was beautiful, old brick, a fountain in the backyard, and far more house than we needed. "It's a bit much, though, don't you think?"

"Okay..." She clicked another link, a house just a few blocks from the law school, a Victorian, small, attractive, but less than twenty feet from its nearest neighbor.

"Oh no," I said. "Look how close those houses are to each other. We'd be able to hear them argue."

"Why are you picking everything apart?"

"I'm not, it's just…"

"We need to get going on this," she said.

"I know, but you don't just click on a computer screen and pick a house. We have to research."

"We're not looking for perfect. All we need is a house that doesn't have this damned study in it. We need a place with no memory of what happened. Frankly, I'd like that too. Why are you being difficult?"

"I'm not being difficult, but you walk in here and spring this on me. I need time to—"

"We don't have time." Dee took a step back so she could face me squarely. "We can't be picky."

"Buying a house is a big deal—"

"No, Boady, it's not. Losing Emma is a big deal. A house is just a house. We need to make an offer before the hearing on Monday."

"How does this not piss you off?" I asked.

"What?"

"Anna Adler is forcing us to move out of our home—a home we love. She's pushing us around and you're all in. Every time you concede to her demand, she wins."

"She doesn't win unless she keeps Emma away from us. Don't you see that? You heard what Ms. Dennis said. We're pushing a stone up a pretty big hill. I'm beginning to think…"

"What?"

Dee shook her head.

"Say it."

"Do you even want Emma back?"

"Of course I do," I said.

"You're not acting like it."

"What do you mean? I'm…" I picked up a stack of corporate reports and waved them in the air. "I'm plodding through four years' worth of this crap, looking for Adler's ulterior motive. Do you have any idea how mind-numbing that is?"

Dee spoke quietly, her soft words like the warning growl of a cat. "You're looking through those because you want to beat Anna Adler in court, not because you want Emma back. Those aren't the same thing."

"If we win in court, we get Emma back. They are the same thing."

She leaned back down and pulled up a list of houses that she had saved. "Any one of these would be fine with me," she said, her voice dripping with sadness. "Do what you need to do, but pick one and let me know."

Why couldn't she see that we were working toward the same goal? Finding Adler's ulterior motive would carry far more weight than moving to a new house. The judge might not even care that we made the move.

Dee left the study without saying another word, and I remained in my chair, limp, deboned, barely able to lift my finger to the mouse. Over the years, I had proven to be a far-from-perfect husband, but she loved me through it all, picking me up every time I fell. And in return, I continued to let her down.

The list of houses filled my computer screen. I clicked one, then another, and another. In the end, it was the house in Lake Elmo that held the most promise: spacious, a large study, and room for Rufus and Emma to run in the yard. I went upstairs to the spare bedroom that Dee used as a home office. She sat at her computer, looking at more houses. I put my hands on her shoulders. "You're right," I said. "We should get the house in Lake Elmo. It's best for Emma."

She didn't turn around. "Are you sure?" I could hear doubt in her voice, and knew that it wasn't doubt about the house.

"Yes, I'm sure. Get the process going and I'll sign wherever you tell me to."

She reached back and lifted my hand from her shoulder and placed it against her cheek. "Thank you," she whispered.

I kissed the top of her head and returned to my study and to my stack of corporate minutes, flipping through six months' worth to get a handle on how many of Adler's proposals Gordy had rejected. In half a year, he had rejected thirty-six. At that rate, he would have rejected nearly three hundred over the course of four years. Three hundred! This was going to be an impossible task.

My cell phone rang and I was happy to answer it. "Hello."

"Mr. Sanden, it's Dr. Cohen."

"Is everything all right?"

"Yes, I guess so, but...Elijah got into a fight today."

"Is he okay?"

"His face is in pretty bad shape, but no significant injuries."

"What happened?"

"That's the thing; he's refusing to talk to us about it."

"Okay," I said.

"I asked him if he would talk to you and he said he would."

"You understand, I'm two hours away."

"I know."

"And it's Friday."

"I'd understand if you said no, but he seems to trust you."

Christ! Two hours to St. Peter. Talk to Elijah—maybe an hour—and then two hours back.

"The Jarvis hearing's only a week away," Dr. Cohen said. "He doesn't have much time."

"Okay. I'll be there in a couple hours."

"I'll get things arranged on this end," Dr. Cohen said. "And Mr. Sanden...thank you."

I ended the call and went to the bottom of the stairs. "Dee? I gotta go do something on that Innocence Project case I'm working on."

She called down from her office, and although I couldn't make out exactly what she said, it sounded like "Drive safely," but maybe that's what I wanted her to say.

CHAPTER 24

Dr. Cohen filled me in as she walked me to Elijah's room. They'd found him curled up on the floor in a common area, his face badly bruised. There were no other patients around, and the assault took place where the security cameras had a blind spot. She knew nothing more than that.

Elijah's room was small and sparse, laid out like a dorm room with a bed, a closet, and a little desk and chair—a Bible lay open on the desk. Dr. Cohen remained in the corridor; I went inside and closed the door behind me.

Elijah lay in bed, the left side of his face badly bruised, his left eye hidden behind a swollen cheek. He had a cut on his lip that had been treated with superglue, and when he smiled at me, it caused him to wince. He lay beneath a thin blanket, his blue pajama top buttoned to the neck. I pulled the chair away from the desk and sat down beside him.

"Are you okay?"

"It's good to see you, Mr. Sanden," he whispered, without moving his lips.

"Dr. Cohen said that you won't talk to her."

Elijah didn't respond.

"You need to tell her what happened."

"I can't," he said.

"Why not?"

"Dr. Cohen is a good person, but she's a doctor. She will have no choice but to share my words with the others. I can't have that."

"If you can't talk about it, why send for me?"

"You are my attorney, are you not?"

"Yes, I guess I am."

"And as my attorney, you are bound by confidentiality. Anything I share with you remains a secret."

I leaned forward, resting my elbows on my knees. "I'm here because they want to know what happened to you—who did this. Why tell me if I can't talk about it?"

"It was my fault," he said. "I don't want anyone getting in trouble for what I did, but it's important that you know what happened. That's why I asked you to come."

"What was your fault?"

"This." He slowly lifted his hand from where it lay on his chest and pointed at the bruise on his face.

"Did you get in a fight?"

"You will keep what I say a confidence?"

"I have no choice," I said. "I'm your attorney."

"It was not a fight. A fight takes two people."

"Who did this to you?"

Elijah raised his gaze to the ceiling as though he had to think. "When you came here for that first visit, you were brought to the conference room by a young man with a crew cut and a tattoo of a lion on his left arm."

I thought back and remembered the security counselor with the crew cut, but hadn't noticed the tattoo. "I remember."

"His name is Jake."

"He did this?"

"Yes."

"Elijah...how could this possibly be your fault? They're here to protect you, not beat the crap out of you."

"I spoke out of turn. I revealed what I should not have."

"What are you talking about?"

"God had sent me a revelation. I should not have shared it. It was imprudent."

"What revelation?"

"Jake has a wife, but he has lain with another."

"Jake beat you up...because he's having an affair?"

"I told him that God was watching—that God does not approve."

"I need to tell Dr. Cohen. That man should not be allowed anywhere near you."

"He isn't angry with me; he's angry with who he has become."

"That's not the point. If Jake doesn't have what it takes to do his job right, he shouldn't be watching over someone like you."

"Someone like me?"

"Like it or not, Elijah, you are here because you are vulnerable. He's supposed to take care of you."

"In loco parentis?"

"You know that term?"

"It means 'in place of the parent,' does it not?"

"Yes, it does. He's supposed to protect you, not beat you up."

"And if the protector fails in his duty...if he cannot rise to the level of what is required of a parent, what happens then? Should he be fired? Or should he be given a chance to change?"

Emma's face flashed through my mind, jarring me. I tried to push the thought aside. "Jake needs to be..." I stammered as I tried to get back to the subject at hand, but the thread of our conversation had become tangled. "There has to be accountability. He was way out of line."

"Some people don't handle it well when you hold a mirror up to them."

"Let me tell Dr. Cohen, so she can protect you."

Elijah moved his covers back and worked to sit up. The way he favored his left side, I could tell that he had taken a blow or two to the ribs. "She will fire him," Elijah said through the pain. "I do not want that. I will try to be more careful...clearer, when I talk to Jake again. He must confess his sin and ask his wife for her forgiveness."

"You do that and he'll just beat you again."

"Then I will turn my other cheek."

"At least defend yourself next time."

"Do not envy the violent or choose their way, Mr. Sanden."

Elijah spoke like a man of peace, and for a moment I forgot that he had been committed as a dangerous psychopath, accused of crushing a man's skull with a rock. When I remembered that point it raised a couple questions, so I asked.

"When you first went to the Church of the New Hope, you brought a stone with you, a remnant of an old homeless shelter. Why?"

"I was sent to seek the lost. Jalen Bale was lost. I brought the stone to remind him of who he had once been."

"Pastor Mammon told me that you and Bale used to meet in his office and talk for hours."

"Yes, we talked a lot. Some walls take longer than six days to knock down."

"What did you and Bale talk about?"

"We talked about many things and nothing."

"Did you talk about his preaching—his sermons about the prosperity gospels?"

"Those are not the words of the Lord. Such smooth talk deceives the hearts of the naïve."

"I saw the video...the one of you condemning Bale."

"It was not I who condemned Jalen. I do not judge. That is the purview of God."

"What you said sure sounded like a threat—at least the jury thought so."

"What shall it profit a man to gain the whole world but lose his soul?"

"Bale told Mammon that he was doing your work. What did he mean by that?"

Elijah considered my question, then said, "That must be some other Elijah. I am but a servant. I give no commands. If a man were to wash my feet, I would wash his in return."

"What was Bale working on?"

"A true man of God will fix that which is broken. He will—"

"Stop. Please." I knew that his religious babble was part of his mania, but I needed him to be clear. "Elijah, you have a Jarvis hearing coming up in one week. If I can't get some movement on this case, they're going to run electricity through your brain. Are you aware of that?"

He spoke in a tone barely above a whisper. "I am not a fool, Mr. Sanden. I am aware of what they plan to do."

"Do you care?"

He looked at me with great sadness. "What happens to me is in God's hands."

"If that were true," I said, "I wouldn't be here. Now, tell me what Pastor Bale was working on."

"Jalen was writing a sermon. He told me it was to be his final sermon."

I thought back to the file and the trial transcript. There had been no mention of a final sermon. "What do you mean, 'final sermon'?"

"That's all he said, nothing more."

"Did you read it?"

"I did not."

My phone buzzed in my pocket. I pulled it out to see Dee calling. I excused myself and left his room. Dr. Cohen was still in the hallway, but she was talking to another doctor down at the far end. I closed Elijah's door and took the call. "Hi, honey."

"How much longer are you going to be?" she asked. "I have the purchase agreement filled out. If you come home and sign it, we can have the offer in today."

"I'm about done here," I said. "I can be home in a couple hours."

"A couple hours? Where are you?"

"I'm at the Security Hospital in St. Peter."

"You drove to St. Peter...when we have so much to do?"

I felt like a child caught skipping out on his chores. "I'll be there in two hours," I said. "I'll hand-deliver the offer tonight, if that's what you want."

"What I want is for you to see Emma as a priority. Is that too much to ask?"

"Emma is my priority," I said. "But I can't drop everything else."

"Is that case in St. Peter more important than your kidnapped daughter?"

"Nothing is more important than getting Emma home. I promise we'll be a family again." But even as I said this, I thought about Elijah getting his brain zapped with electricity. I was a frayed rope in a tug-of-war.

"I'm done here," I said. "I'll be on the road in a couple minutes. We can have that offer signed and delivered tonight. Two hours isn't going to make a difference."

The line went dead. I checked the screen just to make sure that she had actually hung up on me. She had.

I walked back into Elijah's room. "I have to go."

Elijah now stood beside his bed, the covers draped over his shoulders. "Boady?" he said. "May I call you Boady?"

Only half listening, I replied, "Sure."

"I know you see me as a crazy man, but could I ask one small favor?"

"Favor?"

"May I..." He raised his hand slowly, carefully, as if venturing to pet an angry dog, and touched his fingers to my sternum. He closed his eyes like some carnival mystic. When he opened his eyes again, he looked grief-stricken. "I'm so sorry," he said.

I brushed his hand away. "Sorry about what?"

"You have a child…lost…such pain."

He stunned me into silence for a second. How did he know? Then I remembered my phone call with Dee. What had I said that allowed Elijah to piece it together? I had said that Emma was my priority, that we would get her back and be a family again. Had that been enough?

Dee had said more, called Emma our daughter. Were Elijah's ears keen enough to hear her on the phone too? Was that why he was standing when I came back in—had he been listening through the door? I'd had my back turned to it.

It explained so much. He was performing a cheap parlor trick—a charlatan reading body language and eavesdropping. That must have been how he picked up on Dr. Cohen's pregnancy, too. His superpower wasn't reading minds or talking to God. It was above-average auditory perception.

"I will thank you not to eavesdrop on my private conversations," I said, feeling his intrusion like a slap across my face.

"Boady, children are a gift from God. They are a reward from him."

I snapped. "What do you know about it, Elijah?" I couldn't stop my voice from rising. "Exactly how many children do you have?"

His eyes floated toward the ceiling. "Seven billion, eight hundred and sixty-eight million, seven hundred and seventy-two thousand, nine hundred and…" He snapped his fingers. "Twelve."

"Well, you're going to need a bigger house, I guess."

Elijah received my sarcasm with a gentle smile. "Being in the same room with a child isn't what makes you a father. When Solomon faced his dilemma with the two mothers, he ordered that the baby be split in half, knowing that the true mother would give up everything for her child. It is that willingness to sacrifice that makes one a father, not proximity."

"So sayeth your Bible?"

"That is true for everyone...even a skeptic like yourself."

"I have to go," I said.

"Yes," he said. "I know. Just keep in mind that the prodigal you seek will return and bring you peace."

I shook my head as I turned away.

As I left his room, it occurred to me that Elijah had gotten it wrong. The biblical story of the prodigal son wasn't about a child taken away. The son in that story left on his own accord. And the word *prodigal* didn't mean a missing child or a runaway; it meant a spend-thrift. Nothing in that parable applied to what I was going through with Emma.

Dr. Cohen and the colleague she had been talking to earlier were still in the hall. It was as if they were waiting for me to come out of Elijah's room—and it turned out they were.

CHAPTER 25

The man with Dr. Cohen had black hair, stiff with product. The way he combed it up and back made him an inch taller than his five-foot-six-inch height. He wore the dark suit of a man who wanted to be taken seriously, but his skinny pants were wrapped tightly at the ankles, making his brown shoes look clownishly large. When he saw me leave Elijah's room, he strode toward me like Napoleon himself.

"Mr. Sanden, I'm Dr. Stewart Handler, Elijah's primary."

I looked at Dr. Cohen, who had followed Handler up the hall. Her eyes flashed a warning.

"Did he tell you what happened?" Handler asked.

"He did," I said.

Handler motioned for me to walk with him, giving us distance from Elijah's door. When we turned a corner, he stopped and said, "And…"

"And what?"

"What did he say? Who was Elijah fighting with?"

"You're the one who wants to do the electroshock therapy on him, aren't you?" I said.

"ECT is the consensus of the team."

I looked at Dr. Cohen. "Is that true?" I asked.

"Dr. Cohen is no longer the primary; I am," he said. "Her talents were needed elsewhere."

"So if you can't find consensus in the team, just change the team?"

"It's the best option available—not that I have to justify my medical opinion to you."

"ECT is barbaric."

"Ah, you're one of those."

"One of those what?"

"You saw *One Flew Over the Cuckoo's Nest* and now you're an expert on ECT."

"Did I claim to be an expert?"

"No. And yet you seem to think that your opinion on the subject matters."

"ECT will erase him...or do I have that wrong?"

"Mr. Sanden, I've written two papers on the effectiveness of ECT. You're talking to one of the preeminent doctors in the field. It's not the medieval torture people think it is. In fact, it's one of the most effective treatments for patients like Elijah who don't respond to less aggressive options. I've achieved remarkable results with ECT."

"But not every case is a success," I said, as a vision of Richard Gullivay's dead body came to me. "You can't count just the successes. It's like pitching a game of Russian roulette without mentioning that sometimes the gun fires."

"This treatment will help Elijah. He's a very sick man."

"ECT will take away the one thing that makes him who he is. How is that helping him?"

"Mr. Sanden, to the untrained eye Elijah may come across as meek, but I assure you he's quite violent. He's responsible for the death of one man and now...this fight."

"You ordered the ECT long before this fight. It has no bearing on your plans."

"Why don't you tell me what happened and let me decide?"

"Nothing I say will stop the ECT. If Elijah started a fight, you add that to the list of reasons to shock him. If he didn't...well, you'll proceed as planned."

"If you want to help Elijah, you need to tell me what happened. Between the two of us, I can save him. You cannot."

"The attorney-client privilege prevents me from discussing my conversations with my client."

"I see. Well, I think we're done here."

"On that we agree."

Handler turned and walked away. I went the other way, heading to the visitors' entrance, Dr. Cohen walking with me.

"I didn't get you in trouble, did I?" I asked.

"Handler's not my boss. He can bitch and moan, but he can't harm me."

"Elijah didn't do anything wrong," I said. "I can't say what happened, but I can say that he's not at fault."

"I didn't think he was. Have you made any progress in his case?"

"Nothing beyond the little bit I already had."

"You're not going to be able protect him from the ECT, are you?"

I stopped walking. "I still have time."

"Not much."

I started walking again. "Who knows, maybe Elijah might summon a miracle." I chuckled at the lame joke, but Dr. Cohen did not.

At the visitors' entrance, I said goodbye to Dr. Cohen and was headed for the door when I saw Jake sitting at a desk next to the metal detector. I went to his desk and he looked up at me.

"I'm Elijah Matthew's attorney," I said.

His eyes turned nervous as he ran through the possibilities of what I might know.

"Tomorrow you will ask for a transfer to another unit," I said, "or better yet, another hospital. You will not be on the same unit as Elijah ever again, do you understand?"

He didn't answer. He didn't have to. I turned to leave but stopped before walking out the door. Elijah didn't want vengeance. He didn't even want protection. What he wanted was for Jake to come clean—confess his sin to his wife. Who was I to demand anything different?

I returned to Jake, who now looked upon me as though I were death itself approaching. "Or," I said, "you can tell your wife the truth. Ask for her forgiveness. Those are your only two choices. Do you understand?"

Jake gave a subtle nod, never speaking a word.

CHAPTER 26

I arrived home just before nine that night to find the main floor quiet, the purchase agreement for the new house spread out on the dining room table. I looked it over—standard stuff. We were making an offer contingent on the sale of our house. I signed.

Dee came into the room just then, no words passing between us. She took the purchase agreement and headed out the door to deliver it to the seller's agent. As her car pulled out of the driveway, the air in the house felt as still as a dead man's heart.

I walked around, gazing at the walls, and woodwork, and fixtures, the accoutrement of a home that would soon belong to someone else. I loved this old house, so genteel and refined, a wise old lady who had kept watch over St. Paul since the days of the horse and buggy. How many Christmases had she hosted? Easters? Weddings? So many happy times.

But there had been tragic times as well. I found myself avoiding my study, not wanting to awaken Ben's ghost again. With Emma gone, the old house seemed emptier than ever before.

I walked again to Emma's room, where Rufus lay on her bed. He started to get up, but I put a comforting hand on his head and petted him until he lay back down. I took a seat beside him and listened to him breathe, the darkness of the room amplifying the tiny whistle of his exhalations.

For the past month, at least, Emma had known the secret that Dee and I had kept from her. How many times had she lain in that bed and thought about me, just down the hall, the man who let her father die—the man who couldn't be bothered to call her my daughter? I was supposed to make her feel safe, loved, after her own father had let her down in that brutal way. I too had failed her. What hell that must have been.

I don't know how long I sat there before I heard Dee coming up the stairs. I thought about leaving Emma's room, but I couldn't seem to stand up. Rufus whimpered, causing Dee to stick her head in the door and flip on the light.

"What are you doing?" she asked.

"Thinking," I said.

She walked in and sat next to me on the bed, taking my hand in hers, warm and soft, a peace offering. She said, "Want to talk about it?"

I stared at the floor and let the silence settle in around us before I spoke. "I was absent from her life. Even before Anna started poisoning her against me, I was gone."

Dee didn't disagree or ask me to explain, which made me feel even smaller.

"Look around her room," I said. "You see traces of Rufus and you…Jennavieve…but I'm absent."

"What about that?" Dee asked, pointing at the book of Greek myths. "You gave that to her."

"I gave her the book so that I wouldn't have to go out on the porch at night. I didn't like the cold."

"But you did tell her stories. She loved spending that time with you."

"That was two years ago. I've let her down every day since."

Dee put her hands on my shoulder and leaned in to me, her chin and lips resting beside my ear. "It was hard for you."

"It shouldn't have been," I said sharply. "I saw her as my ward. I called her that so many times. I'm the one who put up the wall between us."

"Emma's a teenager. Feelings are everything to her. Words like *guardian* and *ward*...she wants a family, not a babysitter. And...you just see everything through the prism of the law. You can't help it."

"No, it's more than that."

I twisted my wedding band around my finger like I was turning the dial on a safe, waiting for the tumblers to hit just right so that I could find the words. Nothing came, so I just started talking, hoping that what I said might make sense.

"I look at Emma and I see Ben. She has his chin and his smile. I can't help but remember how he was, back in those early days. But I also get stuck reliving that night when I'm alone in my study. I see what's about to happen; it's all moving so slowly. I want to believe that there was nothing I could've done, but...that's not true. I could have stopped it. I could have saved Ben's life, but I didn't. I let him die—and in exchange, we got Emma."

"You don't owe Ben a thing." Dee spoke with a harshness that bordered on scolding. "Ben killed Jennavieve. He killed Emma's mother—you can't ignore that. Why do you think he brought a gun into this house? He was willing to kill you, too. What happened to Ben is on him—not you."

"I know that—I mean, in my rational mind, I understand that."

"Then let him go. You survived. Emma survived. Focus on the living."

It felt good to talk to Dee, to lay out my baggage about Ben. Her comforting words warmed my chest like fine brandy. I owed her so much. "And I let you down. I'm so sorry for that."

"You didn't let me down."

"This was our chance to have a family, to—"

Dee cupped my chin and turned my face to hers. "Do you think..." I saw a flash in her eyes and I couldn't tell if it was anger or hurt. But then her expression softened.

"Do you think I want Emma because we lost our other children? Do you think that I see her as a replacement for Julia?"

"No...I..."

"No one will ever replace Julia in my heart. I will never heal from that. I don't want to. Having Emma here was never about replacement. Emma is a wonderful and special girl. She's beautiful, and kind...and I want to be there for her because I love her—for the person she is."

I stared at the menagerie of trinkets on Emma's dresser: a ballerina jewelry box, a handprint in clay that she made at camp, a theater program she got the night we saw *Wicked*. I wanted to claw back time and live those days over again. I had been blind to what stood before me every day, seeing the ghost of my dead friend instead of the promise of a child. I had been indifferent when I should have felt blessed. And now there seemed little that I could do to fix it.

"If we get her back," I said, my words floating on the air like a whispered prayer, "I promise I won't make those mistakes again."

CHAPTER 27

In the morning, I shut myself in my study, the corporate reports again stacked in the center of my desk, a boulder waiting to be pushed up a hill. My heart sank just looking at them. I picked up the first one and began listing the rejected projects on a spreadsheet.

The first year held sixty-nine rejections and only eight projects agreed to by Gordy. That ratio, by itself, was fodder for our court battle, but I needed more. I held out hope that somewhere in that stack lay proof that Anna planned to replace Gordy with someone who would do her bidding. If I could find it, we could argue that Anna's petition was nothing but a scheme to cheat Emma out of her authority.

As I trudged through the second year of notes, I came upon a name that rang a bell—the Prodigal Project. There was something about that name—I had seen it before.

I scanned my spreadsheet and found it. Anna had presented that proposal to Gordy at their first corporate meeting. Had she taken a second swing at the ball? I read the note and yes, she had—and again, Gordy had rejected it.

I ran a check of the spreadsheet to see if there were any other projects that repeated. The Prodigal Project was the only one. I then flipped through the third year of corporate minutes and found it again, in a meeting one year ago. That time, however, it wasn't Anna who pitched the idea. According to the minutes, a man named Louis DeChamp had been the presenter. Three years in a row she came to the table seeking funding for this project, and every year it was rejected.

I paused as Elijah's words echoed softly in my ear. *The prodigal will return.* I dismissed it with a light chuckle. I had fallen for a conjurer's trick. Elijah had simply gotten into my head.

When I was in high school, I had been forced to take religion classes every year, and in one class the students were given pictures of magazine advertisements for various brands of alcohol. My picture was of a glass of whiskey on the rocks. The lesson was about subliminal messages and how advertisers would hide things like naked women in the ice cubes of the drink to make men desire the liquor. We were then told to find those hidden pictures.

As students around me started raising their hands to signal that they had found the hidden nudity, I raised mine as well. I was sure that I saw a pair of breasts in the ice cubes of my drink. I wanted to see them. I didn't want to stand out as the only student who couldn't recognize a woman's breast, so I saw them. In my forty years since then, I have never once seen boobs in an advertisement for a glass of whiskey.

Elijah hadn't predicted a damned thing. He had simply replicated the trick that Nostradamus had perfected: scrabble words together and wait for some coincidence in the future to vaguely match up. I returned to my task, searching the internet for Louis DeChamp and getting hundreds of hits. A reputable theater director, he had received accolades for his productions around the country. Six years ago, he had set up residency in Minneapolis and had recently produced a musical adaptation of *Equus* at the Guthrie Theater. A little more digging and I discovered that he was the artistic director for a theater troupe called the Chamberlain Players.

Theater? Anna was well known for being a patron of the arts, hosting galas, even for the Guthrie, but what was DeChamp doing pitching an investment to Gordy?

Having no plan, I called the number for the Chamberlain Players, but then my brain started churning. DeChamp was an ally of Anna's, so why would he talk to me? I was about to hang up when a man with a slack voice answered. "Yeah?"

"Um…is this the office of the Chamberlain Players?"

"It's the studio, yeah. Whatcha need?"

"Is…Louis DeChamp available?"

"He's teaching a class. You'll have to call back."

"When's a good time to reach him?"

"I'm not his secretary. I was just walking past the phone. You'll have to try back later."

"Well, do you know when he'll be done teaching that class?"

"They'll probably break for lunch at one. No guarantees. Listen, man, I gotta go." He hung up.

One o'clock. I had an hour to find the studio and come up with a cover story that might get DeChamp to talk to me.

I dug through my top drawer and found my trusty old digital recorder, the one I used back when I practiced law and needed to record a witness. I was sure there had to be gadgets on the market that were easier to hide—surely they made a phone app now—but this was what I had, and I had to act fast.

I put the recorder in my shirt pocket, slipped on a jacket, and tested it. My voice came across muffled. I tried again without the jacket and it worked better. What if DeChamp saw the recorder there? I glanced at the clock. I would have to take that chance.

CHAPTER 28

The studio for the Chamberlain Players had once been a modest-size church, old but well-kept. The belfry was still intact, but the spire had been removed. The windows had been paneled over with wood and painted white to match the rest of the exterior. Above the door hung a small sign. The door was unlocked, so I entered.

To my left was a ticket window and to my right a small office. Ahead of me were three doors leading into the nave of the church. I was about to open one when I heard voices coming from a smaller door near the ticket window. Behind that door, steps led to a basement. I tiptoed down, stopping near the bottom, where I could hear what was going on but not yet be seen.

A man was directing a performance. "Don't be afraid of silence," he was saying. "When it's used well, it can be more powerful than the line. Give the audience the opportunity to feel the emotion of the scene. Let it breathe. Now, Danika, I want you to pick it up after Lars lets go of your hand, and this time hold for a count of five before saying your line."

I snuck back up the steps and slipped into the nave to wait for the class to end.

Before me, a stage occupied the area where the sanctuary had once been. Klieg lights mounted to steel pipes framed a proscenium arch. The pews had been replaced with seats bought secondhand from a movie theater. I tapped my foot on the tile floor and listened as the sound filled the room. The acoustics were good. In the small choir loft behind me they had set up sound and light boards. All in all, it was a nice little theater, a perfect forum to showcase a one-act play or maybe something experimental.

I took a seat in the back where I could listen for the actors coming up the stairs. I checked and rechecked the recorder in my pocket as I rehearsed my cover story, trying to anticipate the questions DeChamp might ask. I confess that I felt a bit foolish. I wasn't a private investigator. This was well outside my comfort zone.

Just before 1:30, I heard the movement of amateur performers climbing the steps, taking a break from their weekend acting class. I turned the recorder on and walked to the entrance, watching a stream of twenty-somethings make their way up from the basement. The last to come up the steps was DeChamp, whom I recognized from his picture online: early forties, more handsome from a distance than up close. He looked at me as though I were a puzzle piece put in the wrong box.

"Excuse me, Mr. DeChamp," I said. Now it was my turn to do some acting. "Could I have a moment of your time?"

He stopped but didn't approach, so I walked to him. "My name is Tom Grayson," I said. "I'm with Fredrickson and Bain Publicity. It'll only take a minute."

A very attractive young woman waited for DeChamp at the exit. He nodded to her. "Go on ahead, I'll catch up." Then he turned his full attention to me. "Publicity, huh?"

"I'm working for a mutual friend, and I was hoping to get your take on her project."

"What project might that be?"

"The Prodigal Project."

I could see that I caught him off-guard in the way that he narrowed his eyes and slightly tilted his head. I half expected him to deny any knowledge, but he said, "And by mutual friend, we're talking about..."

"Anna Adler," I said. "She's asked us to put together a publicity proposal for the project and...well, quite frankly, I have questions."

He motioned with his head and led me back into the theater. When the door closed, he asked, "Why is she getting publicity involved now?"

"That was one of our questions as well. She came across as a little impatient to get things started."

"A little?" He gave a chuckle that seemed genuine, but he *was* an actor.

I said, "When she told me that you were attached to the project, I thought I would get your take. In my experience, the client doesn't always have the most objective view, if you know what I mean."

"Yeah, I get that. And with that show in particular there are some serious blind spots."

A show? "Why do you say that?" I asked.

"It's her baby. I mean, it's one thing to put money into a show from an established playwright...but when you're the writer *and* the financier...I don't know."

Anna had written a play? "I'm confused," I said. "I got the impression that you were on board. Your involvement was going to be one of our main selling points."

"Don't get me wrong, as the director I'll do everything I can to turn it into something good, but between you and me...it's a vanity project. You are going to have your work cut out for you."

"So...why are you doing it?"

"Why are *you* doing it?" he parroted back. "It's work. If she wants to finance a play she wrote, I say more power to her. It puts people to work. When you add it all up, we're talking about a cast and crew of what...twenty-five? Thirty? And that doesn't take into consideration the costume designers, set carpenters...people like you...If she wants to spread her wealth around for the rest of us, well, who are we to say no?"

He shot me a conspirator's smile, and I returned it. "Exactly," I said. "But her funding...I understand there's a bit of a glitch."

"Yeah, but..." He glanced around the empty room, I assumed for effect, as we were the only ones in the building. "From what I hear, that guy'll be gone soon, maybe by the end of summer."

"That would be Gordy Baker?"

DeChamp again narrowed his eyes at me.

"I know all about him," I said. "Anna can be an open book when she's excited about something."

"I met him once," DeChamp said. "Quite the stick in the mud."

"And Anna thinks he'll be gone by end of summer?"

"Anna said I can take it to the bank."

"And will you...take it to the bank?"

"What do you mean?"

"I mean...have you started preproduction? Are you casting yet?"

He looked at me as though I had said something so obviously foolish that he need not explain any further. But after a pause, he said, "You don't start spending money until you have it in hand. If you work in this business, you should know that."

"I...thought maybe..."

His smile fell away. "What's the name of your firm again?"

I almost repeated the name of the fake firm I'd given him, but a simple search with his smartphone would have proven me a liar. I had the evidence I needed. Now I had to keep Louis DeChamp quiet about our meeting until I had time to serve him with a subpoena. The best defense is always a good offense, so I decided to try to get him off-balance.

"I gotta tell you, Louis, I'm a little disappointed."

His brow wrinkled. "What do you mean?"

"I did some checking on you. Quite the résumé. To put that all on the line to direct this...what did you call it...a vanity project? Some might say you're selling out."

"We all make compromises," he said. "I don't see you turning down Anna's money."

I smiled. "Mr. DeChamp, I'm a publicist; I polish turds for a living. This is my wheelhouse." I stood to leave before he could push any further, but I left him with parting words that I hoped would keep him from talking to Anna about my visit. "I'll keep our little talk to myself. No reason for Ms. Adler to find out that neither of us has faith in her project. Wouldn't want to kill the fatted calf before we get our due."

He simply stared dumbly at me. I tipped an imaginary hat to the man and slid out the door.

On the drive home I listened to the recording twice, DeChamp's voice clear and resonant, his betrayal of Anna Adler as sweet to me as a lover's kiss.

I called Erica and left a voice mail at her office.

"Hey, Erica. I have Anna's ulterior motive. She's going to fire Gordy Baker to finance a pet project—a play she wrote. I have a guy on tape saying that Adler promised to have funding for the project by the end of summer. The only way that can happen is to remove Gordy, who still has Emma's proxy vote. I'll fill you in on the details later. See you Monday."

As I approached my house, I saw the For Sale sign already up in the front lawn. Like discovering a dent in your car in the grocery store parking lot, I experienced a sharp, visceral response, but let it pass quickly. I had signed on for this. Emma needed to be with us, not Anna. I realized that now more than ever before.

By the time I parked, I had filled my head with dreams of showing Emma our new house. I pictured the three of us eating popcorn in the large TV room, watching some rom-com they'd picked out. I thought of Emma chasing Rufus around the huge yard, throwing his favorite ball as far as she could. Maybe we could put in a pool; Emma could invite her friends over. This would be a home with no ghosts, no bullet hole beneath a plaster patch.

Then I thought of the emptiness that would fill the new house if we didn't get Emma back.

We wouldn't lose her—not now. I had DeChamp on tape; that had to give us a leg up. But there was still much more to do. We needed to change Emma's mind, not with gifts or manipulation as Anna had done, but through honesty, love, and respect.

We were catching up, but we still had a long way to go.

CHAPTER 29

I awoke the next morning, my spirit light, as though I had paid off a great debt. I had a recording of Louis DeChamp laying out Anna's plan. I had also completed the spreadsheet identifying three hundred and eighty-one ideas rejected by Gordy Baker—proposals he'd declined because they weren't in Emma's financial interest. Between those two exhibits, I felt we had a fair fight ahead of us.

I rolled out of bed feeling more hopeful than I had in a week. And because it was Sunday, I decided to go to church.

The service at the Church of the New Hope was set to kick off at 11, but when I arrived at 10, people were already lined out the front doors and down the steps. As I approached, a cool breeze carried the scent of irises and buttercups. Once in line, however, the scent of flowers surrendered to deodorant and Dollar Store perfume. I stood behind a klatch of women in flowered dresses and bob haircuts. Two of them looked so much alike that they could have been sisters, the only discernible difference being that one of them had a strong Southern drawl.

They were talking about Lucas Mammon. The woman with the Southern accent was insisting that Pastor Mammon had to be gay because there was no way a man that beautiful could still be single. Her friend, a woman who chomped a piece of gum as she spoke, replied, "He just hasn't met the right woman yet."

"It's not fair," the Southern woman said. "God puts a man like that on stage and tells us not to have impure thoughts."

They both giggled.

The people in line ahead of them came in all shapes and sizes, although the general hue was decidedly white, and the thirty-something female demographic was heavily represented. I pondered whether the Church of the New Hope would have that same following if the pastor was a troll of a man, bent and blistered, his haggard clothing pulled from donated stock. Or better yet, what if the preacher was a dark-skinned man, say a Middle Easterner, and instead of pacing across a palatial stage he stood on a simple mound of earth? I wondered how many in this mob would stand in line to hear *that* man speak.

As the line worked its way up the steps, I saw a placard informing me that a seat in the center front required a donation of forty dollars, and a seat in the mezzanine, twenty dollars. When it was my turn to "donate," I asked, "Do I have to make a donation to see the show?"

The girl behind the glass looked at me as if I were asking directions to a street that didn't exist. "Excuse me?" she said.

"If I want to sit in the back, do I have to pay?"

"No, sir," she said, a sweet smile replacing the confusion. "You only have to make a donation if you want a premium seat."

"You understand, though, it's not a donation if it's required."

"No, it's a donation. You don't have to pay if you don't want to."

"And I can sit anywhere I want?"

"No, sir. If you don't make a donation, you have to sit on the sides or in the back. They're all good seats though."

"A donation is a voluntary contribution. What you're doing here... is selling tickets."

"So...do you want to donate?"

"Give me a ticket first and then I'll tell you."

She looked confused again. "I can't give you a ticket until I know what your donation is."

I smiled. "I'll take one of the free ones."

The concourse buzzed with conversations as people milled around before the show. Ushers wearing royal blue vests manned the doors to the auditorium, taking tickets and directing people to their seats. Children ran through the space playing a game of chase, their mothers letting them expel energy before forcing them to sit still.

The merchandise booths were stocked full, people selling God's blessing in the form of T-shirts, and magazines, and holy water. One booth sold Bibles ranging anywhere in price from twenty dollars up to ninety-nine bucks—and if you wanted one signed by Pastor Lucas Mammon, the price jumped another hundred dollars. I paused to watch an old woman dig coins from her purse, counting and arranging her pittance in stacks of a dollar each until she had enough on the table to buy a book. The guy manning the booth happily took her money and handed her a paperback titled *Wealth Through Giving*.

I strolled through the crowd, taking it in, feeling a bit like a tourist, hiding the fact that I spoke a different language—one born of skepticism and logic. At the far end of the concourse a wall of windows looked out over a beautiful courtyard, a stone path winding through a manicured lawn to a wedding trellis covered in purple wisteria blossoms. As I stood wondering how much a wedding there might set a person back, a finger tapped my shoulder. It was Lawrence in a royal blue jumpsuit, a small bucket of cleaning supplies in his other hand.

"You come to see the show?" he asked.

"Had to witness it for myself."

He lowered his voice to a whisper. "You know that file you wanted—the one Pastor Mammon told me to fetch?" He looked around to see who might be watching. "I got it downstairs. I was fixin' to call you, but…here you are."

We walked casually to the elevator. When the doors opened, he gave a quick look around before we slipped in. As the doors closed, he said, "I'm not supposed to take people downstairs."

In the basement, Lawrence led me down a long, windowless hallway to a door marked *Maintenance*. Immediately inside was a small locker room with eight lockers and a bench for changing. To the left, an opened door led to a storage room, shelves full of cleaners, towels, mops, and tools. A door straight ahead led to Lawrence's office, a room of spartan décor. He kept it tidy, the desk clear of papers and clutter, his chair simple, plastic, the kind of chair you'd find in a school cafeteria. He picked up an accordion folder from a table behind his desk, an elastic band wrapped around it to hold the flap shut. He handed it to me.

"This is it?" I asked.

"That's the file that Pastor Mammon gave me when he was cleaning out Bale's things."

"I'm curious," I said. "Why did you put it into storage instead of throwing it away?"

Lawrence pulled a folding chair from behind a filing cabinet and opened it for me. We sat. "I don't know…" he said. "I liked Pastor Bale. I guess I wanted to keep his things around for a little while longer. I know he was dead and wasn't coming back, but I just wasn't ready to accept it. Pastor Bale had some boxes down here where he kept his stuff: old sermons, calendars, plaques that the city gave him back when he ran the shelter. I just put the file in there for safekeeping."

"Did you know Bale back when he ran the shelter?"

Something seemed to catch in Lawrence's throat, but he cleared it and said, "That's where we met."

"Were you…homeless?"

He nodded almost imperceptibly. "It's a long story."

"I'd like to hear it…if you don't mind."

He picked at the dirt beneath his fingernails as he considered. Then he said, "When I was a kid…I was stupid and reckless. Hung out with the kind of guys who just seem to find trouble." He looked up at me. "No, that's not right. No one ever led me where I didn't want to go. I found my own damned trouble. One day I got into a scrap about…something or other…I can't quite remember anymore."

Lawrence dropped his head and stared at the back of his knuckles as if that was where his story was written. "I beat a kid pretty bad. Hit him in the temple so hard…caused his brain to bleed. I did seven years in Stillwater for it." He flexed his hands into fists and squeezed a tremor away. "When I got out, no one would give me a job. Couldn't afford a place to live, so I took to the streets. Drank. Got into fights. One night I see this guy sitting on a park bench eating a hamburger and…"

He glanced up at me and then dropped his head again as if in shame. "If you don't know what it's like to be hungry and broke, you'll probably think I'm a monster, but I pulled a knife on that guy and told him that if he didn't give me his hamburger, I was going to cut his throat. And you know what he did?"

"Gave you the hamburger?"

Lawrence smiled. "Yeah, he most certainly did that. But then he reached into his back pocket and pulled out his wallet. I hadn't planned on robbing him. I just wanted his food. He pulled out eighty bucks and handed it to me along with a card. Said he was a pastor at a homeless shelter in South St. Paul."

Tears welled up in Lawrence's eyes. "He said I should stop by if I ever wanted another hamburger."

Lawrence stopped talking as ghosts of that night seemed to fill the air around him. He swallowed hard and said, "Pastor Bale took me in. Gave me a job cleaning up at the shelter. Found me a place to stay. He was a good man."

"You've been with him for a long time."

"Longer than just about anybody."

"Longer than Lilith Cain?"

Lawrence's lip curled and his face became hardened, but he didn't answer.

I asked, "Do you…not like Mrs. Cain?"

Again, he didn't answer, but now he looked at me to size me up. He opened the center drawer of his desk and pulled out a simple manila envelope. "I was planning on giving this to you." He slid the envelope across his desk. "I found it when I was digging though Pastor Bale's stuff yesterday."

The envelope, thin, had once been sealed and taped shut. On its face someone had written the letters *JBC*.

"Whose initials?" I asked.

"My guess would be Jessica Belle Cain, Lilith's daughter."

I thought back to the picture of Lilith at the ground-breaking ceremony—she'd been holding an infant. I peeked inside the envelope and saw a single sheet of paper. I slid it out.

What I saw confused me at first. It appeared to be a report divided into four columns. The first column was a list of letters and numbers that made no sense to me. The second column was blank, and the third and fourth columns were a scattering of numbers.

I looked at the column headings and my confusion fell away. It was a paternity test from seventeen years ago. Column one identified the genetic markers being examined. Column two was blank because the test did not include the mother's DNA. Column three identified the subject child with the initials JBC. Column four identified the alleged father as Jalen Bale.

At the bottom of the page, I read, *Probability of paternity—0%.* I was confused again. I held it up to Lawrence. "What does this mean?"

"My guess is that Pastor Bale thought he might be the father of Jessica Cain. He did this test to find out."

"Bale and Lilith Cain…were a couple?"

"Not officially. I mean, Lilith was married. Still is."

"Let me ask you something." I leaned forward, one conspirator talking to another. "It started out as a homeless shelter…then a small church…then…" I waved a hand. "This place. Did all that money come from Lilith?"

"What she didn't donate herself, she raised. She just showed up at the shelter one day looking for a cause to support."

Hiding money in charities is a good way to protect it from recapture by the government.

"Had the affair been going on this whole time?" I asked.

"After Mr. Cain got arrested for that fraud stuff, Lilith disappeared for a while. I figured things were over between her and Pastor Bale. I didn't see her for more than a year, not until after they sentenced Mr. Cain to prison."

"He got twenty years, if I remember right."

"Then Lilith came back…and she had baby Jessica with her."

"And did their affair pick up again?"

"I try and stay out of other people's business, but…yeah, it picked up again."

"Did Elijah know about the affair?"

"We never talked about it, but…probably."

"You didn't tell the police about Bale and Lilith…when they arrested Elijah?"

"No, sir, I did not."

"Why not? It could be a motive for Bale's murder."

Lawrence leaned his elbows on the desk and stared hard at his hands. "I've been asking myself that question for four years now. I'd like to say I kept quiet because I wasn't sure about the affair, but… yeah, I knew. But you gotta understand, I'm an ex-con. I have a rap sheet that includes aggravated assault. I didn't want them hanging anything on me."

"So you let them hang it on Elijah?"

He dropped his head. "You can't shame me more than I've shamed myself, Mr. Sanden. They said that Pastor Bale wrote Elijah's name in blood. I figured…I mean…I'm trying to make amends."

"You weren't the only one who knew about the affair, Lawrence. Lilith never mentioned it, nor did Mammon. Don't beat yourself up."

"I appreciate that."

"Is Lilith up in her office now?"

"She might be. It's hit-and-miss with her."

"I think I'll drop in and see her."

"They lock the elevator doors on Sundays so people don't wander up there."

"Can you unlock it for me?"

"I'll lose my job if she finds out."

The room fell silent as I contemplated how to get around the locked elevator. Then the big man's lips inched up into a smile. "But it's like I said, I'm trying to make amends. If you need to go upstairs, I'll get you there."

CHAPTER 30

L ilith Cain's office was on the opposite end of the building from
Mammon's, and where his was old wood and leather, hers was
glass and chrome...and empty. Through the glass I could see an outer
office for an assistant, the desktop sleek and milky white, resting atop
silver legs—no drawers. The room had a sofa and two chairs, white
leather, gleaming as though they had never been used.

Beyond the assistant's space was another glass wall with blinds
opened enough to see Lilith's desk, another huge glass tabletop with
legs that angled inward as though they were partially folded, an
added touch to make sure you knew that the thing was expensive.
Also no drawers. Where did they keep their files? Maybe there were
hidden drawers in the walls or some space-age cabinet that popped
out of the floor, pretentious crap paid for by the hopeful parishioners
below.

I was mid-debate on whether to wait or leave when I heard footsteps behind me. A young woman with dark hair pinned up to look
both messy and intentional walked down the hall toward me from the
direction of the elevator. She wore a knee-length cocktail dress with a
dropped neckline—not the attire women wore to church back when I
sat in the pews. She had dark eyes and an attractive face that currently
messaged, *I belong here and you don't.*

Yet despite the New York chic, she walked with the awkward
gait of a teenager, and as she drew closer, I saw why—she was a

teenager, the hair and the dress simply a disguise to make her appear older. I tucked the file Lawrence had given me under my left arm.

"Can I help you?" she asked. Her sharp tone let me know that helping me was not the point of her question.

"I'm here to see Lilith Cain," I said.

"Do you have an appointment—and before you answer, keep in mind that I make her appointments."

"Then you know that I don't."

"How'd you get up here? No one's allowed up here."

To keep Lawrence's name out of it, I said, "I had a meeting with Pastor Mammon." I held up the file as if that answered her next, unasked question.

She tipped her head, appraised me, and in that movement, a subtle twitch in her left eye drew my attention. It was there and gone in a second. She then said, "You're that guy."

I waited, and when she didn't say more, prompted her with, "You'll have to be a little more specific."

"The guy who's messing around with Pastor Bale's...death. The guy who thinks that Elijah didn't do it."

"Boady Sanden," I said, holding out my hand. She didn't take it.

"He's guilty, you know."

"Do you expect Lilith soon?"

"Her name is Mrs. Cain," she said. She unlocked the door and walked into the office. I slipped in behind her.

"Okay, do you expect...*Mrs. Cain* here soon?"

"You haven't told me your business with her."

"That's because it's my business."

"My mother doesn't always come on Sundays. She's not big on crowds."

"Your mom?" So this was Jessica Belle Cain.

"Yes, my mom." She curled her lip into a snarl the way teenagers do, and pointed at Lilith's office. "I'm her daughter, so that makes her my mom."

"Well, hello, Jessica."

She took a long moment to walk behind the desk and sit down. "You know my name," she said.

"Among other things." There was something about her attitude that made me want to put her off-balance.

"Like what?"

"You don't mind if I wait here, do you?" I sat on the gleaming white leather sofa.

"Like I said, I don't think she's coming in today."

"But you're not sure."

"Elijah threatened us. You know he's crazy. Why are you digging this all up again? It's really none of your business."

I opened the folder and started looking through it, ignoring Jessica's question. I found a packet of glossy brochures with a picture of the old homeless shelter on the front. Unfolded, it held several more pictures inside, of people being helped: old, young, men, women, children. The shelter was a modest structure with two lines of beds running the length of the building. Another picture showed the small kitchen. On the back page were the statistics of how many people had been served that year and a plea for donations to build an addition with a chapel and showers.

Jessica said, "I think you should wait downstairs."

Had Lilith built this new church through fundraising—or had she been hiding her and Ed's stolen money? When I pulled some more papers out of the folder, a thumb drive fell onto my lap. I picked it up and examined it.

"What's that?" Jessica asked.

"Just some stuff your mother worked on before you were born. It's what I came to talk to her about."

"Who gave you that?" She sounded almost distressed at my having her mother's old file on my lap.

"Pastor Mammon said I could look at it." Technically that was true, although Mammon had not specifically given me permission to take the file with me.

"That belongs to the church."

"Technically it belonged to Pastor Bale; it was his before this church existed."

"But it's ours. It's here, now, and possession is nine-tenths of the law."

That nearly made me chuckle. "First of all," I said, "I'm a law professor, and that old adage is nothing but rubbish. Second…" I held the file up. "I have possession."

I expected her to fire off another pointless argument, but instead she had turned her head and looked out through the glass and into the hallway. When she did, her left eye again caught my attention. It didn't track with her right eye. Where her right eye gave a sideways glance, the iris of her left eye turned upward. She gave a small shake of her head, a move so subtle that I almost missed it. I turned to look over my shoulder and saw Lucas Mammon in the hall, frozen in his tracks. When he saw me, he turned and walked away, trying to be casual in his retreat.

Jessica returned her attention to me, her pale cheeks flushed red, her breath catching in her chest as if she had just been holding it. She wore the look of a woman caught committing a sin. I took a shot. "Does your mother know about you and Lucas?"

"What are you talking about?"

I just smiled.

"I think you should go. My mother's not coming in today."

"How old is he? Thirty-five?"

"He's thirty-two…and I'll be eighteen in—" She stopped and stood behind her desk; her knuckles pressed into the white marble desktop. "You know what? It's none of your fucking business, is it? This is my church—my office. If you aren't out of here in two seconds, I'm calling the police."

I raised my hands to signal my surrender. "I'm going," I said. I picked up the file and tucked it back under my arm. As I walked to the door I said, "It was a pleasure meeting you."

She didn't respond.

CHAPTER 31

<u>**Direct examination of Jessica Cain by
Ms. Addams, cont.**</u>

Addams: Ms. Cain, when you say you felt
           uncomfortable around the Defendant,
           did he do anything to make you feel
           that way?

J. Cain: He used to say Bible quotes to me, like
           he was judging me or something.

Addams: What kind of Bible quotes?

J. Cain: Like one time, I asked him to clean up
           the microwave in the upstairs galley.
           I was trying to boil an egg and…well,
           it kind of exploded. I passed him in
           the hallway and told him about it, and
           he said, "One day, the Lord Almighty
           will humble those who are proud and

conceited." It was like he was calling
me conceited because…I don't know. He's
the janitor. Cleaning up things is
his job.

Addams: Were there other things he said?

J. Cain: Yes, all the time. He'd say things like
"The meek shall inherit the earth," or
"The Lord detests the prideful. They
will not go unpunished."

Addams: And did you take that as a threat?

J. Cain: Of course I did.

Addams: There was an incident that you told
investigators about that happened in
the basement of the church. Can you
tell us about that?

J. Cain: So I was in the basement looking for
something, and I walked past
the janitors' room, and I hear a
voice, so I stop to listen, and it's
Elijah.

Addams: The Defendant?

J. Cain: Yeah, the Defendant. He was upset, kind
of crying almost. At least that's what
it sounded like to me.

Addams: Just tell the jury what you actually
            saw or heard.

J. Cain: Sure. He said, "Is there any other way,
            Lord?" And he sounded so…Well, it made
            me curious so I peeked in.

Addams: What did you see?

J. Cain: He was on his knees and there was a book
            on the floor in front of him—a Bible.

Addams: When you say he was on his knees…like
            he was sick, or…

J. Cain: Like he was praying. And he said, "I
            beg thee, Lord, do not make a bed for
            him among the slain. But if it is thy
            will…thy will be done."

Addams: What happened then?

J. Cain: There's an intercom in that locker
            area, and Lawrence, the head janitor,
            called Elijah to go do something. I saw
            Elijah put a bookmark in the page he'd
            been reading. I hid around the corner
            until he left, then I went back in and
            looked at his Bible.

Addams: Did you ascertain which page his Bible
            had been opened to?

J. Cain: Yes.

Addams: And what page was that?

J. Cain: He was reading Malachi, chapter four.

Addams: Your Honor, may I approach the witness?

Court: You may.

Addams: Ms. Cain, I'm showing you what has
            previously been marked exhibit
            eighteen. It's been identified as
            Elijah's personal Bible. Is this the
            page he had bookmarked?

J. Cain: It is.

Addams: Could you read that opening passage for
            the jury?

J. Cain: Sure. "The Lord Almighty says, 'The
            day is coming when all proud and evil
            people will burn like straw. On that
            day they will burn up and there will be
            nothing left of them.'"

Addams: What did you think he meant by that?

Pruitt: Objection.

Court: Sustained.

Addams: Then tell me, how did it make you feel
            to read that?

J. Cain: I felt threatened, like he wanted to
            kill us all.

Addams: Thank you, Ms. Cain. I have no further
            questions.

Court: Defense counsel, your
            cross-examination.

Cross-examination of Jessica Cain by Mr. Pruitt.

Pruitt: Thank you, Your Honor. Ms. Cain, you
            never mentioned what you were looking
            for in the basement that day.

J. Cain: I don't remember; it was almost a
            year ago.

Pruitt: But you remember what page of the Bible
            you read.

J. Cain: I do.

Pruitt: There are other verses in Malachi,
            chapter four...verses that follow
            what you read in court just now,
            verses about God raising good

people up like the sun. Did you
read that when you snuck into that
locker room?

J. Cain: I don't remember.

Pruitt: It says that the good people will be
free and happy as calves let loose
from their stalls. Does that ring a
bell?

J. Cain: I don't know.

Pruitt: Elijah Matthews never once said Pastor
Bale's name, did he?

J. Cain: Not that I remember.

Pruitt: And he didn't read any particular
passage out loud, so you don't know
which verse he actually read—if any.

J. Cain: Not the actual words, but—

Pruitt: In fact, you have no direct proof that
he was reading anything at all. You
simply saw the Bible on the floor.

J. Cain: That's the page with the bookmark.

Pruitt: You didn't like Elijah because he found
you to be proud and conceited.

J. Cain: I was his boss. He had no business
talking to me like that.

Pruitt: You were his boss? You were thirteen
years old. You were only there because
you worked for your mother. He was
a grown man who you treated like a
servant.

J. Cain: It was his job to clean up messes.

Pruitt: But it was your mess. He calls you
proud and you get back at him by coming
here and slinging speculation and
conjecture.

J. Cain: I felt threatened.

Pruitt: If you were his boss, why didn't you
just fire him?

J. Cain: I...um...

Pruitt: You didn't fire him because you weren't
his boss.

J. Cain: No, but—

Pruitt: So you lied to the court—to this jury.

J. Cain: I wasn't his boss, but—

Pruitt: But you considered yourself his
             superior. You looked down on him and
             he committed the unforgivable sin of
             calling you out for your pride.

Addams: Objection. He's badgering the witness.

Court: Sustained.

Pruitt: I have no further questions, Your
             Honor.

CHAPTER 32

The next morning, I awoke from a dream that I couldn't quite remember, a dream that had left its weight. The day had come for our hearing; Dee and I would soon find out if we were to ever see Emma again. I sat up and put my feet on the floor just to feel the reassuring gravity.

We were due in court at four thirty that afternoon. Is that what my dream had been about—Emma's hearing?

I walked to the bathroom and splashed water on my face, resting my elbows on the vanity, waiting there as the droplets fell back into the basin. I had never felt so powerless. We didn't have a guardian ad litem report yet or a psychological report to counter what Anna had hit us with. We were throwing ourselves on the mercy of the court, begging for a visit with a girl who didn't want to be with us.

With my eyes closed, I found a hand towel and dried my face. When I opened my eyes, Dee stood in the doorway, her robe hanging loose on her shoulders, her fingers holding the lapels closed over her heart. I walked to her and pulled her in, wrapping my arms around her, clasping the flannel of her robe. She leaned in and held me. Neither of us said a word.

We ate a breakfast of toast and cereal barely speaking, for no words could relieve the dread that hung over us. As we were rinsing our bowls, Dee finally said what I had been thinking. "I don't think I can sit here and wait. I'll go crazy."

"I know."

"I have a potential listing in Woodbury. I'm gonna see if they have time to meet. It'll take my mind off...everything."

I had considered going back to the Church of the New Hope, maybe catching Lilith to ask her a few questions. But really it was Elijah that I wanted to see. His Jarvis hearing was ticking closer and I now knew something that Ben hadn't: Jalen Bale and Lilith Cain were lovers. Did Elijah know? And what about that passage from Malachi—the one about putting the proud to death—had he really been reading that? What had he meant when he prayed that God not make a bed for Bale among the slain?

I called ahead to make sure that Dr. Cohen could get me in to see him. I wasn't sure if Dr. Handler might get in the way of my visit. She worked it out and when I arrived Elijah was already in the conference room, sitting alone at a small table, an open Bible in front of him.

I sat down across from Elijah. "Good book?" I asked, hoping he would get the pun. If he did, he didn't show it. "How're you feeling?"

"Today, I soar on the wings of angels."

He smiled at me, but I saw nothing for him to be happy about. His left eye, still red from a ruptured blood vessel, peeked out from a swollen, purple face. Beyond that, he was locked in a psychiatric hospital and facing the prospect of having his mind prodded with electricity. Maybe there was something to be said about living a life of delusion.

"So why the high spirits?" I asked.

"Jake came to see me this morning."

A jolt of anger pulsed through me. I had made it clear that he was to leave Elijah alone.

"He apologized," Elijah said. "He was contrite and low, his heart in his hand." Elijah looked like he was about to shed tears of joy. "He asked his wife for forgiveness and ended his lying. Isn't it amazing what God can do?"

What God can do? It had been my threat that had motivated Jake. "I suppose you see this as a miracle," I said.

"There are no miracles, my friend. God's hand is in everything; it's only when we can't explain it that we call it a miracle."

"Well, I can explain this one. Jake apologized because I told him to. He knew that his job was at stake. God had nothing to do with it."

Elijah smiled like a man explaining a riddle. "God works through the agency of men—even men like you."

"Believe that if it helps," I said. "I'm just here to do my job, which"—I pulled the trial transcript out of my case—"brings me to my questions."

"I will do my best to make the path straight."

"Jessica Cain testified that she had been eavesdropping on you when you were in the basement—in the janitors' locker room. Remember that?"

"I remember."

"You didn't know she was there?"

"Because I am a prophet of God, you think I should be all-knowing?"

"Isn't that how it works?"

He smiled as if tickled by a joke that went over my head. "No, it is not."

"So, God didn't mention that Jessica Cain was listening to you."

"No."

"I find that oddly convenient."

"Why is that?"

"A little heads-up would have been helpful in that moment."

"But then I wouldn't have been sent here," he said. "I wouldn't have met you." He closed his Bible and held my gaze. "Love drives out fear, Mr. Sanden. Love protects."

"What does that have to do with anything?"

He shrugged and gave an impish smile. "Maybe nothing. Maybe everything."

"Stay with me, Elijah; this is important. Jessica Cain testified that you were reading from the Book of Malachi—chapter four." I flipped through the pages of the transcript to find that passage.

"That is true."

"Where Malachi talks about burning the proud."

"Those are the words of God as Malachi spoke them."

"She also testified that she heard you say..." I ran a finger down the transcript page to the quote. "'I beg thee, Lord, do not make a bed for him among the slain. But if it is thy will...thy will be done.' Did you say those words?"

Something dark moved through Elijah.

"Did you say that, Elijah?"

He nodded but didn't speak.

"What were you talking about?"

"What shall it profit a man if he gains the world but loses his soul?"

"I don't know what that's supposed to mean. Were you talking about Pastor Bale?"

"I walk, but it is the Lord who sets my path. Sometimes I am sent to save a life, and sometimes I am sent to save a soul. The place for those who worship wealth is a lake of fire and sulfur. It is a second death."

I lifted my hands in a kind of *I give up* motion. "So yes or no...were you talking about Pastor Bale?"

"What is more important, Mr. Sanden, a man's body or his soul?"

I huffed my frustration, although I didn't mean to. "Can you just answer my question with a simple yes or no? Were you talking about Pastor Bale?"

"Yes."

"Thank you." I felt like I was trying to capture a feral cat. "My next question is, did you know that Jalen Bale was having an affair with Lilith Cain?" I held up my finger before he could speak. "And please, just yes or no."

"Why is that important?"

"Tell me yes or no and I will tell you why it's important."

Again he looked grieved to give an answer. "Yes, I was aware of it."

"Okay. So, what I'm doing here is trying to get your case reopened. I have what is arguably an alibi—you at the library—although a good prosecutor will be able to poke holes in it. I need to bring in other suspects with motives for killing Bale. Lilith Cain is married. That brings her husband into the picture. Lilith may have had a falling-out with Bale—that brings her in as a suspect. We might have two alternative perpetrators here that the original detectives didn't know about."

I expected Elijah to be excited about my strategy, but he took the news like a man listening to a bus schedule. "I see."

"But there's a problem," I said. "Because you knew about the affair, the prosecutor will add that to your motivation for killing Bale."

"My motivation?"

"The Bible says that adultery is a sin, right? It's on the list of the big ten. You being a man of God and all, you can hardly overlook something that clear-cut."

"All sins are forgivable. God forgave David for his…affair with Bathsheba."

I knew the story of Bathsheba. I had read it back in college. I had read it again when my daughter Julia was born dead. That story had caused me to throw my Bible across the room. David saw Bathsheba sunbathing on a rooftop and decided he would have her. When he got her pregnant, David killed Bathsheba's husband. And yes, God forgave David, but only after killing their infant child.

"Yeah, God forgave David," I said, unable to keep the edge of anger out of my voice. "But he killed the child—an innocent baby. Tell me, Elijah, why did that child deserve to die? What sin had that baby committed?"

"As the heavens are higher than the earth, so are God's ways higher than man's—His thoughts higher than ours. In other words, the Lord works in mysterious—"

I slammed my hand down on the tabletop to stop Elijah from talking. Something burned hot inside my chest. I wanted to yell at Elijah, grab him by the collar and shake him. I gripped the sides of the table to stay in my seat.

"The Bible can justify anything you want it to," I said, the words seething through my teeth. "You want to say that up is down? You'll find a passage for that. Talking donkeys, giants, rivers of blood, slavery, murder, it's all there. Jephthah killed his daughter—he gets a pass. Lot had sex with his daughters, and hey, no harm no foul, because he was drunk. Do you have any idea how many of my rape clients I could have kept out of prison if that were a defense? People use the Bible to justify war and torture. You want to beat the hell out of your gay neighbor? The Bible has your back."

I let go of the table and leaned in, my chest filled with a rage so powerful I could barely breathe. "God kills babies…babies who didn't do a damn thing wrong. Well, it's fucking bullshit!" Spit flicked off my tongue as I punched the words.

Elijah's face held no expression, as unmoved by my rant as if I had been speaking a language he didn't understand. I settled back into my chair and stared at him, waiting for him to utter another feckless Bible quote.

Instead, he said, "I know you're hurting, Mr. Sanden, and I wish there was something I could say to comfort you, but…I don't understand why children die any more than you do. My heart breaks every day for what could be. But I'm only a man. I hear God's words and I obey."

His soft tone broke my anger. He hadn't been the one to take Julia away. It wasn't fair that I unload on him. When I spoke again, I held my temper in check. "Elijah, you're a schizophrenic. Look around you. Everyone here thinks they talk to God. You're not a prophet. You're a man who needs help."

This made him smile. "And God has sent you to help me."

I gave up. Nothing I said would break through the wall of his delusion. "Yeah," I said. "I'm here to help you."

"I appreciate what you are doing," he said. "And as a token of my esteem for you, can I offer you something?"

"What's that?"

He looked around as though someone in that empty room might overhear him, a playful gesture on his part. Then he leaned in and said, "I don't disagree with you...about the Bible saying all kinds of different things—being used to justify evil deeds—but I know a secret about the Bible. There is a way to read it that can lead you in truth. It's a secret that God Himself whispered in my ear."

I decided to play along. "I'll bite. What's the secret?"

"Do you own a Bible, Mr. Sanden?"

I thought of the two Bibles I had at home: one a family heirloom handed down from Dee's great-grandmother, a beautiful leather-bound antique with gilded pages. The other Bible was my beat-up paperback with a broken spine, the one I had once thrown across the room. "Yeah, I have a Bible," I said.

"Bring it the next time you visit and I will share my secret with you."

He stood, brushed his hands down the front of his shirt as if to wipe the sweat from his palms, and held out his hand. "I have an appointment to go to," he said. "I'm sure you have more important things to tend to as well."

I had not asked all of the questions I wanted to ask, and those few I had managed to get out had worn me down, the slog of communicating with Elijah being a challenge worthy of Sisyphus. I shook Elijah's hand, his fingers frail against my palm, and didn't object as he walked out of the conference room.

CHAPTER 33

My drive back to St. Paul took me within ten minutes of the Church of the New Hope. With three hours before the guardianship hearing, I figured I could pass the time sitting at home staring at the walls, or I could swing by the church and maybe catch Lilith Cain. I called the church and the automated phone message told me to press 5 for her office. I obeyed and Jessica answered, her voice perky until I announced my name.

"Mrs. Cain isn't in. Can I take your number and have her call you back?"

I gave her my number but held no hope that I would get a return call. The only way I was going to talk to Lilith was if I cornered her.

There were no cars in the church's parking lot, but a narrow access road led to a small reserved lot in back. I found three cars, two BMWs and a Mercedes, each with a personalized plate. One of the Beemers had a plate that read *LILITH* and the other read *JESSIE,* so it was no great challenge figuring out who those belonged to. It also told me that Lilith Cain was inside. The Mercedes had a plate that read *PASTOR.*

I drove back to the main lot, called the church, and again followed the automated trail to Lilith's office.

"Hello, Jessica," I said in my most polite voice. "Could I speak to your mother, Lilith?"

I heard a huff and then, "She's not here. I told you that I'd have her call you when she gets in."

I went to the entrance and tried all three of the doors. Locked. I thought about contacting Lawrence, but he had risked his job already. Then an idea came to me. If I could get Mammon to invite me in, I could ask him a couple questions first and then wander down the hall to Lilith's office. With my third call to the church, I followed the automated voice commands to Mammon.

"It's Boady Sanden," I said. "I was wondering if I could stop by and ask you a couple more questions."

"Um...I'm not sure I have the time," he said. "I have...um...a meeting and...after that...some other stuff."

"It won't take long, only a couple questions." There was a pause, so I added, "I'm at your front door."

Another pause, this time followed by a sigh. "Okay, but only a couple questions. I'll be right down."

Mammon opened the door with no greeting, no smile.

I followed him to his office, passing where a receptionist or assistant might have staffed the front desk. Once we took our seats, I asked him about that. "This is the second time I've been here, and I've noticed that..." I half turned and pointed to the outer office with my thumb. "You don't have an assistant."

"I don't see how that's any of your business."

"I only ask because in reading the file from Elijah's trial, I noticed that Bale had no assistant either."

"As pastor, I have an entire staff at my disposal." He did a sweeping motion toward the corridor beyond his door. "I have an accountant, a scheduler, a publicist...just about anything I want."

"Yet Lilith has her daughter working for her. I would think that you might have more need of an assistant than Lilith."

Mammon smiled and shrugged. "It's a family business. You know how it is. A parent finds a place for her kid even if it's not vital to the operation. Jessie's a good person."

I thought back to the look that had passed between them when he showed up outside Lilith's office. I pressed on.

"What's the deal between you two?"

"She's a coworker."

"That's all?"

"You said you had a couple questions for me?"

I crossed one leg over the other, a posture of confidence I used to take in jury trials, my way of telegraphing to the witness that I knew more than they thought I did.

"Why didn't you tell the police about the affair between Pastor Bale and Lilith Cain?" I asked.

Mammon opened his mouth, a glint of deceit in his eyes. He was going to lie to me, but the glint faded. "Why are you trying to stir up trouble? Where does any of this get you? Bale is dead and Elijah killed him."

"Why didn't you tell the police about the affair?"

"What good would it do? Jalen Bale was my friend. He was dead. All it would have done was sully his reputation...and put a cloud over Lilith and the church. It had nothing to do with Jalen's death."

"You can't believe that," I said. "A man dies and the fact that he's having an affair with a married woman doesn't seem important to you?"

"It wasn't important because they broke it off." Mammon spat the words out.

"When?"

Mammon just shook his head as though he had said more than he was supposed to.

"Did you know about the DNA test?"

Mammon's face flushed red; he didn't have to answer. I said, "Bale thought he might be Jessica's father."

"Who told you about that?"

"When did it end?"

Mammon couldn't seem to get past the tangle of lies that knotted up in his throat, so I added a nudge of encouragement, words that I knew came from one of the Gospels, although I couldn't remember which one. "Remember what Jesus said: 'The truth will set you free.'"

His nostrils flared and his eyes narrowed, but after a few seconds his features softened. He tapped a finger on the desk as he pondered something. When he finally spoke, he looked out the window, not at me.

"Jalen wasn't just my friend; he was my mentor. When he introduced me to Lilith, I thought there was something between them, but I ignored it. Then Lilith disappeared for a while. She was going through all that rigmarole with her husband. I honestly thought the affair was over. We were all shocked when Lilith showed back up with a baby. That's when Jalen confessed to me about the affair."

"And Bale thought the baby might be his?"

"It made sense. Lilith got pregnant just before they arrested Ed, so Jessie could have been either man's daughter."

"And Jalen did the paternity test."

"Not right away. He agonized over it for months. He kept asking Lilith if he was the father, and she kept telling him no. Finally, he demanded that they do a DNA test. I think a part of Jalen was disappointed that he wasn't the father."

"But at some point the affair started up again?"

"Lilith can be a hard person to say no to. She's the one who pushed Jalen to build this place and leave the shelter he'd built in South St. Paul. If he'd never met Lilith, Jalen would probably still be passing out soup."

"So, when did it end?"

My question hung in the air as Mammon wrestled with his answer. When his defiance died away, he said, "Jalen broke it off about... a week before he died."

192

As a trial attorney, you develop a poker face. If a witness went rogue on the stand, you had to hold your composure, but I'm sure my jaw dropped a bit hearing Mammon say that.

"A week?" I tried to keep my voice calm and even. "Bale broke off… an affair two decades old…a week before he was murdered…and you didn't bother telling this to the police."

"It wasn't important. It had nothing to do with—"

"That's not your call." My words seethed. "You don't get to decide what's important and what's not."

"Jalen was my friend. His reputation—"

"They set their sights on Elijah Matthews because he'd made cryptic threats against Bale—an easy motive. But the affair gives Ed Cain a motive to kill Bale. Now you say that Bale broke it off with Lilith one week before his death. That makes her a perfect suspect, too. Jesus Christ!"

"Jalen wrote Elijah's name in blood. What more proof did they need?"

"Anyone could have written that."

"You weren't here. You didn't see how Elijah stalked around."

I stood and walked away from the desk, turning toward the shelves stacked with treatises on how to live a moral life. This jerk just didn't get it.

Mammon said, "He used to pop up out of nowhere, say little quips like 'He who has money will never have enough,' or 'Lead us not into temptation.' Every time I saw Elijah, he had some little jab. 'Thou shalt not covet.' He probably said that to me a hundred times."

I had reached the end of the shelves, and so I turned. "And what was it that you coveted?"

"What?"

"'Thou shalt not covet'…what did Elijah think you were coveting?"

"Elijah was a nutjob. I didn't covet anything. He's insane—the court said so."

The sound of someone entering Mammon's outer office came through the closed door. I stopped talking and waited.

The door opened with me hidden behind it. "Hey, handsome, you ready?" It was Jessica Cain.

"Jessie, I have..." Mammon gestured to where I stood behind the door. "Company."

When Jessica saw me, her smile fell away. "What are you..." She looked at Mammon and back at me, her left eye again not tracking with the right. Without another word, she turned and walked out, slamming the door behind her.

"Was it something I said?"

"She's not a fan," Mammon said. "You're dredging up some painful memories for her. Elijah tormented her when he was here."

"Called her prideful," I said. "I read her testimony."

"He basically threatened her, saying that the prideful should be punished."

I wondered in that moment which Mammon had coveted more, Bale's pastorship or Jessica. She had called him handsome, not a standard greeting between coworkers. I walked back to my chair and sat down.

"She's what, seventeen?" I asked, knowing the answer already.

"She'll be eighteen next week."

"That thing with her eye..." I said. "I teach field sobriety tests to my students—it's kind of a hobby of mine. There's one called the horizontal gaze nystagmus. You know...where the cop moves a pen in front of your eyes. I know that there are certain palsies that can cause an eye to be lazy like that. Is that what Ms. Cain has?"

"Not that it's any of your business, but Jessica had a condition called Duane syndrome. She's very self-conscious of it, so for that lunatic Elijah to call her prideful...well, it was a lie—an insult. Why we didn't fire him..."

"You didn't fire him because Pastor Bale wouldn't let you fire him."

Mammon nodded.

"Did he ever insult Bale with a Bible quote?"

"Not that I know of. The relationship those two had never made much sense to me."

"Bale's killer took his laptop. Can you think of any reason why Elijah would do that?"

"Elijah was—is—insane, legally. Who can guess the workings of a madman?"

"What did Bale use the laptop for?"

"The usual: research, social media stuff. He wrote his sermons on it."

"I understand Bale was working on his final sermon when he was killed."

"Final sermon?" Mammon shook his head. "What are you talking about?"

"That's what he told Elijah. He never said anything like that to you?"

"No...but..."

"But what?"

"That last week...before he died, something was wrong. He wasn't himself."

"What do you mean?"

"I was here late one night—just finishing up some work—and his lights were on, so I stopped by. He was sitting here at his desk, working on his laptop. He looked like crap. He hadn't showered or shaved in a while. He had bags under his eyes like he hadn't been sleeping. That was the night he asked me to find that old file of promotional stuff."

"Did he say anything else?"

"Yeah, we talked for a bit. I asked him if he was okay and he said he was on his way to being okay."

"Any idea what he meant by that?"

"I thought he had the flu or something. I asked him what he was working on so late and he said...a sermon about bones."

"Bones," I repeated.

"That's what he said."

"Did he explain what he meant?"

"No."

"Just out of curiosity, was this before or after he ended his relationship with Lilith?"

Mammon gave my question some thought. "I'm pretty sure that was after...yeah, maybe a day or two after."

"Anything else?"

Mammon thought for a second and said, "When I was leaving, he mumbled something under his breath. I recognized it from Proverbs. He said, 'The house of the wicked will be destroyed, but the tent of the upright will flourish.'"

"Did you ask him to explain that?"

"Honestly, I just thought he was overtired...or maybe feverish. We never talked about it."

I had spent more time with Mammon than I had planned to, and now that Jessica had seen me, it wouldn't be long before Lilith knew that I was in the building. I needed to talk to her. "I appreciate you seeing me, Pastor." I stood. "Sorry if I interfered with your lunch date."

Mammon didn't stand. "It wasn't a date."

"You know, just because it's technically legal doesn't make it right."

"You need to leave."

"I'll show myself out."

I left his office and walked down the hall to Lilith's office. Through the glass wall I could see that it was empty, as was the outer office where Jessica normally sat.

I was about to make my way back to the elevator when I saw an exit sign above a nondescript metal door. I tried it, and it opened to a stairwell, the concrete steps painted an ugly gray. At the bottom of the steps, a door led out to the reserved parking lot where Lilith's and Jessica's cars had been parked.

Their cars were gone.

CHAPTER 34

Dee and I met Erica in one of the small meeting rooms that lined the hallway outside the courtroom, a space barely big enough to hold a table and four chairs. I had seen Anna's lawyer scamper into another of the small rooms down the way. I doubted that they'd brought Emma to the hearing, but if they did, she would be in that room with them.

"I got an email from the judge's clerk this morning regarding the final hearing," Erica said. "A slot opened on the judge's calendar two weeks out." She studied my reaction, which fell somewhere between surprise and concern. Nothing moved that fast in St. Paul.

"Two weeks?" I was about to say that it wasn't enough time, but Dee stepped into the conversation.

"Can we be ready by then?" she asked.

"I have the psychologist lined up. She's reviewing the report of Anna's expert and says she can shoot some pretty big holes in it—especially now that you're moving out of your house. As for the guardian ad litem, I think he can have a report completed in time. The only other witness is that guy you found. What can you tell me about him?"

"Nothing right now," I said.

Erica looked confused. "I thought you said you had a witness."

"When we go in front of the judge, she'll ask you for your witness list. Give her the name of our psychologist and guardian. Tell her that we plan on calling a third witness but you don't have that person's information yet. That will be a true statement."

Erica didn't look happy.

"Once we have a date for the hearing, we can subpoena the witness. I don't want his name out there until he's under subpoena. Anna might send him out of the country."

"What about the two weeks?" Erica asked. "What's your feeling on that?"

I was about to say that it was too soon, but Dee piped up. "If we have our ducks in a row, why wait?"

I said, "We need time with Emma. Get her to see that we're the better choice."

Dee turned to Erica. "Will you get us visitations today?"

"There's no guarantee."

The room went silent as Dee held the floor. She sat down in her chair as though the weight of her decision demanded it, her fingers clutching the edge of the small table.

I had my thoughts on the matter, legal points and strategy, but those were empty casks next to the flood of emotion pulsing through her veins. I gently put my hand on her back, my pinky resting on her right shoulder blade to let her know that I would support whatever she decided.

"The way I see it," she said. "If you can get us some visits with Emma…we should know where she stands pretty quickly. She'll either feel the connection or she won't—and if she doesn't…I'm not going to manipulate her into coming back. Emma has to want to come back. A visit or two will tell me all I need to know. And if we don't get visitation…well, then it really doesn't matter how long until the next hearing."

Erica looked to me for confirmation. I nodded.

"Okay then," Erica said, glancing at her watch. "We might as well head into court."

It felt odd not being the attorney in charge of the case, to sit quietly at counsel table not speaking my piece. But I have to admit, Erica knew her stuff. She started with an attack on the validity of the ex parte order, the part of the case we fully expected to lose. She laid out the timeline for Anna's experts, making it clear to the court that Adler had been working on her scheme for over a year.

"The Sandens didn't have to grant Ms. Adler visitation after they were named guardians," Erica argued. "Ms. Adler repaid their generosity by undermining them at every turn. But the Sandens were looking out for Emma's best interest. They wanted her to have contact—a relationship—with her aunt. They did this even though they knew that Ms. Adler might someday launch the frivolous attack that brings us here today."

Smart. Lay the groundwork for our theory here so that the judge will have that in her head before we even show up for the final hearing.

I glanced at Anna to see how she was taking it. She wore a dark suit, tailored but understated, an attempt to downplay her wealth. She needed the court to believe that none of this had to do with business or money, a façade that would come crashing down once we put Louis DeChamp on the stand.

As Erica had predicted, the judge was not willing to second-guess another judge's ex parte order, and let it stand. It was official. Emma would stay with Anna until the final hearing decided the case. Anna had control over Emma and all of her assets. She could choose a new conservator now if she wanted to, one who would rubber-stamp her vanity project. But if she was smart, she would wait until after the final hearing. Any move now would expose her scheme for what it was.

Then came the argument for visitation.

"Your Honor, over the four years of Emma living with the Sandens, she became a part of their family. Then Ms. Adler went to work undermining that relationship. Ms. Adler manipulated Emma, using the tragedy of Emma's father's death to turn her against Mr.

and Mrs. Sanden, manipulating her into signing that affidavit. We are asking that the court grant reasonable visitation between now and the final hearing."

Erica paused before proceeding to her next argument, as if contemplating whether or not to make it, but she proceeded. "Your Honor, when this case is laid out at trial, you'll see that Ms. Adler isn't doing this because she loves her niece. She's doing it to gain control over Adler Enterprises, a company that Emma—through her conservator—now controls. That's the real reason—"

"Objection." Adler's attorney stood and raised his hand. "This is wildly inappropriate. There is no evidence whatsoever to support counsel's bald-faced accusation. I demand that she apologize to Ms. Adler at once. This court—"

"Mr. Weisman," the judge interrupted. "You'll have your turn to argue. Your objection is overruled. Ms. Dennis has the right to state her position. When we have the evidentiary hearing, she will be put to the task of backing up her allegations. For now, the court will receive it for what it's worth."

"Thank you, Your Honor," Erica said.

"And Ms. Dennis," the judge continued, "I have no patience for attorneys who submit baseless allegations, so I will advise you that you'd better come prepared to prove your assertion with evidence."

"I will, Your Honor," Erica said.

Adler's attorney, Mr. Weisman, went for the easy counterargument, pointing out that Dee and I still lived in the same house where Emma's father had been killed. The grounds that supported the original order had not been abated.

Erica asked for rebuttal.

"Two things," she said. "First, if the court deems it appropriate, the Sandens are agreeable to have visits at a location other than their home. That will alleviate Mr. Weisman's concerns. And second, I neglected to mention this earlier, but the Sandens are moving out of their house. They've put a contingent offer down on a new home in Lake Elmo. Once their house sells, the problem that seems to be at the heart of all this will be eliminated. They love Emma so much that they are willing to give up their home to be with her."

Anna broke out of her poker face for just a moment before regaining her composure. She leaned to Weisman and whispered something. He shrugged his reply.

When it was his turn to speak, Weisman pointed out that the problem wasn't only that Ben Pruitt died in my study, but that I had been there—that Emma blamed me for not saving her father's life. "That little tidbit can't be solved by moving to a new house," he said.

"That may be true," the judge said, "but Mr. Sanden has had a relationship with this child for four years. I'm granting visitation. It will be set up at a location away from the Sandens' home. I'm going to authorize two visits each week until the evidentiary hearing. The visits will start at four p.m. and end at eight p.m. Parties will transfer the child in the parking lot of the Ramsey County Sheriff's Office. Is that agreeable?"

"Yes. Thank you, Your Honor," Erica said.

"Now, if counsel would come back to my chambers, I want to discuss the dates for those visitations and schedule the evidentiary hearing."

Erica and Weisman disappeared with the judge through a door behind the bench, leaving Dee and me alone in the courtroom with Anna, who sat rigid in her chair, hands gently clasped together on the table, her head frozen atop her long neck. If I hadn't seen the woman blink, I would have thought her made of plastic—or stone.

Dee sat with her eyes fixed on the door behind the judge's bench, a worried mother waiting for her daughter to come home. I imagined her thoughts were the same as mine. How would Emma react to us? To me? Would Emma even speak to me?

I glanced at Anna again. She hadn't moved an inch. Neither had

Dee. Were they sweating too, or was that just me? There was no water pitcher on the table. That realization turned my mouth dry. Why hadn't they put water on the tables? And what was taking Erica so long?

The door behind the bench opened and the attorneys reentered the courtroom, Erica walking to our table to pack her papers into her briefcase, her face blank. She tipped her head toward the exit, and Dee and I stood to leave, the three of us returning to the small conference room.

"The first visit with Emma will be tomorrow evening, the next on Friday. After you pick up Emma at the sheriff's office you can go anywhere in the city except your house. Have her back to the sheriff's office by eight."

"Thank you," Dee said, her voice trembling with relief.

"Yes, thanks, Erica. You did great."

Erica looked at me coolly. "I went out on a limb in there. Bring me the goods. I need a witness that will make it clear that Adler is out for the money. If we don't have that, we're sunk."

I smiled, reached into the pocket of my suit jacket, and pulled out a piece of paper with a name and address on it. "His name is Louis DeChamp. He's a theater director. I have him on tape saying that Anna Adler promised to finance a play she wrote. She needs Adler Enterprises to put up the money, but Gordy has refused it. DeChamp came right out and said that Anna's going to replace Gordy Baker before the end of summer."

"And you have this on tape?"

"I do. I'll make you a copy."

Erica smiled. "We may win this thing yet."

CHAPTER 35

That evening Dee and I celebrated our little victory by baking game hens for supper and splitting a bottle of chardonnay. During supper my phone buzzed with a text from Erica telling us that Louis DeChamp had been served his subpoena, and I breathed a sigh of relief. Outside it was one of those picture-perfect Minnesota nights, the June sky clear and luminous, the gibbous moon lifting over the dome of city lights, fireflies flashing in the yard.

Before going to bed, I went to my study, determined to make a copy of Louis DeChamp's recording for Erica. I pulled the guardianship file from my briefcase and played a few seconds of the conversation, careful to hit play and not delete. The last thing I needed was to screw up that recording, the centerpiece of our case. The sound of DeChamp's voice made me almost giddy.

In the bottom drawer of my desk, I kept a tangle of old chargers, RCA adapters, headphones, and the like. I dug through the wad of cords in search of the one that would connect my recorder to my computer. But after twenty minutes of pulling and twisting at my Gordian knot, I couldn't find it. I dropped the tangle back into the drawer and surrendered. My lovely mood had been spoiled.

I put the recorder back into the file and returned it to my briefcase, pulling out the accordion file I had taken from the church, laying the brochure out on my desk, and plugging the thumb drive into my desktop computer.

The drive contained two files: a large one designated *Raw Footage* and a smaller one titled *Edited*. I opened *Edited* and while my computer buffered, I read the old brochure. It laid out the plan for the addition to the homeless shelter: showers, an expanded kitchen, and, upstairs, a modest church. The pictures in the brochure showed some of the residents looking wan but hopeful.

The little buffering wheel had been circling on my computer for ten minutes. Something wasn't working. A problem with the thumb drive? Why can't technology just work when you want it to? But then again, the thumb drive was nearly two decades old. I copied the files to my computer and tried again. This time the file opened.

The file titled *Edited* contained a two-minute video of Lilith Cain interviewing people at the shelter. The video was well produced with clips of residents mixed in with Lilith explaining the goal of expanding the shelter. She was understated, yet persuasive.

Then I opened the larger file titled *Raw Footage*. It consisted of short interviews with the residents, footage from which the edited clips had been cut. The first interview was with an old man, his mental illness so acute, he could barely speak. After that, Lilith interviewed a woman with two children who told about getting kicked out of their home.

Because this was raw footage, unedited, Lilith would sometimes give instructions to the cameraman, Lucas Mammon. I found nothing earth-shattering about the footage, yet this had been what Jalen Bale had asked for that night Mammon found him disheveled in his office—the night he was working on his final sermon. There had to be a connection, but so far, I didn't see it. Did he merely want to be reminded of who he had once been? Reconnect with the people he had once served? Possibly, but something told me that there had to be more to it.

Movement in the doorway pulled at my attention. Rufus stood watching me and something about his stance looked off. He leaned forward slightly, his head lowered. I paused the video.

"Hey, boy," I said, holding my hand out as if to pet him. He didn't move. That's when I noticed his hackles were raised.

"Rufus?" I leaned toward him, my elbows on my knees, my finger pinched like I held a treat. He pulled his lip into a snarl.

"Buddy, you okay?"

With that, he let loose an angry growl followed by a string of threatening barks. My heart jumped in my chest. I was suddenly afraid to move. Then I noticed a slight shift in his gaze. He wasn't looking at me—he was looking at the window behind me. As I turned, I heard a crash outside.

I jumped to my feet, my chair falling backward. Beyond the glass I saw only darkness. Rufus charged the window, barking. I ran from the study, out the front door, and stopped on the porch to look and listen. I saw nothing and at first heard nothing, but then—footsteps to my left, running away. I ran off the porch and through the yard, stopping at the street.

I could no longer hear the footfalls. Had they cut through a yard? Hidden behind a car parked on the street? I started down the side-walk, but thought twice of it. When I was in college, a kid in my dorm had gotten stabbed when he followed an intruder out into the night.

I didn't give chase, but I didn't go back inside either, not right away. I slipped behind an oak tree and waited. Ten minutes later, the street remained quiet, so I walked around the side of the house and found what had made the crashing noise. A hanging planter outside my window had been knocked to the ground. Someone had been spying on me.

CHAPTER 36

Neither Dee nor I slept well that night. The officers who responded to my 911 call did a walk-around, shining their flashlights at the broken flowerpot, and surmised it was likely not an attempted burglary. "With both of you at home and the lights on, it's more likely some kid peeping in the window," the officer said.

I rejected his explanation. Erica had served a subpoena on Louis DeChamp, which meant that Anna now knew about my visit to the theater. I pictured Anna's stubby little butler with his nose pressed against the glass of my office window, his ears perked as I played a snippet of DeChamp's recording. At least sending her henchman to spy on us had exposed her nervousness.

I double-checked the locks on all of the doors and windows before going to bed. I even stacked pan lids against the doors so that any movement would cause a commotion. We dragged Rufus's bed from Emma's room to ours, parking him near the doorway. Then I pulled my nine-millimeter from the safe in the closet and laid it on the nightstand next to me. If the prowler returned, I would be ready.

The next morning broke quietly. I rolled over to find Dee awake and staring at the ceiling. "You okay?" I asked.

I expected her to say something about the night before, but instead, she said, "I was just wondering…how Emma's going to react to us tonight. I'm sure that Anna's spent the last week telling her lies."

I put an arm around my wife's waist and tenderly kissed her cheek. "Once she sees you, she's going to remember how much she is loved."

"And how do you think she'll react to you?"

That was a better question, one for which I had no answer. "I think she'll be a different girl than the one I used to read to on the porch," I said.

"We need to be gentle with her," Dee said. "She'll be defensive and wanting answers."

I looked at the clock on my nightstand. "I have nine hours to put something together," I said with more certainty than I felt. "I'll be ready by the time we pick her up."

In the meantime, I could check on another witness in Elijah's case: Ray Gideon, the ex-cop who'd found Bale dead. I had so much ground to cover in Elijah's case, and the days were quickly ticking away. According to the police reports I'd read, Ray had lived in the Phillips neighborhood of Minneapolis, but that had been years ago. I took a chance and drove over in the hopes that he might still be at the same address.

When I pulled up, I rechecked the address to make sure that I hadn't misread it. The place looked like it had been condemned. A two-story house converted into a duplex, it had weeds as high as my thigh where the tiny front lawn should have been. The house itself seemed to lean toward the morning sun, although that was probably an optical illusion created by the uneven slate siding. A balcony on the upstairs unit lacked a rail, and the concrete steps leading up the wooden front porch were split and buckled down the center as though crushed under the weight of some great beast. Everywhere I looked, rot had the building in a death grip.

I stepped onto the porch, avoiding the weaker boards, and rang the doorbell for the downstairs unit, half hoping that Ray Gideon had escaped to a safer abode in the years since the trial. I rang again and still heard nothing.

I went to the car, dug his police statement out, and called the number he'd had back during the trial. As I stepped onto the porch again, I heard the chime ring on the other side of the door. He answered his phone.

"Ray Gideon?" I asked.

"Who wants to know?"

"Come to your front door and find out."

The man who opened the door seemed to match the decay of the duplex. In his late fifties, he wore tattered khakis held up by suspenders over a dirty T-shirt. He was barefoot, unshaven, and smelled of old beer and sweat. He looked at me as though I might be a bill collector. I held out my card. "Boady Sanden. I'm a lawyer with the Innocence Project."

His eyes narrowed slightly as he studied my card. "Okay. So?"

"I'm looking into a case you were involved with—the Elijah Matthews case. I was hoping to ask you a couple questions."

He looked at the living room behind him: a floral-print couch, its foam cushions pushing out through torn seams, a coffee table strewn with beer cans and dirty plates. He appraised me again, apparently deeming me worthy to enter Shangri-La, and invited me in, shoving a pile of clothes from the couch to make room for me to sit. I hesitated. A brown stain, which could have been spilled coffee or something far worse, bloomed in the center of the cushion. I touched the spot to make sure that it was dry before I sat.

"The Innocence Project," Ray said. "You're the guys who go around springing murderers out of prison."

"We free the wrongly convicted," I said. "I understand you used to be a cop?"

"In Jamestown, North Dakota. Spent twenty years on the force. Got as high as detective. Had my life wrapped up in a bow until... well, I suspect you read the file."

"Your daughter."

"Christina. She disappeared one night with no warning, no note. I kind of thought she snuck out to be with her boyfriend and forgot to come back. I was so damned mad. She was sixteen. You do stupid things when you're sixteen."

"Had you had a fight?"

"No. There was no fight. I mean, there was always tension. You have a daughter?"

I caught myself about to explain Emma's guardianship, but stopped and said, "Yes."

"Then you understand."

I didn't, but I nodded anyway.

"When Christina didn't come home that first day, I went looking for her. That's when everything went to hell. She was nowhere. Her boyfriend hadn't seen her. She wasn't with her friends. She was just gone. We put up flyers and got the state police involved, but none of it helped. Time just kind of stopped moving at that point."

Ray's words trailed behind his thoughts like smoke from a cigarette, hollow and wispy, the pain that had once been raw now little more than an echo.

"A man don't know the weight of grief until he loses a child. I had no idea where to look, so I stayed in North Dakota, hoping...waiting. Months passed, then years. I lost her mother to cancer five years back. Took up drinking. Got fired from my job. I was mad at the world in a way that had me thinking about killing myself. The only thing that kept me from pulling the trigger was the possibility that I might see Christina again."

A cockroach scampered across the coffee table in front of us. I pretended not to notice, but Ray picked a shoe off the floor and slammed it down on the bug, juices and body parts sticking to the table as he lifted the shoe away. "Sorry about that," he said. "I'm trying to make ends meet with my pension, and that ain't much. Things are a lot more expensive here than in Jamestown."

"You came here looking for Christina?"

"Four years ago. One of my buddies on the force helped me with some face-recognition technology. We put pictures of Christina into the computer and..." He stood and walked to a dining room table, overflowing with papers. He pulled something from the pile and brought it back to the couch. It was the brochure that Lilith Cain and Lucas Mammon had put together back when they were trying to add on to the shelter. "We found this."

He opened the brochure and pointed to a picture of a teenage girl in the background of the shot, sitting on a cot, with dark hair and a faraway stare in her eyes, a blanket wrapped around her shoulders. "That's Christina. I knew it the minute I saw her. I had almost convinced myself that she was dead, her remains scattered in some field in North Dakota, but now I had proof that she had made it to the Twin Cities. I dropped everything and came here to look for her."

"That's a fairly old picture," I said. "A cold trail."

"It's all I had. She'd left North Dakota and made it to Pastor Bale's shelter. Those people were my last hope."

"So you went to see Bale?"

"I bought a ticket to go see him preach at that big church. Sat up front. That was the day that Matthews guy jumped up on stage and called Bale a false prophet. It was quite a show. After things died down, I found my way upstairs...to Bale's office."

"The elevators are locked on Sundays. How'd you get up there?"

Ray smiled. "You learn a few things about locks when you're a cop."

"Breaking and entering."

Ray looked at me sideways. "Are you here to interrogate me? 'Cause if that's the case—"

"No." I held my hands up in mock surrender. "I applaud your resourcefulness. You had a missing daughter. I'd have done the same thing." That wasn't true, but I needed Ray to talk.

"There ain't much a man won't do when it's their child in danger."

"Someone told me that Jalen Bale was kind of...messed up that day."

"He looked like crap." Ray rubbed the scruff on his chin as he spoke. "Like he'd gone ten rounds with the devil himself. I felt bad for the guy given what happened on stage that morning, but I had my own business to tend to. I showed him the brochure and told him about Christina. I can't say I had his full attention, though. He told me he didn't remember her, but he had some old files. He promised to give 'em a look."

Voices in the apartment above us erupted, a man and a woman yelling. I couldn't make out everything, but the gist of the argument was that he had just gotten home from his night out with the boys. That apparently didn't sit well with the woman.

"Fucking assholes," Ray said. "I'd move to a nicer place, but this is cheap. If I watch my pennies, I can make it on my pension without getting a job. That way I can spend my days walking around town, hoping to bump into her. I know it sounds ridiculous. She'd be... thirty-four years old now. I probably wouldn't even recognize her if she walked past me, although I'd like to think I would."

"According to your statement to Detective MacDonald, you asked Bale for a job. Why do that if you wanted time to walk around town?"

"What if they were running a trafficking ring out of that homeless shelter? In my line of work, I've seen it all. Bale wasn't getting a pass just because he claimed to be a preacher. I offered to be his bodyguard. Figured with that Elijah fella around, he might need one—but he didn't bite."

"And as his bodyguard, you might have had access to his old records."

"That church and the people in it were the end of the trail. I don't buy that they didn't know anything more about Christina. It was a long time ago, sure, but someone had to know something. They had to have some kind of record system. I thought…if I could get a job there, I could snoop around."

"Maybe check out their computer records?"

"Sure…why not?"

"What was Bale's reaction to your pitch?"

"He just stared at the wall, like he wasn't even listening, so I wrote my information on a piece of paper and left."

The man in the apartment above us must have gotten tired of defending himself, because he slammed his door so hard it shook the whole building. Ray and I paused to listen as he stomped down the stairs, cussing with every step.

When things quieted again, I said, "But Bale *had* been listening."

Ray rubbed his thick hands together, nervously. "I guess so. He showed up at my door here two days later. He still looked like shit. He hadn't shaved. Looked like maybe he hadn't slept, either, and I think he was wearing the same clothes. Truth is, he acted like he was having a mental breakdown. I invited him in and offered him a drink, thinking he could use some water. Instead, he asks for a beer."

Ray stepped out of his memory and turned to me. "Speaking of which…Would you like one?"

My first thought: *It's nine thirty in the morning.* My second thought: *He's talking; keep it going.* "Sure," I said.

Ray went to the fridge and withdrew two cans of light beer, then returned to the couch.

"So, we're sitting here," Ray said, "just like you and me—and I'm thinking he's here because he had news about Christina. But instead… he asks me the strangest question. He asked if I thought it was possible that Hitler could be in heaven. I mean…what the hell? I thought it was a joke, but he was serious. He said, 'If Hitler begged for forgiveness just before he blew his brains out, would he go to heaven?'"

"What did you say?"

"Well, my first response was, 'Why the hell are you asking me?

I'm no religious scholar.' But when he persisted, I said that a man can't hardly ask for forgiveness if he doesn't put a stop to the sin first. Hitler shot himself in his bunker but didn't lift a finger to stop the war. People were still killing and dying in his name. He could have rectified at least that little bit of his clusterfuck if he really wanted forgiveness."

"What did Bale say to that?"

"He started crying and said that I was right...that a person can't ask for forgiveness without doing something to fix the evil he'd created. That's when he handed me this."

Ray reached beneath the brochure on the coffee table and pulled out a picture. As in the brochure, Christina sat on a cot with the blanket around her shoulders, but this was a close-up. Her smile was weathered and her eyes heavy with stress as she stared straight into the camera.

Ray poked at the picture. "This proves I was right. They had more stuff on Christina. I knew it. I pressed him—asked if I could look at their records. I begged him to give me a crack at those computers. I used to be a detective. I could find her trail; I knew I could. But he just looked at me like I was some kind of lunatic. Said he was doing all he could."

"What do you think he meant by that?"

"Cover-up. There was something going on; I could see it in his eyes. But when I pressed the issue, he got up, took his beer, and left. I was so pissed, I thought about calling the cops and reporting that he was driving with an open container—that's illegal here."

"The thing that doesn't make sense to me, Ray...is why did you go to Bale's office the night he was killed?"

"He invited me."

"Out of the blue? For no reason?"

"If you're looking for a reason, you'll have to ask him. All I can say is he told me to be there at six."

"You were a cop, Ray. Who do you think killed Bale?"

"I know you got your job to do, but you're wasting your time. Elijah Matthews killed Jalen Bale. That's all there is to it."

"The problem with that," I said, "is that Elijah had no reason to take Bale's computer."

Ray looked confused.

"The killer took a laptop from Bale's office. Why would Elijah take it?"

"I don't know. Is that important?"

"Maybe Bale was killed for what was on his laptop."

"Like what?"

I shrugged. "Old records."

"What are you implying?" Ray set his beer down and shifted to better face me on the couch.

"I'm just thinking this through logically...the way a detective might."

Ray picked my card up from the coffee table and read my name. "Mr. Sanden," he said slowly, "I don't like being accused of something I didn't do." He crushed my card in his fingers. "I think you should go."

I stood and let myself out.

CHAPTER 37

Cross-examination of Raymond Gideon by Mr. Pruitt, cont.

Pruitt: So after you hit a dead end with Pastor Bale, you decided to talk to Lilith Cain.

Gideon: She made the video. I figured she might remember Christina.

Pruitt: But Mrs. Cain refused to meet with you.

Gideon: She was never around.

Pruitt: She wouldn't take your calls?

Gideon: No.

Pruitt: But you found your way to her office on the morning of Pastor Bale's death.

Gideon: Yes, I did.

Pruitt: Explain how you managed to get upstairs
            when all the doors were locked?

Gideon: They weren't all locked. There was a
            back stairway that was open.

Pruitt: According to numerous witnesses, that
            staircase is always locked.

Gideon: It wasn't that day.

Pruitt: In your training as a police officer,
            were you ever trained to pick a lock?

Gideon: Are you suggesting that I broke in?

Pruitt: I'm asking if you've been trained to
            pick locks—and remember I have your
            personnel file from Jamestown.

Gideon: Then you already know the answer. Yes,
            I received that training.

Pruitt: So you took a staircase up to Lilith's
            office, a staircase that is always
            locked. When you made it to Mrs. Cain's
            office, how did she respond?

Gideon: She seemed upset. She didn't want to
            talk to me.

Pruitt: She told you to get out or she would
            call the police.

Gideon: Yes. She said that.

Pruitt: In fact, she screamed it.

Gideon: I only wanted to ask her a few
            questions.

Pruitt: And when she threatened to call the
            police, you left her office.

Gideon: I did.

Pruitt: Where'd you go?

Gideon: I went back down the stairs.

Pruitt: And it's your testimony that you ran into
            Pastor Bale at the bottom of the steps?

Gideon: The stairs led to an exit and a small
            parking area reserved for the pastor
            and a few others. Pastor Bale was just
            on his way in.

Pruitt: And that's when you say he asked you to
            come back that night?

Gideon: Yes. He wanted me to come to his office
            at six o'clock.

Pruitt: He wanted you to come back after the church was closed for the day.

Gideon: He said he'd leave a door unlocked.

Pruitt: Did he tell you why he wanted to see you?

Gideon: I thought maybe he reconsidered giving me that job.

Pruitt: Yet there is no record that any such job had been approved by the elders.

Gideon: I wouldn't know about that.

Pruitt: And there is no phone record of Pastor Bale asking you to come there.

Gideon: There wouldn't be because he told me face-to-face.

Pruitt: Did anyone see you talking to Pastor Bale?

Gideon: Not to my knowledge.

Pruitt: Detective MacDonald could not find one shred of evidence to corroborate that Bale invited you there that night.

Gideon: That doesn't change the fact that it happened.

Pruitt: You believed that the Church of the New Hope was hiding evidence about your missing daughter?

Gideon: There had to be some kind of record.

Pruitt: You were obsessed with finding your daughter.

Gideon: Like any father would be.

Pruitt: Might there be evidence of your daughter on Pastor Bale's computer, perhaps?

Gideon: I have no idea.

Pruitt: But if you could just get a peek at that computer—maybe link up to the church's server—you could look for yourself. All you had to do was hide somewhere in that big empty church until everyone was gone. Once you got your hands on Pastor Bale's laptop, you'd have all night to look through their files.

Gideon: I didn't do that.

Pruitt: But Pastor Bale showed up and
           surprised you.

Gideon: I know what you're trying to do, Mr.
           Pruitt. You need to point a finger
           at anyone other than your client.
           But Pastor Bale was the last link I
           had to my daughter. Throw mud at me
           all you want, but ask yourself this
           one question: Why would I kill the
           only person who might help me find my
           daughter?

CHAPTER 38

When I was a child, my mother took me to a traveling carnival. I don't remember that my father was there, but he must have been, because my mother rarely left the house after he died.

I don't remember much about the carnival, either—where it was, what rides they had—but I do remember the funhouse. It was long and narrow like a mobile home and lit up like Christmas. My mother bought a ticket and ushered me to the entrance, telling me that she would be waiting for me when I came out.

Excited, I walked into darkness. This didn't faze me at first. Sure that the fun part lay just ahead, I took a couple steps and bumped into a wall. Why were there no lights? I turned and—thump—another wall. Why would they put a wall there? Turned again and another wall. Panic began to creep its way up my spine. It didn't make any sense. Every direction I tried was a dead end. Then it occurred to me that I had somehow walked into a closet. I had walked into a place I wasn't meant to be, and I was trapped.

I began screaming and banging on the walls. Tears filled my eyes. I couldn't breathe. I pictured the carnival leaving town with me entombed inside one of its attractions. I pounded harder, yelled louder.

Finally, a pair of hands reached out of the darkness and pulled me backward. A few steps and I stood in light again at the entrance, my mother running toward me.

Years later, I would go through a funhouse with Dee holding my hand, the whole experience feeling a bit silly. But I never forgot the disorientation of that first try, and as I drove to visit Elijah, Jalen Bale's murder had me back in that same dark hall.

Lucas Mammon had received a big payday out of Bale's death, his promotion to pastor of a multimillion-dollar ministry coming with a mansion, a Mercedes, and a lot more. Was it Bale's wealth that Elijah thought Mammon coveted? Or did he covet Jessica Cain? That thought turned my stomach, because Jessica would have been thirteen when Bale was murdered. If my worst suspicions were true, Mammon would be guilty of first-degree criminal sexual conduct. He'd be facing better than a decade in prison. That secret would be a powerful motive for murder.

And then there was Lilith Cain, Bale's lover, with an affair starting before Jessica was born and continuing until a week before Bale died. A jilted lover is a dangerous thing, but so is an affair with a married woman. Lilith's husband might have been in prison, but he wouldn't be the first inmate to reach out beyond those walls to take revenge.

And what about the sermon? Was the bone sermon that Mammon remembered the same one that Elijah referred to as Bale's last? What did bones have to do with any of it? What did it mean?

I felt like I was hitting my head against wall after wall, stumbling through the dark. I needed to talk to Lilith, and I wanted to talk to her husband, Ed, but first I needed to talk to Elijah. I needed to ask him about Bale's sermon again. The theft of the laptop had to be tied to that sermon.

When I arrived at the Security Hospital, Jake manned the security desk. He searched my briefcase without making eye contact, taking out my tattered old Bible and flipping through to make sure that I hadn't stashed any contraband in its pages. For my part, I stared at him hard. When he passed me through, he whispered, "I did what you said...with my wife. I just wanted you to know."

I didn't answer. I didn't want him thinking he was off the hook.

Jake escorted me to a library instead of the conference room. In the library, Elijah sat at a table across from another patient, the man's head bowed low, Elijah leaning in as though whispering. Jake called Elijah's name, and when he saw me, he put his hand on the other man's shoulder, patted twice, and said something that raised his friend's head. The second man wore a gentle smile and an eye patch over one eye.

I remembered Dr. Cohen telling me about the patient—John—who had tried to blind himself. John gave Elijah a hug and then Elijah joined me and Jake at the library door and we headed to a conference room.

"I wasn't expecting you today," Elijah said.

"What? God didn't tell you that I was coming?"

He smiled. "Some things are beneath God's infinite attention. Did you come for your lesson?"

"My lesson?"

"You wanted to learn the secret to understanding the Bible."

The man was facing a hearing in three days and his thoughts were on teaching me a biblical lesson.

"I brought my Bible," I said at last.

When we arrived at the conference room, I walked in but he stayed in the corridor for a few seconds talking to Jake. When he finally came in, I opened my briefcase, pulled out my old Bible, and handed it to Elijah. He examined it with the intensity of a clockmaker. A tear ran most of the length of the spine. He ran a finger down the tear and then opened the book to where the split had separated the pages like a fault line. It was the story of David and Bathsheba—and the baby that God killed.

"This is the book of a man who has suffered a great loss," he said.

"It's the book of a man who has little patience for hokum," I said.

I was about to say more when the door opened and Jake entered, carrying a roll of packing tape. It made me wonder what Elijah had whispered to Jake. Did Elijah plan to repair my torn Bible? No, because he hadn't yet seen it, so he'd had no idea that the spine was torn.

Jake gave the tape to Elijah and returned to his position in the hallway, watching us through the window in the door.

Elijah opened my Bible and began flipping pages. "You were right," he said, "when you said that the Bible can be used to justify almost anything. It contains powerful words, but also great confusion." He stopped turning pages at the Gospel of Matthew. "What is God's word and what is put there by men seeking to hold authority over their fellow man? Old laws, new testaments, horsemen of the apocalypse—it can be overwhelming. But here is the secret…"

He lifted a page by its corner and gently tore it free. Having thrown that book across a room, I was no fan of the Bible, but seeing him tear a page out felt unsettling. He carefully folded it until what remained was a single column about an inch in length. He taped the passage to the front cover of my Bible and then wrapped the packing tape around the Bible once, twice, three times, sealing the book shut. He handed it back to me, and I read.

For I was hungry and you gave me something to eat, I was thirsty and you gave me something to drink, I was a stranger and you invited me in, I needed clothes and you clothed me, I was sick and you looked after me, I was in prison and you came to visit me.

I looked at Elijah, not sure that I understood.

"The secret to understanding the word of God can be found in that one passage. It's all there. Conform your life in all things—in all ways—to those words and you will understand God—and not just when it suits you, but always, in every aspect of your life. If you pass a man hungry on the street and don't help him, nothing in the rest of the Bible can save your soul. If you spend your week fighting those who cross a border in search of food or safety, nothing you say or do in church on Sunday will matter.

"You are not permitted to cut the tape until you live according to those words from the Book of Matthew. You don't get to read or cite anything from the Bible until you have fully committed to that passage. You see, Mr. Sanden, the rest of the Bible is meaningless if you are not taking care of your fellow man."

I felt cheated: no secret code, no word jumble that spelled out the eternal truth, not even a mash-up between the Book of Revelations and current events. "Good one," I said, dropping my taped-up Bible back into my briefcase.

We sat at the table. The swelling in his cheek had diminished slightly, although he still talked with a slur from the pull of the contusion. "Is Jake being decent to you?" I asked.

"Jake has a long journey ahead of him, but he has taken that first step. He is being good to me."

"Remember that sermon that you said Pastor Bale was working on...the one you thought would be his last sermon?"

"I remember."

"I asked Pastor Mammon and he didn't know about any final sermon, but...he found Bale working late one night, not long before he was murdered. Bale said he was working on a sermon about bones."

Elijah smiled inwardly, the way a mother might upon receiving a gift from a child.

"Does that make sense to you?" I asked.

"It does."

"What was Bale talking about?"

"For a long time, Jalen refused to see that he had strayed. He was getting close to the truth, but he believed himself to be doing God's work even though he lived in a great house and had all that money. He argued that his church sent hundreds of thousands of dollars to charity. He argued that he needed the church to be big so he could keep doing that."

"Isn't there something in the Bible about it being easier to pass a camel through the eye of a needle than for a rich man to get into heaven?"

"Matthew chapter nineteen, verse twenty-four. We talked about that often. We also talked about Jesus saying that the temple had become a den of thieves. As Pastor Bale's stubbornness wore away, I read to him a quote about the true meaning of giving to the poor. I told him, 'A bone to the dog is not charity. Charity is the bone shared with the dog, when you are just as hungry as the dog.'"

I took a guess. "Is that from Proverbs?"

"No, it's Jack London."

"I like that," I said.

"Then it will be my gift to you."

"And you think that was the sermon that Bale was writing when he was killed?"

"Jalen lived in a great house, drove a nice car. He had all that our society said a successful man should have. In the end, though, I think he understood that it is not charity if one gives only what they are comfortable with. There is such suffering in the world: hunger, disease, sickness. That passage I taped to your Bible ends with 'That which you do for the least of my brothers you do unto me,' but the inverse is also true: That which you withhold from the least of my brothers you withhold from me. True giving demands sacrifice."

"Was he going to tear down the church? Is that what his final sermon was about?"

"The house of the wicked will be destroyed and the tent of the upright will flourish," Elijah whispered, almost to himself.

"He was going to destroy a multimillion-dollar enterprise, expose it for the fraud it was, and go back to being the humble man who served soup to the poor."

"I suspect so."

"His final sermon was a nuclear bomb."

"No, not a bomb," Elijah said. "Just the opposite. It was salvation itself."

"The laptop." I looked at Elijah to see if he had made the connection.

He stared at me and blinked his confusion.

"He was writing that sermon on his laptop—a sermon that would tell the world that the temple was nothing more than a den of thieves. Whoever killed him took the laptop to hide the evidence. That's why Pastor Bale was murdered."

"If you say so."

"It has to be."

Elijah stared at his hands and again spoke quietly. "And when the chief priests and scribes heard Jesus, they began looking for a way to kill him, because they were afraid of him."

CHAPTER 39

At home, I got dressed for our visit with Emma, my long-sleeved shirt itching against my skin. I switched it out for a blue polo. That also felt wrong, too casual. I settled on a short-sleeved button-down that made me look like an accountant from a 1950s television show. It would have to do.

Dee, sensing my nervousness, walked up behind me and put her arms around my shoulders. "Just remember, what she needs more than anything," Dee said, "is love. She needs to know that we'll always be there for her, no matter what."

In planning the outing, I had suggested taking Emma to the Mall of America, to see a movie, maybe ride a few of the rides at the amusement park.

"You're not some divorced dad trying to buy off your daughter. We're a family. We're going to act like a family. Talk to each other. It's supposed to be a beautiful evening, so we'll go to Como Park and have a picnic."

Her logic and her tone were unassailable.

Dee packed a dinner of turkey sandwiches, fruit cups, and brownies while I sweated like a nervous groom. It had been only a week since I last saw Emma, and yet I felt like I was getting ready to meet a stranger.

At the last minute I tossed my laptop into the backseat.

"What's that for?" Dee asked.

"We can show her the new house," I said.

"We're not buying her off," Dee said. "I'm not stooping to Anna's level. If we make this a fight over who can give her more, we'll lose. When she gets her inheritance, she'll be wealthier than both of us. If I can't have her here because she loves me—us—then…I would rather she be with Anna."

"In case she asks," I said. "I won't say a word about the new house unless she asks."

"Only if she asks."

The Ramsey County Sheriff's Office was a mere seven-minute drive from our home, its parking lot surprisingly tranquil, with shade trees and grass framing the edges. Anna stood with her lawyer at the rear of her Mercedes. I almost didn't recognize Emma.

When she'd left us to go shopping with Anna, she was a skinny kid with strawberry-blond hair, freckles, and pale cheeks. She had been wearing blue jeans and a pink blouse. The girl who waited for us in that parking lot looked like a miniature version of Anna. Emma was still small and skinny, but she had cut her hair short and dyed it black. She wore dress slacks, black shoes, and a red jacket with the collar turned up. And was that makeup on her face?

I said nothing but Dee muttered, "Oh my."

I parked the car and we walked over, stopping ten feet shy. Dee lifted her arms expecting a hug, but Emma, with her arms folded across her chest, didn't move. This was the little girl who, six months ago, sat on Dee's lap as we binge-watched Christmas TV specials. Dee had pulled her out of school over Valentine's Day to go to a spa, the two of them coming home with matching manicures. Now Emma could barely bring herself to look at us. What had Anna done to her?

Dee let her arms sink to her sides. "Hello, Emma," she said.

"Hi." Emma glanced up as the words left her lips and then dropped her gaze back to the ground.

"I love the new look," Dee said.

Anna cut in. "You'll have her back at eight sharp?"

"On the dot," I said.

Dee walked to Emma, touching a finger to her arm, and guided her to our car. The two of them sat in back while I drove.

I wanted to say something—to break the ice—but I worried that whatever I said would be wrong. I wanted her to know that I wasn't the monster that Anna painted me to be, but how could I wade gently into a conversation that ended with the death of her father? Instead, I pretended to concentrate on my driving.

"We've missed you," Dee said.

Emma didn't respond.

"We're going to Como Park," Dee said. "I brought a picnic basket. I thought we could spread a blanket out beneath a tree and just... enjoy the beautiful evening."

"Remember when we took you sledding there?" I added. "That was a fun day, wasn't it?"

In the rearview mirror I caught Dee glaring at me. I had become that divorced dad. I decided to keep my thoughts to myself.

Como Park, nearly four hundred acres within the city of St. Paul, had a lake, a golf course, a band shelter, a zoo, and an enormous conservatory filled with beautiful flowers and exotic plants, but what we sought was a simple shade tree. I parked along the street and carried the basket of food, following Dee and Emma as they walked slowly through the grass until they found a spot beneath a silver maple overlooking the lake in the distance.

I spread the blanket while Dee and Emma strolled toward the pavilion and the sound of folk music. I wanted to join them but had not been invited.

When they returned, Emma wore a cautious smile that disappeared when she drew near me. They sat on the blanket, Dee next to me, Emma opposite, her body turned so that she didn't have to look at me.

I passed out the food and we ate. On any other day, I would have thought the sandwiches delicious and the fruit salad perfectly curated, but sitting in the shade of that tree, with Emma wanting to be anywhere other than in my presence, the food seemed tasteless.

Dee tried to work me into the conversation, asking me to talk about Rufus or tell Emma about the case I was working on. I tried to sound enthusiastic, but the chill emanating from Emma sapped the vigor from my words, so I decided to eat my food in silence and hope that Dee could break through to Emma despite my presence.

When we finished the meal and I started packing up the leftovers, Emma finally seemed to reach a decision. Blurting out what had been on her mind all evening, she looked at me squarely and said, "Did you even try to save my dad?"

My mouth went dry. I tried to swallow, but the dust in the back of my throat denied my effort. I looked at Dee, who seemed as surprised as me. We held each other's gaze, and in her eyes I saw encouragement but also fear. This bridge needed to be crossed if we were ever to have a chance at getting Emma back.

"Your father was my friend," I said slowly. "At one time we were close enough that he named me your godfather."

Emma watched me with unwavering eyes.

"I didn't want to believe that he killed your mother. I couldn't believe it. That's why I took his case. I was convinced we would get an acquittal—and we were on the verge of it...but everything fell apart."

After all the fretting I had done, there had really been only one path. I would tell Emma the truth—all of it. I continued. "I had discovered something...a piece of evidence that proved that your father had killed your mother. That's why he came to my office. He wanted to talk me out of revealing what he'd done. If I kept his secret, he would be alive today, but your mother's killer would have walked free. If I didn't, he knew he would go to prison. I told him I had no choice. And that's when he pulled out his gun."

I took a drink of water, my hand steady now, my gaze fixed on Emma's face. Her eyes were wet with tears ready to fall.

"What your father didn't know was that a friend of mine—a police officer—had been standing outside my office listening. He came in to try and stop Ben. Your father shot at the officer and the officer fired back. That's how your father died."

"That's not what Aunt Anna said." Tears trickled down Emma's cheeks. "She said the cop shot Dad in cold blood first. She said you set him up."

Anna had been shrewd in how she had misled Emma, corrupting the truth just enough for it to be believable.

"Your father…died by suicide," I said.

Emma's brow scrunched up in confusion. She shook her head slowly. "That's not true."

I wanted to reach out and hold her, but I dared not cross that line. "He was facing prison for the rest of his life. The world was about to learn that he had killed your mother. You were going to find out. Ben decided that he couldn't live in that world."

"You're lying." Emma was crying hard now, her face in her hands.

"Emma, your dad's last words were that he wasn't going to prison. That's when he fired a shot. Into the wall. I believe he missed the officer on purpose. He knew that the officer would react without thinking. They call it suicide by cop. I'm sorry."

Dee went to Emma—to hold her—but Emma pushed Dee away.

"Anna said you'd lie about it. She said you'd make it Dad's fault." She lifted her face and looked at me with rage in her eyes. "You killed him."

Dee put a hand on Emma's leg with the care one might use on a wounded animal. "No, Emma. Boady's telling you the truth. He didn't want—"

Emma turned to face me, eyes red with anger and pain. "Tell me this," she said. "Could you have saved him? Could you have done anything that would have kept him alive?"

I choked back my answer.

Had I done everything possible? Maybe I should have called Ben's bluff and simply walked out the door and risked getting a bullet in the back. Maybe I could have talked him out of his plan, convinced him to hand me the gun. As I considered those possibilities, I could not answer Emma's question the way I wanted to—the way that would make her forgive me.

"I don't know," I said. "I don't know if I could have done anything to save him."

"Because you didn't try. You didn't try!"

She stood and ran away from us. I got up to chase her, but Dee held me back. "I'll get her," she said. "You go walk around the conservatory or something. I'll call you when it's okay to come back."

I wanted to argue, but Dee took off at a run to catch up with Emma. I felt hollow. This wasn't the way our day with Emma was supposed to go. I packed up the blanket and basket and carried them back to the car. Then I found my way to the conservatory.

McNeely Conservatory was an enormous glass castle that housed all manner of vegetation that couldn't survive outdoors in Minnesota. In the summer, it was a big draw for weddings. In the winter it drew people in need of a reminder that the entire world wasn't buried under snow and ice. I entered and wandered blindly until I found myself in a wing overrun with palm fronds, elephant ear leaves, and bamboo. The path I had followed ended by a fountain surrounded by benches. The fountain resembled a large birdbath and had a bronze woman standing atop, her hand reaching skyward. The benches looked like a good place for me to sit and contemplate what had just happened, so I did.

"I really fucked that one up," I said to the woman on the fountain. "I was supposed to make things better...but I made them worse."

The woman offered me no solace.

"What else was I supposed to do? Lie to her? Tell her you died a valiant death?" I wasn't talking to the woman anymore. "You died a coward. You were supposed to protect her. That's what a father does; he protects his child from evil. But how could you protect her from evil when you *were* the evil?"

I stood and paced angrily, my hands clenched into fists, spit flicking from my lips as I ranted. "You were never her father. A real father could never have done what you did. You heartless prick. You know what? I'm glad you're dead. The world's a better place without you. Emma is better without you."

I stopped pacing and faced the woman again. "I'm done with this guilt—with thinking that you're out there somewhere looking over my shoulder. I'm done kicking myself because of you. Damn you and your memory. I'm gonna find a way to give her the happiness she deserves—the happiness you stole from her. I'm gonna make things right."

Movement to my left caught my attention. At the other end of the path stood a young couple, on a date maybe. They stared at me nervously, then turned and left.

Alone again, I sat on the bench and bathed in my anger. Minutes ticked away unnoticed until my phone buzzed. It was a text from Dee.

> I'm going to take Emma back to the sheriff's office—alone. It's better that way. I'll call you when I'm on the way back.

It was the last thing I wanted, but I replied: *Okay.*

CHAPTER 40

On the drive home, Dee told me how the evening had gone in my absence.

"She's hurting," Dee said. "Everyone she's relied on has let her down. She thinks that we betrayed her."

"Now she knows," I said. "Ben was a liar, and murderer, and an absolute shit of a father. It can't get any worse for us from here on out."

"You're not going to like this," she said.

"What?"

"When I took Em back, Anna said she wants us to bring Rufus to the next visit...to live with them."

"No!"

"He's Emma's dog and—"

"He belongs with us. Emma belongs with us. I'm not giving Rufus to that..." I took a breath and let my anger pass. "I'm not giving Rufus to Anna; he's part of this family. So is Emma, and Emma's coming home."

I pulled into our driveway and parked outside our tiny garage. It was a cloudless evening, and except for the soft hum of music coming from one of the houses on the back side of our block, the neighborhood was quiet. Neither Dee nor I moved to get out of the car right away. I wanted to stay in the darkness—in the peace of the night—for just a few seconds more before going into a house where I had made so many mistakes.

Staring ahead at the garage door, I asked Dee, "Back when we first started dating, did you ever think we'd be in such a mess?"

She thought for a bit and then placed her hand on top of mine, which rested on the console between us. "Boady, a fairy tale is easy to start. It's the happily-ever-after that's hard. It may not happen, but we'll do everything we can to get there."

I gave her hand a squeeze.

We got out of the car and I carried the picnic basket to the house, with Dee following me. I was about open the door when I saw something shiny at my feet. I paused to look and saw a shard of glass lying on the brick step. Where had it come from? My confusion gave way when I saw the fissures in one of the panes of the door, the cracks fanning out from a hole that had been punched through.

I held my hand up behind me, touching Dee's shoulder, stopping her. I put my finger to my lips, pointed at the broken glass, and watched her expression change as she connected the dots.

We backed away from the door, and it was then that I heard a whimper come from inside the house. Rufus?

"Get in the car," I whispered. "Back out of the driveway and call the police."

"What about you?"

"I'm going in. I think Rufus is hurt."

"No," Dee said. "We both go to the car or we both go inside."

I looked hard into her eyes. She needed to see that I was not going to budge. "No argument. I need to check on Rufus."

She hesitated only a second more but got into the car and backed out of the driveway.

I tested the knob. Unlocked. If someone had been inside when we drove up, they would have heard the engine. I picked up a paving stone from the edge of the flower bed and held it shoulder height. The door croaked a long slow wail as I eased it open.

Rufus whimpered again, low and mournful.

I stepped inside, brick raised and ready, and listened, but heard nothing beyond his soft whine. The setting of the midsummer sun spread a dim glow through the house, casting shadows over the many places an intruder could hide. I stepped through the mudroom, pausing at the kitchen to let my eyes adjust. That's when I saw Rufus lying in a pool of blood, a trail staining the floor as though he had dragged himself across the kitchen. His left hip glistened red. He looked up at me, with such hope and despair.

I dropped my stone and ran to his side, spotting the bullet hole before I made it to my knees.

"Jesus!" I put my palm against the wound and he gave a light yelp. With my other hand I lifted his head to mine, our foreheads pressed together. "It's going to be okay, boy. I'm here."

Blood seeped around the edges of my fingers as I applied pressure. I grabbed a towel hanging from a drawer handle and folded it into a makeshift bandage. Then I picked him up and ran out the door.

Dee stood on the street in front of the car, a phone to her ear.

"Open the door," I yelled as I ran toward her. She opened the passenger-side door and I laid Rufus on the seat. "He's been shot."

"Oh my God!" Then into the phone she said, "The intruder shot our dog...Yes...Okay." She put the phone to her chest. "They want us to go someplace safe."

I took my phone out and typed a search for the nearest veterinary emergency room. I found one twenty minutes away in Arden Hills. I called them.

"My dog's been shot. Can you see him tonight?"

"We have a full-service emergency room," the calm voice on the other end said.

"My wife will be bringing him in. One second."

I pulled up the maps app and punched in the address and handed the phone to Dee, taking her phone from her hand. "I'll deal with the police. You save Rufus."

With fear in her eyes, she nodded, took my phone, and hurried into the car. As she pulled away, I spoke to dispatch. "This is Boady Sanden. I'm the homeowner. Are they on the way?"

"We have a unit dispatched. I would like for you to move away from the house until officers arrive."

"I'll wait here," I said.

Somewhere to the east, a siren rose in the night sky.

CHAPTER 41

Luckily, police response in my neighborhood is lightning fast. I had four squad cars there within five minutes. One officer stayed with me getting the details of the broken windowpane and how we'd found Rufus. The others scoured my house, looking for an intruder. It took fifteen minutes before they radioed that it was clear for me to enter.

In the kitchen, two officers examined the side door where the intruder had broken the glass, one of them collecting the shards and putting them into an evidence bag. A sergeant asked me to walk through the house to see if anything was missing.

I first went upstairs to the safe we kept tucked behind the clothing in our bedroom closet. Its contents appeared untouched. Next was Dee's four-foot-tall jewelry box. Dee didn't have enough jewelry to fill all eight drawers, so she used a couple to store her childhood coin collection, but it all appeared to be in order.

I walked through our bedroom and then Emma's, trying to discern if anything seemed different, but nothing struck me as being out of place.

Downstairs, I did the same thing in the kitchen, dining room, living room, and front parlor. Had they broken in just to shoot my dog?

The last room I checked was my study. I doubted anyone would break in to steal my law books or the old desktop computer, but where was my laptop? It wasn't on the desk. My breath caught in my chest

until I remembered that I had taken it to the park with us. The shelves
of books appeared undisturbed. The drawers of my desk hadn't been
touched.

I shook my head and was about to leave when I saw it, the bare
spot next to my desk where my briefcase should have been. I tried to
make sense of it. "They took my briefcase?" It came out as a question.

"Your briefcase?"

I pointed to the side of my desk. "It was here when we left. I'm
sure of it. Why would they take my briefcase?"

"Can you describe it?"

"Black. It's a trial case so it's bigger than your average case...
about..." I held my hand out to measure the size. "Maybe ten inches
wide."

"What was in it?" the sergeant asked.

"A couple files," I said. I ran through the inventory in my head.
I had Elijah's trial file and transcripts, the promotional file from the
homeless shelter, and Emma's guardianship file. "I can't imagine who
would want—"

Something cold opened up in my chest. DeChamp's recording
was in that case—the only copy. "Son of a bitch!"

"What?"

"Anna Adler. She's behind this—she has to be."

"Who's Anna Adler?"

I walked around the desk just to make sure that I hadn't set my
case down somewhere else. *Goddammit!* "She's on the other side of a
custody case I'm involved in. I had evidence in that briefcase that...
Christ!"

"Anna Adler?" The sergeant wrote the name on a small notepad.

"Or her henchman," I said.

"Henchman?"

"She has a butler or bodyguard—George."

"You know George's last name?"

"No, but—" Then another thought hit me. "She knew we'd be gone," I said. "My wife and I had a visitation with…with our daughter. Adler knew we'd be out of the house tonight."

"Do you know where we can find Ms. Adler?"

I gave the sergeant Anna's address and phone number. "Don't be surprised if she kicks you out of her house or lawyers up. She'll never admit to any of this."

The sergeant folded the notebook and tucked it away. "I'll make a report and have one of the detectives follow up. So…the only thing taken was that briefcase?"

"As far as I can tell, yeah."

The sergeant nodded to the other officers who were standing just outside the study. "We're done here."

As I walked the officers to the side door, we stepped past Rufus's bloody trail. "You took pictures of that?" I asked.

"We did," the sergeant said. "Sorry about your dog."

As the last of the squad cars pulled away, my phone chimed. It was Dee. "He's out of surgery," she said. "The doctor said he's going to live. It's too early to know if there's any nerve damage."

"It was Anna Adler," I said. "She stole my briefcase. I had DeChamp's interview in there."

"Don't you have a copy?"

"I was going to make one, but…no."

In the long silence that followed, my anger climbed. True, I should've made a copy, but who would have thought Anna would stoop to burglary?

"What do we do now?" Dee asked.

"We fight back. I'm not sure how, but if this is the war Anna wants, it's the war we'll give her."

"They're going to keep Rufus for observation," Dee said. "But…I don't want to stay in that house tonight. I can't."

I understood exactly what Dee meant. The house seemed too large, too empty, too vulnerable. We had been violated.

"We can stay at a hotel," I said. "How does the Hyatt sound?"

I heard her sigh in relief on the other end of the line.

I said, "I'll pack your things and meet you there."

CHAPTER 42

Hotel pillows, even at a place as nice as the Hyatt, have always felt to me as though they are stuffed with cotton candy, or spiderwebs, or some other ethereal filler far too slight to support a human head. I folded and wadded my pillow all night, seeking comfort but finding none. Next to me, Dee fidgeted well into the morning, and when dawn broke and we both rose, she wore the stress of her long sleepless night like a burlap robe.

I suggested that she take advantage of the amenities, thinking that some time on a massage table or in a sauna might do her some good.

"I can't," she said. "I'm showing our house today. I need to clean up the blood."

"I'll take care of that," I said. "You stay here and relax."

She sat on the edge of the bed in the T-shirt and shorts she'd slept in. "You know I can't do that."

I sat down beside her, put an arm around her shoulders, and pulled her in to me. "It's going to be okay," I said, although I didn't yet know how. We no longer had DeChamp's admission on tape. We could call him to the stand, but Anna would make it worth his while to deny what he'd told me. And without the tape we couldn't prove that he was lying. Our trump card was gone.

"I need to stay busy," she said, her fingers rubbing warmth into her knees. "I'll clean up the house...get someone to fix that broken pane...maybe check on Rufus. If I don't keep busy, I'll go crazy."

I kissed her temple to let her know that I understood.

I showered first and was dressed by the time she came out of the shower in a towel. She looked at my semi-business attire and asked. "What are you going to do?"

"Drive to Yankton, South Dakota."

"Yankton? What's in Yankton?"

"A federal prison camp and a man who's been lurking in the shadows of that Elijah Matthews case."

"Who's that?"

"The husband of one of the church founders. He has a motive that the original investigation missed."

"Can't you just call?" She couldn't hide her worry at the thought of me being so far away today. I regretted it too, but time was running out for Elijah.

"I could, but I want to see his reaction to what I have to say. It may not matter, but…the day after tomorrow Elijah's going to be approved to undergo electroconvulsive therapy. But the thing is…I think he might be innocent."

"That's awful." Dee slipped yesterday's jacket over her shoulders to fight off a shiver.

"The part that gets me is…so what if he thinks he's a prophet? If he's innocent, who cares? If he wants to live in a fantasy—let him. Who's he hurting? If they shock him, he'll lose the one thing that makes him Elijah."

Dee sat back on the side of the bed. "I didn't know. Do you really think he's innocent?"

I considered this and answered, "Yes, I do."

"Can you prove it?"

"I'm not quite there yet. It's just not adding up."

"How long is the drive to Yankton?"

"Five hours one way."

"So you won't be home until…after dark?"

"You should stay here another night," I said.

"We have a home and I'm going to stay there."

"If I go now, I can be back before the sun goes down." I patted my pants pockets to make sure I had my phone, wallet, and keys.

"You'll be back by dark?"

I wrapped an arm around her back and kissed her. "I promise."

On the drive to Yankton, I called Erica to tell her about the break-in...and about the theft of DeChamp's recording. I could hear exasperation in Erica's voice as she replied. "If he takes the stand and denies everything, we're cooked—and the judge will be royally pissed."

"I can testify as to what he said."

"You're an interested party. The judge will dismiss your testimony in a heartbeat. You know that, Boady."

"My phone GPS will prove that I was at his theater. If he denies meeting with me, or ever seeing me, we can prove him to be a liar."

"But it doesn't prove Anna's ulterior motive," Erica said.

"And if Anna wrote a play, maybe she copyrighted it. That would be further corroboration of my conversation with DeChamp. And if push comes to shove, we call Gordy to the stand. He knows all about the Prodigal Project."

"It's weak," Erica said, "but it's a start. I'll get one of my associates on the copyright angle. Maybe she created an LLC for the production company. We'll look for that too."

"If we could just prove that Anna was behind the break-in, we'd have her dead to rights."

"But we don't have proof of that, do we?"

"What burglar's going to ignore the safe and my wife's jewelry and take my briefcase?"

There was silence on the other end of the line for several seconds.

Then Erica said, "Professor Sanden, I took your evidence course in law school. Do we really need to have this conversation?"

I shook my head even though I was alone in my car. "No."

"We keep focused on what we can prove...chip away at her case. We'll keep DeChamp under subpoena for now. How did the visitation go?"

I didn't answer.

"Boady?"

"It didn't go well," I said. "She's hurt...and mad at me. I spent most of the visit away from her. She couldn't stand to be near me."

Another pause, then: "Talk to Dee about delaying the hearing. We need time for you to get through to Emma. If we don't have Emma on our side, I don't think we can win this thing."

"I'll talk to Dee tonight."

There was one final long pause in the conversation before Erica said, "We'll come up with something," she said. "I don't know what..."

"Yes, we will," I replied. "We'll find a way to win this case, one way or another. I'm not letting Emma go."

CHAPTER 43

I had been to a few federal prisons over my career, but none like the prison camp in Yankton. There were no walls or even fences. I parked in a lot for visitors and walked to the administration building across a lawn populated with inmates sitting at picnic tables and strolling the grounds. The facility had once been the campus of a small college, and now it housed federal convicts who were waiting out the last few years of their sentences: nonviolent offenders, fraudsters, and con artists like Edward Cain.

I didn't recognize him when he walked into the visitors' lounge. He had aged dramatically since his booking photo, which was the most recent picture I could find. Back then, he had dark hair cut short and neat, the perfect look for a man running an investment scam. Now his hair fell between his shoulder blades, a misty gray, like he'd walked through a cobweb, and although he was five years younger than me, the deep lines in his face aged him beyond my years.

Ed Cain gave me a look of placid curiosity as he approached. "You want to see me?" he said.

"I'm Boady Sanden, an attorney with the Innocence Project in Minnesota. Can we talk?" He motioned to the door and we walked out onto the sweeping lawn.

"It's quite a prison you got here. Honor system?"

"They do head counts."

"You have an out date?"

"With good time shaved off, I'm sitting at eight months, one week, and two days." He pulled a pack of cigarettes from his shirt pocket, popped one from the pack, and lit it. "You want to tell me why you're here?"

"Does the name Jalen Bale mean anything to you?"

"You know it does. He was in business with my wife—that church."

"So you know he's dead."

"Few years back. Yeah."

"Do you know how he died?"

"Yep."

"Out of curiosity, how did you learn about his death?"

"I read about it in the paper. Maybe online. I don't remember."

"Lilith didn't tell you?"

"No."

"She ever visit?"

My segue was clumsy, and he paused to calculate where I might be going. "Not for a while," he said. "What's it to you?"

We came to a picnic table and I motioned toward it. He shrugged and we sat across from each other.

"What about Jessica?"

This time his pause carried scrutiny. He looked me up and down, misgivings etched on his face.

"I can check the visitors' log, if you'd prefer," I said.

"Lilith thinks it's better that Jessica not visit me in prison."

"That's got to be tough," I said, doing my best to sound sincere.

"I hurt a lot of people. I guess I can see her point, but I always did right by my daughter."

"In what sense? I mean…with you being here and all."

"I know people look at me and see a selfish asshole—and who knows, maybe they're right, but when it comes to Jessica…" He shook his head. "She'll have a good life no matter what happens to me."

"I thought the feds recaptured most of the money you took."

"I'm not talking about stolen money. I wouldn't do that to my daughter."

"So what are you talking about?"

"I come from a wealthy family—did you know that?"

"I did not." I would have done more digging, had everything else in my life not been screaming for attention.

"That's probably at the root of my crime. I wanted to show my father that I could do what he'd done." Ed smiled sadly to himself. "I guess I was wrong."

He took a deep drag from his cigarette and exhaled with the breeze. "My father was in failing health when I was being investigated…practically on his deathbed. I was his only heir, but if he left his money to me, I'd end up giving it all to the feds to pay back those investors. And because Lilith's name was on some of the shell corporations I'd set up, she was in the same boat."

"But your father could give his money to Jessica," I said.

"She came along like a miracle. We'd been trying to have a baby for years. Too bad it didn't happen until everything was falling down. When Lilith told me the news, I got down on my knees and thanked God. I could do twenty years in prison knowing that I have a family out there—a daughter—waiting for me."

"You mind if I ask…How much money are we talking about?"

"Enough that she'll never have to worry. It's in a trust. She gets it when she turns eighteen." A big smile spread across Ed's face. "Which is the day after tomorrow. She'll be old enough to visit me without her mother's permission."

"Do you think she will?"

"I'm hoping. I've seen pictures of her, but…Do you have any idea what it's like having a child and not being able to see her?"

I said, "I can't imagine," although I knew exactly what it was like.

"You ever met Jessica?"

"Briefly," I said. "I stopped by the Church of the New Hope. She works for Lilith."

"What did you think of her?" His eyes lit up like he'd just gotten a letter from a pen pal.

I decided to be nice. "She's...feisty. Strong-willed."

"Just like her old man."

"Tell me what you know about Lilith getting involved with the Church of the New Hope."

"Lilith came to me one day saying she wanted to put money into some damned homeless shelter. They were expanding...building a church on the site."

"Was it an investment or a donation?"

"A church can be one hell of a tax shelter. And she got quite the return on her investment." He crushed his cigarette into the empty ashtray on the table.

"My understanding is that Lilith spent a lot of time at the shelter... with Bale."

He narrowed his eyes and leaned in. "If you're trying to get my goat, you'll have to try harder than that."

"Okay," I said. "Did you know about their affair?"

Ed stared at me, unblinking. I tried to read him and what I saw was calculation. He said, "I take it that's why you came to see me?"

"You knew?"

"Not until Bale came to visit me."

I willed myself not to react, but...holy shit! I checked my breathing and tried to present a nonchalant façade. "Bale told you?"

"Not in so many words, but I could see it in his eyes. He told me about the church he and Lilith had built, but he talked about it like... like it was the bridge on the River Kwai."

"I don't understand."

"At the end of the movie, when that Alec Guinness character realizes that he's made a deal with the devil? That church was quite the achievement, but Bale seemed almost ashamed of it, like he'd built it for all the wrong reasons."

"And that was the first time you two ever met? He'd never been to see you before?"

"First time—and I asked him why, after all those years, he felt a need to come. He wouldn't give me a straight answer. He just said he wanted to meet me, but I knew that was bullshit."

"So why did he come?"

The big man stared at me with cold eyes as he pulled another cigarette from the pack and slowly lit it. When he was good and ready, he said, "He came here because he'd been screwing my wife."

"He said that?"

"Didn't have to. I could tell. He apologized out of the blue—just said he was sorry. When I asked why, he hemmed and hawed... couldn't bring himself to admit it out loud. Then he said there was something that he had to do, and it was going to cause a lot of pain. I didn't know what he was talking about, but I'm sure it had to do with Lilith. Maybe he was going to try and get her to divorce me? I don't know."

"That had to be tough," I said.

"In the back of my mind, I guess I expected it. Lilith's a beautiful woman. You can't expect someone like that to go for twenty years without...wanting to be with a man. It made sense that it would be Bale. They worked together. I figured it was bound to happen sooner or later."

"Sooner or later?" I asked. "Did you think...that the affair was something new?"

Ed looked confused.

"Ed...it started before you were arrested."

"Before I..."

That hit a nerve. His eyes darted from side to side as he added things up. His cheek twitched. A vein in his neck darkened. He stood and walked away from the table, stopped, pressed his hands to his forehead. "You're lying," he said.

"I'm sorry. I thought you knew."

"Bullshit!"

"Bale did a DNA test because he thought he might be Jessica's father. I found a copy of it."

Ed held his breath, one small word escaping his lips, "And?"

"He's not Jessica's father."

Ed's shoulders slumped in relief. Then he came back to the table, put his foot on the bench, and leaned down to face me. "Damn you for putting me through that," he said. "You're an asshole."

He picked up his pack of cigarettes and walked away.

I started back toward my car, not sure what to make of our conversation, when I realized that I had forgotten to ask an important question.

I went back to the administration building and found the deputy warden. It took a while, but I convinced him to look up the date when Jalen Bale came to the prison to visit Ed Cain. The man disappeared into his office; when he came back, he handed me a piece of paper with a date written on it.

The date: six days before Jalen Bale was murdered.

CHAPTER 44

As promised, I got back to St. Paul before dark, the shadows of the oak trees in my front yard falling long and thin to the east. Dee greeted me at the door with a hug followed by a short kiss. "A good day?" I asked.

"We showed the house three times, and the second couple didn't want to leave. They looked in every closet and in the attic. I got a text from their realtor about an hour ago. She thinks they're putting in an offer."

I hugged her again. I wanted to celebrate, yet I couldn't help feeling that we were losing something cherished. Over Dee's shoulder I saw the spot where Rufus had lain on the floor. A shiver ran down my spine and I wondered what it must have been like for Emma to walk by my study every day knowing that her father had died in there. For the first time, I was truly glad to be selling the house.

Before going to bed that night, I double-checked the locks, balanced cookware against the doors again, and placed my gun on my nightstand. But nothing woke us in the night.

In the morning, I set to re-creating the files that had been stolen from my study. I could get new transcripts of Elijah's case from the court of appeals, but the police reports would be a little more difficult. The prosecutor's office would have them, but might not be keen to hand a copy over, and if they did it would probably take weeks to come through. Elijah didn't have weeks. His Jarvis hearing was set for tomorrow.

As for Emma's guardianship—I could get a full set of all the paper-work from Erica, but I could never replace the audio recording of Louis DeChamp. I stared at the bookcase in front of me, waiting for inspiration, but all I found were muddled thoughts.

Bale had visited Ed Cain in prison six days before he died. Why? Absolution for the affair with Lilith? But Bale had broken up with Lilith, so Ed had that wrong. And then there was the revelation that Princess Jessica was about to inherit Grandpa Cain's money. Did Mammon know about that?

I was still staring at the bookcase two hours later when my cell phone chimed. I didn't recognize the number and probably wouldn't have answered it had I not wanted a reason to stop staring.

"Hello?"

"Mr. Sanden?" It was a female voice.

"Yes."

"This is Lilith Cain. I think it's time we met."

I sat up, curious. "I think so too. Are you at the church?"

"We'll meet at my house in Wayzata. How soon can you be here?"

"I'll be there in an hour."

She gave me the address; then the line went dead.

I reached for my briefcase, my hand swiping through empty air where it normally sat. I was wearing jeans and a T-shirt. So I ran upstairs to put on a collared shirt and khakis. I was tying my shoelaces when the doorbell rang. We were expecting the buyer's realtor to pos-sibly stop by with an offer on the house, so I didn't put much thought into who it might be, but when I came downstairs, I saw Elijah's sister, Ruth, standing in the front entryway talking to Dee.

Dee turned to me. "There's a Ruth Matthews here for you," she said.

Of all the people I might have expected, she was the last. "Ruth? Is everything all right?"

Ruth was carrying a box the size of a brick in her hand. She walked over to hand the box to me. "This is from Elijah," she said.

I looked at Dee, who smiled graciously at our guest, unaware that this woman, the sister of a man locked up in a psych ward, was someone who believed that her brother was an actual prophet. She was probably every bit as crazy as her brother, if not more so. She had gone to the effort to find our home and deliver a box to me, a box of unknown contents. I took it and felt that it had heft, so it probably wasn't anthrax. A small, venomous snake maybe, angry for having been shoved into that box? "I don't normally accept...things like this from my clients."

"I made it myself," she said, beaming with pride.

So, not a snake. I opened the box to find a crude metal plate about the size of a playing card. It had the same scorched patina as the metal cross that still hung from Ruth's own neck. I picked it up, the leather cord unraveling beneath it. Then I turned it over and read what had been engraved on its face:

> A bone to the dog is not charity.
> Charity is the bone shared with the dog,
> when you are just as hungry as the dog.
>
> *Jack London*

Elijah had said that he would make the Jack London quote his gift to me, but I didn't think he meant literally. "Well...I thank you. Um... it's very nice." It wasn't nice. It was hideous...and heavy. And how the hell did this crazy sister of that crazy man find my home?

"Elijah wants you to wear it on your next visit."

I hadn't planned on going to St. Peter again unless I solved the case. But maybe I *should* go see him. At the very least, if I had any final questions, I should ask them before the shock treatments took his memories away. The Jarvis hearing was only twenty-eight hours away, and I was beginning to understand that I had failed him.

"I'm sorry," I said softly.

"Sorry?" she asked.

"I'm...not having much luck with the case."

She smiled. "You are doing God's work. I have faith in you. Elijah has faith in you."

"Ms. Matthews, are you aware of the hearing tomorrow afternoon?"

"I don't believe that I am."

"It's called a Jarvis hearing. It's to determine whether the doctors can...do stuff to your brother against his will. They want to do a procedure, electric-shock therapy. It can have a dramatic effect on a person. Has your brother ever mentioned that to you?"

"No, but our Lord will provide."

"No, he won't," I said. "This is going to happen. God's got nothing to do with it."

Again she smiled, this time like a teacher gently correcting a misguided student. "Mr. Sanden, God has everything to do with the path Elijah walks. Nothing happens to my brother that isn't part of a plan."

I dropped my head, the words of Thomas Paine reverberating in my mind. *To argue with a man who has renounced the use and authority of reason...is like administering medicine to the dead, or endeavoring to convert an atheist by scripture.*

I took Ruth's hand in mine and thanked her again for the gift.

"Will you be seeing Elijah soon?" she asked.

"I'll drive down today," I said.

"God will guide you there," she said.

I closed my eyes to hold back a word of blasphemy. Then I smiled and led Ruth to the door.

On the porch, she turned and said, "Don't forget to wear the necklace."

I gave a small wave goodbye. "I won't forget."

"She seems...nice," Dee said.

I held out the hunk of metal for Dee to see. "She thinks I'm actually going to wear this."

Dee gave a wry smile and shrugged. "If it makes Elijah feel better, what's the harm?"

Dee was right, but damn, that thing was ugly.

CHAPTER 45

L ilith Cain lived in a house the size of a ski chalet, with white pillars and five gables along the front, all of it protected by a brick wall and a wrought-iron gate. The lawn between the gate and the house was as big as a baseball outfield, filled with shrubbery, and flowers, and stone gardens. *Blessed are the poor in spirit*, I thought, *for theirs is the kingdom of heaven.*

I pressed the button on the intercom. A man's voice, dry and slow, answered.

"This is Boady Sanden," I said. "Lilith Cain is expecting me."

"Yes."

A few seconds of silence passed before the gate slid to the side. I parked in front of one of five garage doors and walked to the entrance, the door opening before I could ring the doorbell. A man with hunched shoulders and a dour disposition beckoned me in. His stiff, dark suit was classic "butler," straight out of a black-and-white movie. His bony face bore no expression as he said, "This way."

He led me across marbled floors to a staircase that descended into a shiny white entertainment room. This, too, seemed ordered from the pages of *Town and Country* magazine: a claw-foot pool table, a cherrywood bar with liquor for every possible taste, niches built into the walls that held fresh flowers. Psychedelic light filtered in through a row of stained-glass windows that ran along the top of the exterior wall. One of the windows depicted St. George and the Dragon, another a golden chalice that I assume had to be Lilith's interpretation of the Holy Grail. We passed by an archway beyond which was a mini theater with large leather recliners facing a screen the size of a Ping-Pong table. The place had the untouched feel of a museum, everything polished and clean. Had Jeeves—or whatever his name was—offered me something to eat, I would have declined for fear of dropping a crumb to the floor.

Jeeves led me finally to a set of double doors, golden oak with a dead-bolt lock. He opened them inward and stood aside to let me pass.

I didn't expect what lay on the other side. Lilith Cain stood with her back to me, a gun in her hands, which she luckily had aimed down a long dim corridor that ended in a paper target. A private gun range? As Jeeves closed the doors behind me, she fired a shot, the clap causing me to jump just a little. Who *was* this woman?

She wore camo pants and a white blouse, her long dark hair up in a ponytail capped with red ear protectors. She fired a second shot, her hands together on the handle of the automatic pistol, her feet staggered one ahead of the other, knees slightly bent, her head tilted ever so slightly as she sighted her target, the outline of a human torso about forty feet away.

By the time she fired her third shot, I understood that this was a show meant to intimidate me. She had probably been waiting in her entertainment center, watching something on her big screen TV, until I buzzed from the gate, my arrival cueing her little production.

At last, she took off her ear protectors and laid the gun down, turning to me with a half-lidded expression of nonchalance. "Why are you harassing my family?" she asked without preamble.

"I'm asking questions," I said. "The pure of heart shouldn't feel harassed by a few innocent questions. For example, I have a question for you—"

"You are not here to ask questions, Mr. Sanden. You are here to answer them." Her voice rose sharply. "Who in the hell do you think you are, coming into my world and stirring up trouble? How dare you talk to my husband! How dare you tell him such filthy lies!"

"Lies?"

"You don't know me. You don't know my family. You're causing people pain for no reason. You—"

"I told your husband that you and Jalen Bale had an affair. Are you saying that's a lie? And before you answer, know that I have the paternity test."

Lilith's next line got tangled in her throat. I could almost read her eyes, debating her next move.

She split the baby.

"You think you know everything because of one little piece of paper?"

"I know that Bale thought he might be Jessica's father. I know that the affair continued and that he broke it off just before he was murdered. I know you have a motive to see him dead and you never told that to the police."

"That's because a lunatic named Elijah Matthews killed Jalen. I'm not going to expose my personal business when the murderer's name was literally written in cold blood."

"Anyone could have written that name."

"But anyone didn't write it. Jalen did. I tried to fire Elijah, but Jalen wouldn't let me. The way he skulked around here...popping out of the shadows, judging people."

"Which Bible quotes did he use to judge you?"

"None of your damned business. Like I said, you are not here to ask questions."

"What are you afraid of?"

"I know a thing or two about you, Mr. Sanden. I make it a point to know my enemy."

"You see me as your enemy?"

She turned back to the firing range and pressed a button on the wall. It summoned the target, pulling it forward on a cable. "You don't give a damn about Elijah Matthews. Deep down, you know he killed Jalen. You only came here to destroy what I've created."

"I know no such thing."

"I see vipers like you every day, people who covet what is not theirs, but remain unwilling to build wealth on their own. So they find other ways to take what they want."

"And what do I want?"

She pulled the target from its clip, and for the first time, I noticed that the three bullet holes were grouped half an inch apart in the dead center. Lilith Cain was showing me what she could do if she set her mind to it.

"You want money," she said. "You've come here to find a secret, something you can use to blackmail me—blackmail my church. You are the worst kind of thief."

"Blackmail? Is that what you think is going on?"

"You picked the wrong woman. I'm not some tender flower to be plucked. I'm steel and fire, and if you fuck with me, you will understand what wrath really means."

"Spoken like a true Christian," I said.

"Obviously you are not familiar with the Old Testament. I will protect what is mine with a vengeance that would make God himself blush...just as you might want to protect Dee and Emma."

Hearing their names coming from her lips sent a chill to my core.

As if reading my thoughts, she said, "Yes, I know all about you...a pathetic little man who couldn't cut it in the courtroom, so you slithered away to teach. Look around you, Mr. Sanden. This is what success looks like. This is what drive and ambition lead to."

She picked the gun up again and held it against her chest, her right hand on the grip, her left caressing the muzzle. "This is my world, Mr. Sanden, and I will defend it to the death. Do you understand me?"

More theatrics. I swallowed my rage over hearing her veiled threat against my family to calmly say, "Is that what you said to Jalen Bale when he kicked your ass to the curb?"

Her face bloomed hot and red. "Get out!" she seethed. "Stay away from my family. And if I see you anywhere near my church again, I'll have you arrested. Do you understand?"

She pushed another button on the wall and Jeeves entered the shooting range, hands folded together. He stood by the door, waiting. I gave Lilith a smile and left.

CHAPTER 46

Cross-examination of Lilith Cain by Mr. Pruitt, cont.

Pruitt: You testified that Pastor Bale's position as an elder in the church automatically transferred to the next pastor; is that correct?

L. Cain: That is correct.

Pruitt: And that was Lucas Mammon.

L. Cain: That is correct.

Pruitt: Fifty percent stake—like Bale had?

L. Cain: Well, not exactly.

Pruitt: Why not...exactly?

L. Cain: Jalen Bale and I started the church
           together, just the two of us. We were
           the only elders. When he died...well,
           things had changed. My daughter was
           growing up and I felt that it was
           important to protect her interest.

Pruitt: So you made her an elder.

L. Cain: Yes.

Pruitt: At the age of thirteen.

L. Cain: Her interest is in a trust.

Pruitt: That's right. And the conservator of her
           trust votes her interest by proxy.

L. Cain: That's how trusts work.

Pruitt: Could you please tell the jury who the
           conservator of her trust is?

L. Cain: I'm the conservator.

Pruitt: So Pastor Mammon became an elder of the
           church, but he gets only one vote to
           your two votes.

L. Cain: Until Jessica is of age.

Pruitt: So, in essence, with the death of Pastor

Bale, you became the sole authority at
the church.

L. Cain: If you are suggesting that I may have
killed Jalen to get control of the
church, you're forgetting that I have an
alibi.

Pruitt: Yes, you were at a fundraiser for
Senator Caldwell.

L. Cain: It was a reception.

Pruitt: At one thousand dollars a plate.

L. Cain: The senator has done some good work
on behalf of religious organizations.
I support those who support living a
moral life.

Pruitt: It's a twenty-minute drive from the
venue where the reception was held to
your church. Is that about right?

L. Cain: That sounds accurate.

Pruitt: And the reception ran from four in the
afternoon until eight that evening.
Were you there the entire time?

L. Cain: I left around seven. I gave the
detective a picture of me taken with

the senator. It proves that I was there.

Pruitt: Yes, but according to the reception's official schedule, pictures were taken upon arrival. What we do not have is any picture of you there when Pastor Bale was murdered. You don't have any pictures like that, do you?

L. Cain: Not that I know of.

Pruitt: Do you have any witnesses who could testify that you were at that reception at six that evening?

L. Cain: I was at the reception. If you think otherwise, I believe it is upon you to provide the evidence.

Pruitt: Your Honor, I object to that last answer as being nonresponsive.

Court: You asked the question, counselor. The answer stands.

CHAPTER 47

I had no urgent reason to visit Elijah, but I felt compelled to drive to St. Peter. Tomorrow he would be approved for electroconvulsive therapy, and if the therapy worked, he would no longer talk to God. There was a part of me that mourned that.

I had just passed the midway point on my drive when my phone buzzed. It was Erica.

"Calling with good news?" I asked, although I knew better than most that getting a call from an attorney rarely carried good news.

"Are you sitting down?"

"I'm driving."

"You may want to pull over."

"What is it?"

"That break-in at your house...Anna Adler has filed an amendment to her petition arguing that you don't have the capacity to keep Emma safe."

"What?"

"She attached an affidavit stating that police officers showed up at her house to question her about the break-in...and that you accused her of stealing your briefcase. She says that she spent that evening on a conference call with some of the regents of St. John's University, working out the details of a scholarship in her father's name."

"I never said she did the break-in. It was probably that henchman butler of hers."

"She's alleging that you faked the break-in because you're losing this case and are desperate to hold on to Emma so you can get to her money."

"That's bullshit."

"Emma told her about the visit—that you weren't there for most of it. Anna's accusing you of sneaking back to your house, faking the break-in, and shooting Emma's dog."

"Why in the hell would I shoot my own dog?"

"Because it's not your dog; it's Emma's. They're alleging that you're so angry at Emma that you shot the dog out of spite."

"I was in the Como Park Conservatory."

"Do they have surveillance cameras?"

"I have no idea."

"I'll call there," she said. "If they do, I'll have them preserve the footage."

"This crap won't carry any weight—will it?"

"It's a well-crafted argument," Erica said. "I have to give them credit for that. They say that because Emma is set to inherit a great deal of money in a few years, she's a kidnapping target."

"Every rich child is. So what?"

"They're using the break-in to argue that you can't protect her. Your house has no security: no fence, no gate, no alarm system or cameras. Your neighborhood is a high-traffic area that allows potential kidnappers to stalk her without standing out. On the other hand, Anna lives in a house with its own gate. She has a state-of-the-art security system and a…She calls him a manservant who has a black belt in ninjutsu, whatever that is."

"She thinks I won't protect Emma?"

"It's ridiculous, I know, but they're spinning every little thing they can. I just wanted to give you the heads-up."

"We got an offer on the house," I said. "The sale won't be done before the hearing, but the judge will know that it's in process. Once the sale goes through, Emma won't have to go back to that house."

"Are you suggesting that Emma should stay with Anna until the sale happens? Concede that Anna's right about Emma's safety?"

"No, but..."

"I'm going to recommend that we push the final hearing back. We need time to get our ducks in a row. Can you convince Dee?"

"Yeah. She'll see the logic. If we can set the hearing just beyond the closing date for the new house, that should negate Anna's argument."

"I agree," Erica said. "Now, about that next visit."

"Tomorrow evening."

"Yeah. It's terribly important that it go well—I mean really well. I can't have Emma kicking you out of the visit. She needs to bond with you. She needs to forgive you."

"But now she thinks I shot her dog—I'm sure Anna's convinced her of that."

"Don't let Anna set the narrative."

"It just feels like I'm walking on eggshells."

"Boady...I know that Emma is your only experience at being a parent, but can I give you a little advice?"

"That's what I hired you for."

"I have a son. He's four years old. We don't always get along. He hates eating vegetables. He refuses to go to bed at his bedtime. It seems like he fights with me at every turn. But I'm his mom. I love him beyond all measure. I would do anything for him, and at the end of the day, he knows that. It doesn't matter that we have friction now and again. Being a parent goes beyond that."

"I can't seem to show her that part of me. She has this wall...a wall that I helped to build." I took a deep breath. "I know I have a lot of ground to make up, and I'll do whatever it takes to make it right."

"Does she know that?" Erica asked.

"She will," I said. "I'm not going to stop trying until I have her back. If that takes days or weeks...or years, I won't stop trying until she realizes that she belongs with us. We're not a family without her."

I don't remember the rest of my conversation with Erica because those last words echoed in my head. *We're not a family without her.* She wasn't my ward—my obligation. She was my *daughter.* How could I move on with my life if she wasn't there? The shy way she peeked around the corner to say goodnight, the oatmeal cookies she made me on Father's Day, her giggle as she watched Rufus run around the coffee table, her quiet whisper as she marveled at the twinkle of a planet in the night sky, the gentle strength of her arms when she hugged me—how could I live without those things?

I wanted her back, not because Dee needed it to happen, and not because I wanted to win the fight with Anna, but because there would be a hole in my heart if she weren't there with us. With her gone, our family wasn't complete.

CHAPTER 48

Arriving in St. Peter, I considered putting on the necklace that Ruth had given me, but decided to leave it in the car. I had no intention of lugging that thing through security if I didn't absolutely have to.

Inside, I waited in the conference room, feeling a bit naked without my briefcase. In nearly thirty years of meeting in jails, and prisons, and now a locked psychiatric unit, I had never gone in without my case.

I tapped out a rhythm on the tabletop as I waited for Elijah. When he entered the conference room, he immediately looked at my chest and then at my eyes, his forehead layered with lines of disappointment. When he drew close enough to confirm that I wasn't wearing the necklace, he turned and walked away.

"Wait," I said. "Where're you going?" It was as if he couldn't hear me.

Dammit. Now I had to cater to the whims of a schizophrenic.

I called Dr. Cohen as I walked back to my car. "Elijah wants me to wear a necklace his sister made for me," I said. "He's refusing to see me without it."

"Okay," Dr. Cohen said. "So wear the necklace."

"It's a steel plate," I said. "It'll never make it through the metal detectors."

"I see. Is it...a weapon?"

"There are no sharp edges or anything. It's just thick…and ugly."

"I'll call the security director and tell them to let you in. Just keep it buttoned under your shirt."

When I returned to the building, a security counselor I didn't recognize waved me in while on the phone, examining the necklace and relaying what it looked like to the person on the other end of the line. Then he nodded me through.

Once more, I waited for Elijah in the conference room, too worked up to take a seat. When he came in, he walked around the table, right up to me, and put his hand to my chest. When he felt the necklace beneath my shirt, he smiled.

"You know, I'm busting my butt for you," I said. "The least you could do is be a little bit helpful."

"You need to open yourself to the answers that the Lord provides," he said.

It's going to be one of those days, I thought. We at last took our seats across from one another. "Elijah, what does that even mean?"

"All will be revealed in time."

"That's the thing—you don't have time. You understand that, right?"

"No one—not you, not I—can say what tomorrow will bring. We are all but puffs of smoke, to appear and then to vanish."

"I know what tomorrow will bring. It's going to bring a hearing where a judge will give the doctors permission to shock your brain with electricity—unless we can pull off some miracle. Is there anything Bale said that you haven't told me? Throw me a bone—anything."

"God tells us that nothing is covered up that will not be revealed. You must be patient."

"Bale said he was doing your work—the work of Elijah. What was your work?"

"I was there to hold up a mirror so that Jalen could see himself. Nothing more."

"You jumped onto the stage when he was giving a sermon and called him a false prophet."

"Like I said, I held up a mirror."

"You hit him in the face with it."

"He refused to listen."

"But you must have gotten through to him. I mean, he was working on that bone sermon."

"Yes." Elijah gave a sad smile. "I must have gotten through."

"If I could find a copy of that sermon…or notes…anything to prove that he was going to expose the grift of his church, I could take that to a judge, maybe get a search warrant for the church computers. He might have saved a copy on the church's hard drive. If I had something like that…I might be able to stop your Jarvis hearing."

He shrugged. "I have had many hearings in my life. What is one more?"

"You've never had a hearing like this one. Their treatment will change you forever."

"The Lord is my shepherd; I shall not want. And though I walk through the shadow of the valley of Death, I fear no evil."

"Elijah, you won't be able to talk to God anymore. Don't you understand that?"

"Mr. Sanden, I will always talk to God."

"But he won't talk back." Now it was Elijah who refused to listen. "That voice you hear—the one that you think is God—it'll be gone… forever. That's the whole point of the procedure."

"You don't understand," he said.

I had rested my hands on the table between us. Now he reached out and laid one of his hands upon mine, the bones of his fingers so frail that they seemed almost hollow. "I will always talk to God," he said. "And God will always answer me. There is nothing any man can do to stop that. I will finish helping those people I was sent here to help. And when the Lord deems it time for me to leave, I will leave."

"You're just going to walk out when God tells you to?"

"I have one last person to help," he said. "When I have finished the task God has set out for me...then I will be free."

I thought about the man with the eye patch, the man Elijah was helping to swim up from a great darkness. Once Elijah no longer talked to God, would helping others still be possible? Would he even care?

"I get it," I said, "but humor me: Is there anything you can tell me that might help me find that sermon? *Think.*"

"The Book of Amos tells us, 'God reveals his secret unto his servant, the prophet.'"

I leaned in. "Elijah, if you're a prophet, now would be a good time for that to happen. I'm at the end of my rope. If you have anything to tell me, I need it now."

Elijah regarded me for a couple seconds as though weighing a decision. Then he scooted his chair back, put his hands on his lap, and closed his eyes.

He took in a deep breath and hummed as he slowly exhaled, his lips moving in silent speech, his eyes darting back and forth beneath his thin eyelids. He repeated this three more times, the hum of his exhalations growing louder.

Upon finishing his last exhale, he popped his eyes open, sharp and alert, an expression of discovery painted across his face. Then his eyes turned dull again and he shrugged. "Nope, nothing," he said.

I had never wanted to punch a client more.

CHAPTER 49

I left the Security Hospital wondering if I would ever return, my investigation now careering toward a dead end. Elijah had an alibi, but not one that was bulletproof. I had a parade of characters who might have wanted Jalen Bale dead, but no evidence that any of them had acted upon those motives. And what probably bothered me more than anything was that Elijah didn't seem to care. God's will be done. If religion is the opium of the masses, then Elijah Matthews was one stoned son of a bitch.

But there was one piece of evidence that I kept coming back to, one that I couldn't explain away—Elijah's name written in Bale's blood. Ben had tried to sprinkle doubt on the case by getting the blood-spatter expert to agree that it was *theoretically* possible—although incredibly unlikely—that a very careful killer could have used Bale's finger to write that name. If Elijah wasn't the murderer...then why did Bale write it?

The killer had used a weapon of convenience—a stone sitting on Bale's credenza—to bludgeon him to death. That wasn't the hallmark of a careful criminal. It stretched credulity to think that someone acting on that kind of impulse would then have the presence of mind to hold Bale's finger and write Elijah's name without smearing any of the tiny blood droplets on the back of Bale's hand.

Again, why would Bale write Elijah's name if not to identify him as the killer?

I let that question float in the air as I rearranged my options: one, the killer wrote Elijah's name to divert suspicion; two, Bale wrote it to identify Elijah as the killer; or three…Bale wrote it but for some other purpose. Was he trying to say that Elijah held the answer? If that was the case, Bale had wasted the last precious seconds of his life, because Elijah wasn't sharing that answer.

Frustrated, I was about to turn on some music when a tiny thought found its way past my capitulation. Could it be a different Elijah…maybe one from the Bible? *God reveals his secrets unto his servant, the prophet.* Maybe there was something in the story of Elijah that Bale wanted us to know, some clue hidden in the Book of Kings that would lead to his killer?

I pulled into a parking lot along the highway and found a podcast on my phone where two men read the Bible. I loaded First Kings and played it, jumping forward ten seconds at a time until I heard the name Elijah. I pulled back onto the highway and listened.

I had read the story of Elijah when I was in college, and remembered the part about him executing four hundred and fifty false prophets, but I hadn't remembered that he had lived with a woman while hiding from King Ahab, and had brought that woman's son back from the dead. I searched for meaning, for likely puzzle pieces, but by the time I got to the end of First Kings, I had found no hidden clues. I loaded Second Kings and listened. Again, I heard nothing that related to Bale's death. Another dead end.

I eased into a turning lane that would take me home, the truck behind me creeping up so close that I could count the bugs in its grill.

What if Bale's clue wasn't in the story itself, but in something that Bale had left in his Bible? Underlined words or a note scribbled in the margins?

My exit approached.

It was a harebrained notion, but in less than twenty-four hours

Elijah would be approved for shock therapy. And stranger things had been kept in Bibles, surely.

"Goddammit," I muttered as I hit my blinker and pulled back onto the highway. I felt like a gullible fool, but I was headed back to the church.

Lilith's words played in my ear as I pulled into the parking lot: *And if I see you anywhere near my church again, I'll have you arrested.* Technically, she didn't say that I was prohibited from going there. All I had to do was get in and out without her seeing me.

I drove around back to the private parking area. Mammon's Mercedes was there, but not Lilith's or Jessica's cars.

I called him. The phone rang three times and went to voice mail. I dug Lawrence's number from my phone's history and dialed.

"Hello?"

"Lawrence, it's Boady Sanden. I need a favor."

Silence.

"Can you get me into Mammon's office? I want to take a look at a Bible in there."

"I can get you in, but…"

"But what?"

"Pastor Mammon's in there right now."

"He didn't answer his phone."

"Don't expect he would. He's drunk as a skunk. Something's going down, and I suspect whatever it is, he's getting the short end of the stick."

"Can you let me in?"

"I don't know, Mr. Sanden."

"This could be important, Lawrence. It'll only take a minute, I promise."

"Okay, but you gotta get in and get out fast. Miss Lilith said I wasn't supposed to be talking to you no more."

"You'll hardly know I was there."

CHAPTER 50

L oud music blasted behind the closed door of Lucas Mammon's office—*Jesus Christ Superstar,* the movie version. My Catholic high school had paid for a special showing at the local movie theater once. I was surprised to recognize the song playing in Mammon's office: "Gethsemane." Jesus in the garden, lamenting his coming fate. Mammon caterwauled with the song, his voice cracking flat on the high notes.

Lawrence, who had delivered me that far, shook his head and left. I would be going in alone.

I knocked, but the caterwauling continued. I knocked harder.

"Go the fuck away!" came from inside.

I knocked again. "Pastor Mammon, it's Boady Sanden. I need to see you. It's important."

Mammon stopped singing. After a second or two he turned off the music. I opened the door to find Mammon leaning on his desk, his hands flat, arms locked, as though bracing himself against a strong wind.

"You okay?" I asked.

"Little dizzy," he said.

"You'd better sit down."

On the corner of his desk a bottle of Jim Beam lay on its side, some of the liquid still dripping down onto the carpet. Mammon navigated back to his chair and plopped down so hard, I half expected to see him pass out.

I walked to the desk and tipped the whiskey bottle upright. The room was a mess: papers on the floor, books pulled from the shelves, the odor of alcohol permeating the air. I could also smell bile and noticed a stain on the front of Mammon's white shirt.

"Rough day?" I asked.

"Fuck you."

"Want to tell me about it?"

"They're screwing me. That fucking bitch is screwing me. She thinks she can…" His head bobbed forward and the thought was gone.

"Lilith?"

"What?"

"Who's screwing you?"

He opened his eyes and looked as though he was surprised to see me in his office. "She's screwing me," he mumbled. "She thinks…" Again his brain shut off.

In the corner of the room a mini-fridge stood open and I could see bottles of water. I grabbed one and poured it over Mammon's head, taking only a little joy in the action.

"What the hell!" He swung at me, missing completely. As he blinked and wiped the water from his eyes, I asked again. "Who's screwing you?"

"Lilith…" He took a breath, and when he let it out it was as if his spine had surrendered. His head dropped so that his chin rested on his chest. "And that little princess of hers," he whispered.

"Jessica?"

He started singing "Gethsemane" again, the lyrics of the song barely intelligible through his slur. "After all I tried for three years… seems like thirty…seems like—"

I opened a second bottle of water and held it above his head.

"No, man. Don't. Please."

"Then stay with me. What are you talking about?"

"I see what's she's doing…she's going to replace me."

"As pastor?"

Breathing seemed to exhaust him. "Where's my bottle?"

"Replace you with whom?"

"The little princess. She's eighteen now. I gotta share the stage with her. I'm not an idiot. I see…"

I wanted to feel sorry for Mammon, but he was a man who preyed on the weak. He took advantage of people who sincerely believed the words he preached. He pried nickels and dimes from their fingers and promised them that God would repay them. Let Mammon drown in his self-centered misery. I didn't care.

"These are Pastor Bale's books, right?" I said.

Mammon didn't answer.

I scanned the shelves and quickly spotted a Bible, a paperback edition, its corners dirtied from years of being held and studied. I pulled it from the shelf and thumbed through looking for First Kings. Finding it, I flipped until I found the beginning of Elijah's story, chapter seventeen. I ran a finger over the text, looking for underlined words or notes in the margins. The pages were worn but unmarked. No hidden message. I continued into Second Kings, skimming through to chapter two where Elijah was swept up to heaven. There were no codes. No notes. It was one more dead end.

"What are you…looking for?" Mammon's words dripped off his thick tongue.

I didn't think Mammon was sober enough to understand, but I explained anyway. "I thought Bale might have written the name Elijah because he left a message in his Bible…in the Book of Kings."

Mammon smiled smugly. "You heathen," he said, then laughed as though he had made a great joke.

"What?"

"You don't know anything."

"What don't I know?"

"Elijah is also in..." He twirled his finger in the air as though homing in on his answer. Then he got tired and dropped it to his lap.

"Where else should I look?" I asked.

"Malachi." He sang the word, taking pleasure in knowing an answer that eluded me. Malachi? That's what Elijah had been reading when Jessica spied on him. I flipped through the Bible again until I found the book, only four chapters long. I scanned the words and found a mention of Elijah in the very last paragraph.

But before the great and terrible day of the Lord comes
I will send you the prophet Elijah.
He will bring fathers and children together.

Still, none of it was underlined; there were no notes in the margin. I put the book back on the shelf.

"I'm sorry for barging in," I said, trying not to succumb to my disappointment. "There's nothing there."

Mammon had slumped deeper into his chair, his eyes closed, and for a moment I thought he had fallen asleep, but then he muttered, "What about the other one?"

"The other what?"

His answer was barely audible, but it sounded like "Bible."

I turned back to the shelf and scanned the titles, starting with the top row, and there, at the end, was another Bible. This one had a red leather cover, its pages gilded in gold. It was the kind of Bible that Dee had inherited from her mother, an heirloom to be cherished, not leafed through and mangled. I pulled it down and opened it, finding the pages thin and crisp. Each chapter began with a capital letter written so prettily that they hardly looked like letters at all. I started flipping through, but it fell open on its own, cleaved by two pieces of paper shoved into the spine.

My heart began thumping as I lifted the papers out and unfolded them. One was a printed email dated three days before Bale was murdered, a reply from a lab telling him that the test results he had requested were attached. The second paper was another DNA test. At the top was a column for the child. There, I saw the name *Jessica Cain*. The next column, however, didn't hold a name. It merely read, *Forensic sample.*

I shot to the bottom and read the results. *Probability of relatedness: 99.98 percent.* I wanted to yell *Eureka!* but in truth, I had no idea what I held in my hand.

I turned to show Mammon, but he had fallen asleep, his head tipped back, a light snore rising from his throat.

As I left his office with the DNA test in my hand, I wondered whether Mammon would even remember that I had been there.

CHAPTER 51

That night, I lay in bed trying to find sleep, fragments of Jalen Bale's life and death floating in the darkness around me. I was back in that funhouse again, bumping into new walls. There had to be a way to connect everything, but damned if I could find it.

What did this new paternity test mean? The test identified the donor merely as a forensic sample. I had seen enough paternity tests in my day to know that that was unusual. It suggested that the donor might not even know that the sample had been taken.

I thought about my visit with Ed Cain. He had smoked two cigarettes in the short time we were together. All Bale had to do was pocket a butt and he'd have Ed's DNA. Had that been the true purpose of Bale's visit? But why would it have been important for Bale to confirm that Ed was Jessica's father?

Could Lucas Mammon be the sample donor? He would have been eighteen or nineteen when Jessica was conceived, old enough to do the trick and maybe young enough—and clueless enough—not to put it together. It would have been easy for Pastor Bale to find a sample of Mammon's DNA to send to the lab. The same with Jessica's sample, although the lab already had her on file from seventeen years earlier.

Jessica had flirted with Mammon. I didn't even want to think about the rotted fruit that family tree might bear. But why kill Bale?

I hit another wall in the funhouse.

Was the paternity test even the reason that Bale died? He was writing a sermon that promised to tear down the temple he had built. But if it was the sermon that got him killed, why scrawl the name Elijah in his blood? It was his last act. It had to mean something, but what?

I woke in the morning still feeling trapped. The sun brought no clarity. I ate a breakfast of eggs and sausage, coffee and orange juice. I read the morning paper, hoping that the distraction might loosen the logjam in my head. When none of that worked, I went to my study to think.

There was one small detail that had kept pulling my attention, a paper cut finding salt. The result of that second paternity test read *probability of relatedness,* not *probability of parentage.* I was pretty sure the reason for that was because they were going off a forensic sample instead of a standardized testing kit, but I wanted to give the lab a call just to confirm.

I retrieved my laptop from my car, where it had been since my devastating visit with Emma. We would have our second visit that afternoon. By then Elijah would have had his Jarvis hearing and been approved for ECT. With that failure tucked securely under my belt, I would have to try to repair the mess I had made of my family. The thought of that battle caused my stomach to knot up.

Once at my desk, I turned on the laptop and typed in the name of the lab, looking for contact information. In my periphery I saw Dee step into the study doorway and lean against the frame.

"I was thinking we should take Emma to the park at Minnehaha Falls today."

"Sure." I nodded.

"I mean, Como Park is much nicer, but after what happened on Tuesday...maybe it would be best to have a new location."

"Uh-huh." There were hundreds of listings for the lab, most of them advertisements that had an email option but no phone number.

"Remember when we took her there a couple years ago? You two walked up behind the falls?"

"Yeah." Why would a lab make it so hard to give them a call? It's not like they're some kind of military secret. They're a lab, for Christ's sake.

"And then we should rent a helicopter and fly to Manhattan and do some shopping?"

"Sure." I'd found a phone number—finally.

"Boady!"

I looked up from my computer.

"What was the last thing I said to you?"

I thought back and had a fuzzy recollection of a helicopter and Manhattan. *Shit*. I decided that not answering was a better course than admitting my error.

"This is important. You need to take this seriously."

"I am. It's just that—" I stopped myself and tried to remember what Dee had suggested. A few of the words came to me. "I know it's important," I said. "I think Minnehaha Falls is perfect."

"Boady, I need you there...not just physically. I need you to be present with us...with Emma."

"I'll be there, body, mind, and soul. I promise." And I meant it. I wished I could tell her just how much I now understood, but with her eyes boring into me, I couldn't find the words.

After Dee left, I dialed the number for the lab, and as the phone rang, I noticed that my toolbar had an icon for the video player. That puzzled me until I realized the last time my laptop was open had been on the night the prowler came to my window, the night when Rufus chased them away with his growl. I had been watching raw footage from the homeless shelter.

I clicked on the video and watched it with the sound off as I navigated the automated answering message from the lab. On the screen, a man in his seventies with a tangled beard around his toothless grin spoke to the person holding the camera. On the phone a tinny voice said, "For information about our testing procedures, press 3." I pressed 3. A woman came on the line.

"Yes, I was hoping you could answer a question about a report I have."

"Sure, what's your question?"

The video on my computer switched from the old man to a mother and child, she in her early twenties and the child barely out of diapers. A woman off-screen reached into the frame and handed the child a stuffed teddy bear. I wondered if the hand belonged to Lilith Cain.

I said, "I have a paternity-test result that reads 'probability of relatedness' instead of 'probability of paternity.' I was just wondering why that is?"

"I would assume that the test wasn't necessarily looking for the child's father. It might be trying to determine if a certain person might be related to the child in any way."

The video's cameraman moved on from the mother and child to a face that seemed oddly familiar. A young woman, dark hair, pretty. She drew my attention and caused me to sit up.

The woman on the phone continued: *Relatedness* could be a father, aunt, grandmother—anyone, really.

I stopped the video. "Um…thanks. I have to go." I hung up on the lab, backed the video up, increased the sound, and hit play.

The woman was looking directly into the camera, and I could tell by the cameraman's voice that it was Lucas Mammon. He asked, "How has the shelter helped you?"

The young woman had a blanket wrapped around her shoulders and seemed frightened, like she had passed through a terrible ordeal. She answered in a quiet voice, "You gave me food and a place to sleep. I really appreciate it."

It was Christina Gideon.

The off-screen woman spoke, and I recognized the voice of Lilith Cain. "Can I ask…what brought you here…to our shelter?"

Christina hesitated, as if unsure whether to answer or not. She continued facing the camera but glanced toward Lilith.

Then she answered the question.

It was as if a bolt of lightning shot through me. I jumped out of my chair, breathless. I knew who killed Jalen Bale—and I knew why.

CHAPTER 52

I folded my computer shut, grabbed the DNA test, and headed for my car, passing Dee in the kitchen on the way.

"Where are you going?"

"To church," I said, pausing at the door to the mudroom. "I have to—"

"Our visit starts at four."

The clock on the kitchen stove read 10:00. "I'll be home in plenty of time for that."

"Boady?"

"I promise."

Outside, I threw my computer on the passenger seat and called the church as I pulled out of my driveway, punching the numbers that took me to Lucas Mammon. He answered like a man just waking up.

"Hello?" His voice sounded as cracked as a desert lake bed.

"Lucas. It's Boady Sanden. I need to see you."

There was a pause, a space where he must have been trying to piece together who I was and why I might be calling. "Not a good day, man."

"It's important."

"Shit." Then the phone went silent except for the sound of his breathing.

"Mammon?"

"I got a meeting. I don't have time."

"Who are you meeting with?"

"Not that it's any of your business, but...Lilith and Jessica."

"Is it about the plan to put Jessica on stage with you?"

"Uh...how'd you know about that?"

He didn't remember my visit last night. "I'm on my way. It's important. I'll explain when I get there." I hung up before he could object.

My second call went to Griffin MacDonald, the investigator who'd handled Bale's murder case four years ago. I had a request for him.

"Why the hell would I care to go to that church?" he asked, his voice rising in irritation.

"Because Elijah Matthews didn't kill Pastor Bale."

"I'm going to hang up on you now, so have a nice—"

"Wait. Just hear me out. Did you know that Bale was on the verge of destroying the church? That he had been working on a sermon that would have brought the whole organization crashing to the ground?"

"I don't recall that, no."

"And did you know that Jalen Bale and Lilith Cain had been having an affair?"

Silence. Then: "No."

"And that Jalen Bale broke it off just before he was murdered?"

"What are you saying?"

"I'm saying that there's a lot about this case that you don't know, but if you help me, we can undo a grave injustice."

"Help you out how?"

"Meet me at the church and bring a picture of the murder weapon—that stone."

"You want me to drop everything...because you think I screwed up four years ago? If you have new evidence, bring it in to me and I'll take a look."

"I have evidence, but I need your help to carry it to the finish line. I need you to meet me at the church."

"What evidence?"

I told MacDonald what I knew and what I believed, laying it out as logically as I could. When I finished, I could almost hear him nodding through the phone connection. "I'll be there," he said.

My last call was to Ray Gideon. I still had his number in my phone from my visit. He picked up on the third ring.

"Ray, you need to get to the church. I'm meeting with Lucas Mammon at…"—I looked at my watch and calculated my arrival time at the church—"ten thirty."

"Why? What's going on?"

"I'll explain when you get there. It's important."

"Is it about Christina?"

"Very much so," I said.

CHAPTER 53

L awrence let me into the church. I asked him to wait for the others and let them in when they arrived, then made my way to Lucas Mammon's office, where Lucas greeted me, reeking of whiskey and sweat. His hair had been finger-combed but remained splayed in disobedient tufts, and his eyes burned red above the dark rings on his pale face. He was trying to pretend that he was up and ready for the day but had woefully missed the mark.

I placed my laptop on Mammon's desk, opened it, and had just fired it up when Detective MacDonald walked in. I introduced myself and then Mammon. Although MacDonald already knew Mammon from the investigation, I could tell he was surprised by the state the man had sunk to, slumped at his desk.

"What's going on?" Mammon finally asked.

"Just a little presentation," I said.

Mammon stood. "What's he here for?" Mammon aimed a thumb at Detective MacDonald.

"Backup."

I cued up the video as the two men stepped to my side on the visitor's side of the desk. Ray walked in looking properly confused. I introduced him all around even though I assumed that he already knew the players, and his suspicious look at Lucas only confirmed that. Then I began.

"As you know, four years ago Elijah Matthews was prosecuted for the murder of Pastor Jalen Bale. Elijah had taken the stage during one of Bale's sermons to accuse him of being a false prophet, and in the Book of Kings, the prophet Elijah put false prophets to death. Add to that, Elijah's name had been written in blood by Bale's own hand—a victim identifying his killer. Elijah's DNA was found on the murder weapon. Granted, so was the DNA of the victim and of an unidentified person. But that was more than enough evidence to—"

The door to Mammon's office rattled open and there stood Jessica Cain, a look of bewilderment on her face.

"Jessie," Mammon said, running his hands through his hair again. "You're early."

"What's going on?" she asked.

"I'm giving a little presentation," I said. "Have a seat. You may find this interesting."

Jessica looked at the four of us as she padded slowly to one of the two empty chairs, her gaze wavering between me, my laptop, and Ray Gideon.

I asked Detective MacDonald if he'd brought the picture of the stone, and he unfolded a photocopy from his pocket and handed it to me. I showed it to Jessica. "I'm curious, do you know what this is?"

Jessica gave the photo a quick glance. "No."

"You've never seen this before?"

She shook her head.

"It used to sit right there," I said, pointing to Bale's credenza.

"Oh yeah, I forgot."

"Did Pastor Bale ever tell you what that stone meant to him?"

"No."

"Did you ever lift it? Feel how heavy it was?"

"No."

"You never picked that stone up?"

"I said no!" Adamant or angry, I couldn't tell.

"One of the things that confused me," I said, "was that the killer

stole Bale's laptop. In those few weeks before he died, he'd been working on a sermon, one that he told Elijah would be his last. He had
been writing it on that laptop. But if Elijah killed Bale, why take the
computer? And if Elijah saw this church as a haven for false preaching,
why not let Bale go through with his plan to destroy it?"

I turned to Mammon. "Then there was that old promotional
file that you and Lilith had worked on. Bale asked you to dig it up,
remember?"

"Yeah."

"Did you know that there was a thumb drive in there with footage from the homeless shelter?"

"Honestly, I didn't look. I just gave it to him."

I forwarded the video to the interview of Christina Gideon. Ray
gasped, seeing his daughter. Tears filled his eyes. "That's Christina,"
he said, his voice cracking to push the words out.

I nodded and hit play. On the screen, Mammon asks Christina,
"How has the shelter helped you?"

Christina answers, "You gave me food and a place to sleep. I really
appreciate it."

Then Lilith says, "Can I ask...what brought you here...to our
shelter?"

Christina stares at the camera as if unsure whether to answer.
Glancing to the side, perhaps at Lilith, one of her eyes drags and then
lifts, not tracking with the other.

Mammon, Detective MacDonald, and Gideon were watching the
screen with sharp attention—but I was watching Jessica. She dropped
her gaze to the floor, her face pale and drawn.

Then Christina answers Lilith's question. "I'm pregnant. I needed
a place to stay."

"Oh my god," Ray whispered. He put a hand on Mammon's desk
to keep from sinking to the floor. "I didn't know." Thick tears streaked
down his face. "Why didn't she tell me?"

I turned to Ray. "When your daughter glanced to the side...one of her eyes didn't track."

Ray looked at me as though I could not have said anything less relevant. "It's a condition called Duane syndrome," he said. "She inherited it from her mother."

I wouldn't have believed Mammon could look paler, but he did. He turned to Jessica, who had slumped forward in her chair, her arms wrapped around her thighs. She rocked slowly but breathed heavily. "Jessica?" he said.

"The thumb drive was corrupted," I said. "I had to transfer it to my hard drive to play it. So did Jalen Bale. He put it on his laptop."

"I don't understand," Ray said.

"Last night I came here—to this office—because I was convinced that Bale had left behind a clue."

"Wait..." Mammon spoke as though he'd been pulled out of a daydream. "You were here last night?"

I nodded, and continued. "I had been operating under the belief that Bale's murderer had written the name Elijah in blood to mislead the investigation...but I was wrong. Bale had written that name, but he wasn't naming his killer. He was telling us to look for Elijah in his Bible. That's where I found this."

I laid the DNA test on Mammon's desk. "I got twisted up thinking that this was a paternity test—a test to determine a father—but it's not. It's a DNA test to determine the relatedness of someone else."

"Who?" Mammon asked.

I turned to Ray Gideon. "That day Bale went to your house, you had a beer together."

"Yeah."

"You said that when he left, he took his beer with him."

"Yeah."

"But it wasn't his beer that he took. It was yours."

"What are you talking about?"

"He wanted your DNA to test his theory." I touched Ray's arm and gently turned him away from the computer screen so that he faced Jessica. "Ray, I'd like to introduce you to your granddaughter, Jessica."

Jessica now looked up; the fear of a trapped animal coiled behind her eyes. Her lip curled into a snarl and she hissed, "He's not my grandfather."

"Because that would take away your inheritance," I said.

"My dad is Edward Cain. My mom is Lilith Cain. I'm not related to this..."

"Bum?" Ray said softly. The word carried twenty years of grief.

Detective MacDonald had picked up the DNA report, his eyes circling from the report to Jessica to Ray as he reworked the case in his mind. I would need him to accept that he had been wrong, and I would need it soon.

I said, "Bale saw Christina's eye in the video—the Duane syndrome. He put it together. When Bale said he was doing the work of Elijah, he was referring to the last lines from the Book of Malachi: 'I will send you the prophet Elijah. He will bring fathers and children together.' He was talking about you, Ray—you, Christina, and Jessica. Bale was bringing a grandfather and a granddaughter together."

"Oh God," Ray whispered.

"Bale wanted you to come to his office to tell you what he had discovered," I said to Ray. Then I walked over beside Jessica. "But he brought you here first, Jessica. He probably wanted to break the news to you gently, give you some time to digest it."

"Jessie?" Mammon said. "Did you..."

"No," she said, pleading.

"He brought you behind his desk," I said.

"No."

"Showed you the video—then the email he'd gotten from the lab with the DNA results."

"I didn't."

"The stone was right there."

"I..." Jessica seemed tangled as she looked from Mammon to me to Detective MacDonald, unable to get out the words she wanted to say.

"There were three distinct DNA profiles on the murder weapon," I said. "Bale's, Elijah's, and..." I gestured to Jessica.

"Jessica," Mammon said, looking sick. "Did you kill him?"

Her eyes begged for something that was beyond her ability to ask.

"A DNA test will prove that you held the murder weapon," I said. "That third DNA profile will be yours, and after you just said that you've never touched it."

"I don't..." Jessica put her hands to her head, pressing her palms into her temples.

"Bale was going to take away your name," I said. "Your identity. Your inheritance. Exposing who your mother was would destroy the church—destroy you—so you struck first."

"He wouldn't stop. I just wanted him to stop. I didn't mean to—"

The door to Mammon's office slammed open. Lilith Cain stood in the frame, rage burning in her eyes. "What the hell is going on here?"

CHAPTER 54

Jessica sprang from her chair. "They know, Momma!" But before she could take a step, Detective MacDonald had her by the wrists.

"Take your hands off her." Lilith's voice boomed like a cannon.

"That's not going to happen," MacDonald said. "She's under arrest."

Jessica broke one of her arms free and swung at MacDonald. He grabbed her torso, lifted her into the air, and dropped her to the floor, pulling her arms behind her as he pulled out his handcuffs.

Lilith started for MacDonald. "Let go of her!"

I stepped in between them and Lilith threw a punch at me. I leaned in, took the punch on the top of my head, and shoved her backward to the floor. I raised my fists to be ready for round two.

That's when it occurred to me that Lilith hadn't bothered to ask why Jessica was being arrested. She knew.

Lilith climbed to her knees, struggling against gravity, and shock, and the tug of her skirt twisted around her thighs. Mammon stepped to my left to make a wall between Lilith and MacDonald.

"Let it be, Lilith," he said.

"Let it be?" she said, rising to her feet. "Let it be? Don't talk to me like that, you little worm."

Ray Gideon, who seemed not to notice the scuffle in front of him, spoke as though he were working through the lines of a riddle. "Where's Christina?" he said.

Lilith regarded him for a moment and then, just that quickly, disregarded him.

"Where's my daughter?" he repeated, staring Lilith down.

I had been working on that question myself. Ray wasn't going to like the answer. It was possible that Christina had agreed to leave the baby with Lilith and had run off to parts unknown, but I didn't think so. Lilith needed a baby, and she needed one fast. Ed had been arrested, so the window for Lilith concealing her fake pregnancy was closing. Without a child, Lilith would lose out on Grandpa Cain's fortune.

I was pretty sure that Christina was dead.

When Lilith ignored Ray a third time, he lifted a marble cross that hung on the wall. Holding it like a battle-ax, he stepped toward Lilith.

I held up my hand. "Not like this, Ray."

He stopped, but the struggle showed on his face, and he still held the cross high. "She knows where Christina is."

"Ray, she's got nowhere to go. We'll know everything soon enough; it's just a matter of time." I looked hard at Lilith. "It's over, and she knows it."

Jessica lay trapped on the floor beneath the weight of Detective MacDonald. I half expected Lilith to surrender, but instead she stepped back. She looked at me and hissed, "I will destroy you for this."

Then she turned and walked out.

"Mom!" Jessica screamed. "Where are you going? Mom!" Mammon sank to the floor, stunned by all that had unfolded.

Ray looked to me, his eyes questioning how we could let Lilith go. "We'll find out what happened to your daughter," I said. "I promise."

Ray lowered the cross slowly, despair weighing his shoulders down. "She killed Christina, didn't she?"

I didn't want to agree with him, but I couldn't bring myself to lie to him either, so I said nothing.

Detective MacDonald lifted Jessica from the floor, her face red and streaked with tears.

I gestured for Ray to look at her. "You have a granddaughter to think about."

Ray approached Jessica slowly. When he stood in front of her, he said with wonder, "You're my granddaughter."

Jessica raised her cold eyes to her grandfather, and spat in his face.

CHAPTER 55

As soon as the elevator doors closed on MacDonald, Jessica, and Ray, my brain jumped to a new track—Elijah's hearing. It was scheduled for 1:30. I wasn't the attorney of record, so I had no standing to put a stop to it over the phone. I would need to drive there and explain to the court what had just happened. If I hurried, I could make it to St. Peter and back home in time for our visit with Emma.

I called the court administrator in Nicollet County as I drove.

"Just to be clear," she said, "you're not the patient's attorney."

"I am not."

"Who do you represent, then?"

"I'm not a part of the hearing at all, but I have important information. If you could just put me through to the judge."

"I would need all the parties on the line. Otherwise, that would be ex parte communication."

That was true and I knew it. "Fine. Which courtroom is the hearing in?"

"They don't hold those hearings here," she said. "The judge appears electronically. The parties and their attorneys gather in a room at the hospital."

Of course. "Do you know which room?"

"He's scheduled for conference room three in Summit Hall."

Summit Hall was where I'd met up with Dr. Cohen on my first

visit. At least I wouldn't have to scramble all over campus looking for the venue. "Thank you."

I was on pace to arrive in time to stop the hearing. The remaining problem was getting into that conference room itself. I called Dr. Cohen.

"I need to stop Elijah's Jarvis hearing," I said. "Another person has been arrested for the murder of Pastor Bale. It happened just a few minutes ago."

"So...he didn't kill that man?"

"No. I'm on my way there now. His hearing is at 1:30. Can you meet me before that? I'll need your help getting my information to the judge."

"Certainly," she said. "I'd be happy to help."

"Meet me outside the gift shop," I said. "I should be there around 1:15."

"I'll see you there," Dr. Cohen said.

I didn't know the judge and she didn't know me. I had no criminal complaint or proof that Jessica had been arrested for the murder of Jalen Bale, but I had Griffin MacDonald's phone number. I could ask the court to call him to confirm the arrest, run the call through dispatch maybe to shore up MacDonald's bona fides. Law school taught no procedure for what I was about to attempt. I would just have to make it up as I went.

I pulled into the parking lot outside Summit Hall and was getting out of my car when I remembered that stupid necklace. The last thing I wanted was for Elijah to refuse to talk—especially after the morning I'd had. I threw the necklace on. Because Summit Hall housed doctor offices and meeting rooms, it had no metal detectors, so I tucked the chunk of metal under my shirt and headed in.

Immediately, I saw Dr. Cohen standing at the entrance to the building frantically waving at me, panic painted across her face.

"They moved the hearing," she said.

"To a different building?"

"The time," she said. "The judge had a cancellation and moved Elijah's hearing up. It's going on right now." Dr. Cohen took me by the sleeve and pulled me inside.

The conference room was across from the gift shop. Through glass that framed the door, I could see Elijah sitting at the end of a long table, his face expressionless. Next to him was a gray-haired man in a blue suit—his court-appointed attorney—and behind them stood a muscle-bound security counselor. Elijah's treatment team lined the sides of the table, Dr. Handler in the middle of the cluster, arguing why Elijah should receive shock therapy.

I wasn't sure what to expect: an angry judge, contempt of court, or a hard takedown by the security counselor. I didn't care. I opened the door and ran in.

CHAPTER 56

Everyone in the room stopped talking and looked at me. The security counselor lurched forward but saw Dr. Cohen walk in behind me, her hand up in an *It's okay* gesture, and wavered. I walked to the end of the table so that the judge could see me.

"Can I help you?" she asked. She made no attempt to hide her irritation.

"My name is Boady Sanden," I said. "I'm an attorney for the Innocence Project. I represent Elijah Matthews in that regard, and I have information that is critical for this hearing."

"This is a Jarvis hearing," she said, as if those words alone were enough to shoo me away.

Dr. Cohen interjected on my behalf. "Your Honor, I used to be Mr. Matthews's primary. What Mr. Sanden has to say here is relevant to your decision on whether electroconvulsive therapy is appropriate for Mr. Matthews. I ask that you hear him out."

Handler stood up. "Your Honor, this is highly irregular. Dr. Cohen is no longer on this patient's team. She has no authority to speak to his treatment. And this attorney…he's undermined my authority with the patient. He has no business being in this room. This is a confidential proceeding."

"You haven't issued your order yet, have you?" I asked.

The judge said, "I was just about to, but if you're not his attorney in this matter, you have no business in this hearing."

"Your Honor, Elijah Matthews is here because he was found to have committed the act of murder. The man Elijah was supposed to have killed was a pastor named Jalen Bale."

"All of that is in his file," the judge said.

"Yes," I continued. "But what's not in his file—and what none of these doctors here know—is that the true murderer of Jalen Bale was arrested less than two hours ago in Minnetonka. Elijah did not kill Pastor Bale."

The room went silent. Handler slowly sat down.

"I'm sorry," the judge said. "What happened?"

"This morning, I presented evidence to Detective MacDonald, the lead investigator in Elijah's case. It proved that a woman named Jessica Cain killed Pastor Bale. MacDonald has placed her under arrest. Elijah Matthews is here due to a false conviction."

"Mr. Sanden, I don't know you from Adam," the judge said. "Mr. Matthews is here under the lawful authority of Judge Cooper's order finding him mentally ill and dangerous. Are you asking me to ignore all that and, what...release him?"

"I'm just asking that you not go forward with the ECT."

"We've held the hearing and his treatment team is unanimous in their recommendation."

Handler had regained his attitude and said, "Mr. Matthews is a sick man. He's been here four years. He needs treatment or his condition will never improve."

I ignored Handler and kept my focus on the judge. "Your Honor, if he didn't commit the crime, then he shouldn't be here. Take the false conviction out of the equation, and he's just another man walking around his apartment talking to the voices in his head. You can't treat him as dangerous if the one thing he's accused of doing that made him so is a lie."

The judge considered my argument and then said, "I come back to the fact that I don't know you. I can't simply take your word for something that significant. Do you have a charging document to show me?"

"I drove straight here from the scene of her arrest."

"Mr. Sanden, I'm not inclined—"

"Your Honor, you have the file, so you know that the original investigating officer was Detective Griffin MacDonald. Call the Minnetonka Police Department and have them patch you through. He can verify everything I've said."

The judge paused again, and this time leaned to her court reporter and whispered, "Get a number for the Minnetonka PD."

Elijah should have been jumping up and down for joy, cheering me on, but he sat there with the calmness of a man watching a movie he'd already seen, as though the voice in his head had tipped him off as to how this all would end. He was truly all in on his delusion.

The judge called the Minnetonka Police Department and got patched through to Detective MacDonald. She put the call on speakerphone.

"This is MacDonald," he said.

"Detective, this is Judge Allister from Nicollet County—you're on speakerphone. I have a rather odd request, if you could indulge me? I was in the middle of a hearing involving a man named Elijah Matthews. You were the investigating officer in his case?"

"Yes, Your Honor, that's correct."

"Well, I have a Mr. Sanden here who says that someone else has just this morning been arrested for the murder of Pastor Bale."

"That's true, Your Honor—Jessica Cain. She gave a full confession on the ride to the law enforcement center. She's with my partner now filling in more details."

The hearing room went so silent that I could almost hear the sweat trickling down Handler's temple.

The judge looked at me, mouth slightly agape, then said, "So...what I'm hearing is that...Elijah Matthews was...wrongfully convicted?"

"That appears to be the case, Your Honor," MacDonald said.

"Well, thank you, Detective. We will proceed accordingly."

"Your Honor," MacDonald said. "Is Mr. Sanden still there?"

"He's here."

"Can I talk to him?"

"You're on speakerphone," Judge Allister said. "He can hear you."

"Mr. Sanden, I'm at Lilith's and Jessica's home right now, executing a search warrant. I thought you'd like to know that I found a briefcase in Lilith's office. It had papers in there that look like they belong to you."

"My briefcase was stolen three days ago," I said.

"I saw the report. We have enough to arrest Lilith Cain. We can hold her on suspicion of burglary while we look into what happened to Christina Gideon. I'll get an arrest warrant issued."

"She's not there...at the house?"

"No. Not at the church, either. Truth is, we don't know where she is. And Mr. Sanden, you should also know that some of your papers were spread out on Lilith's desk—some kind of guardianship case?"

CHAPTER 57

I had it all wrong. I had been so wrapped up in my enmity for Anna Adler that I couldn't see the true reason my briefcase had been stolen. It made sense now.

Jessica Cain had killed Bale for showing her that she was the granddaughter of a broken-down ex-cop. Jessica then stole Bale's laptop to hide the evidence. She hadn't known about the thumb drive until I showed it to her that day in Lilith's office. She had asked me what it was and I had told her. Days later, Rufus spotted someone lurking outside my study as I played that video.

Had it been Lilith outside my window that night, or Jessica? I suppose it didn't matter. Griffin MacDonald had found my file on Lilith's desk, so she was in on it. Jessica might have been the one to hit Bale with that stone, but it couldn't have been very long before Lilith joined the cover-up.

I imagined Lilith luring Christina Gideon to some remote location with the promise of helping her with the birth, maybe paying her medical bills. It explained why Lilith disappeared for a year around the time Ed went to prison. My bet was that Lilith had killed Christina shortly after the poor girl gave birth. So stealing my briefcase would have been a minor scribble in the grand ledger of Lilith's sins.

I entered my home address on my car's GPS map, not because I needed directions, but because the app counted down the miles and minutes to my arrival. Leaving St. Peter, I had an hour and thirty-six minutes of driving and only an hour and thirty-five minutes before Dee and I needed to leave for our visit with Emma. I was cutting it too close.

As I neared the outer suburbs of the Twin Cities, I had made up two minutes on the travel time, but then the numbers on the GPS began to slide the wrong way. Interstate 494 had turned red on my screen—afternoon traffic jams.

Dammit! I looked for alternative routes, but they too flashed yellow and red.

I merged onto the interstate behind a cement mixer going twenty miles an hour. The traffic in the next lane moved slightly faster, so I juked left until I was in the fast lane, going all of thirty-five. Ahead of me, for as far as I could see, cars lined up bumper to bumper, crawling at a pace that made my chest tighten.

My phone rang and I answered it. It was Dee. "Where are you?"

"I'm on my way."

"What time will you get here?"

I looked at my GPS. "It's going to be tight. Right now, I'm showing an ETA of 3:53. That will give us seven minutes to get to the sheriff's office. We should get there right at four."

There was silence on the other end, although I could guess her thoughts: *You promised you'd be here on time. This is important.*

"Let's do this," I said. "Drive down to the sheriff's office on your own. I'll meet you there. If I'm late, it'll only be by a minute—two at the most."

Still, silence from the other end.

"It'll be okay," I said. "We'll leave my car there and take Emma to the park in yours." Even as I spoke, the cars in my lane dropped to twenty miles an hour. My time of arrival ticked into the red. I pictured Anna's attorney telling the judge how I cared so little about Emma that I couldn't bother to show up for my visit on time.

"Try and get there by four," Dee said. "Please."

"Traffic should ease up soon. I might even be there before you." I knew that to be a lie, but I didn't want Dee to worry.

"Okay," she said. "I'll see you there."

I touched the phone to end the call and tapped my brakes to slow yet again, this time coming to a complete stop. I hit my steering wheel with my palms.

How could I make it up to Emma? How could I let her know that I wanted a second chance? That I understood what I had done to her and I wanted to make things right? At this late hour, how would she not see it as an act of selfishness, another empty gesture? I had to be there for her. I was her dad, and this was my last chance to let her know.

The traffic started to crawl again, but at a snail's pace, and I wedged my way into the lane to my right, which appeared to be moving a little faster. A truck behind me laid on his horn to let me know how he felt about my sudden move, but I didn't care. I needed to get to St. Paul.

As I passed over the intersection for Interstate 35, my speedometer read twenty-four miles per hour, but by the time I got to the airport turnoff, we were almost back to the speed limit. I weaved my way toward the Ramsey County Sheriff's Office, my GPS telling me that I would be two minutes late. If I hit a single red light, it would drop my time even more, but Providence seemed to favor me as I charged through St. Paul.

I was almost there when my phone rang again. I answered it, eager to tell Dee that I was thirty seconds out.

"Hi, honey," I said. I was about to say more when the woman on the other end spoke.

"You fucked with the wrong woman." Lilith's voice came across low and ragged.

My blood turned cold. "Where are you?"

She ignored my question. "You stole my daughter from me. Now you're going to feel my pain."

"What are you talking about?"

The line clicked dead. And in that moment, I somehow knew.

CHAPTER 58

The stoplight ahead of me turned yellow. I laid on my horn and hit the gas. The light turned red, but I couldn't stop. Four lanes of traffic converged as I threaded the needle. Veering left to miss a pickup truck, I hit the median. The left side of my car bounced into the air.

I could see the sheriff's office a quarter mile ahead. I dialed 911 with my right hand as I held the steering wheel in a death grip with my left.

"Nine-one-one, what is your emergency?"

"Shooter at the sheriff's office in St. Paul! Parking lot!"

I braked hard as I turned onto the street that ran in front of the Law Enforcement Center, a lawn the size of a cul-de-sac stretching in front of the building, beyond which was the turn to the parking lot.

"I'm sorry, sir. What did you say?"

There were cars scattered throughout the parking lot. Dee stood next to her SUV, talking to Anna's attorney. Adler leaned against her car, looking bored. And in the aisle between, all by herself, Emma stared at the screen of her phone, oblivious to the world around her.

A car coming toward me turned into the lot, moving at a snail's pace—blocking my way. I jumped the curb and headed across the lawn, wheels spinning wildly for purchase in the grass. That's when I saw Lilith. She was at the far end of the parking lot, walking toward Emma, her hand tucked inside her purse.

"Shooter in the parking lot!" I yelled into my phone; then I dropped it to the passenger seat.

My attempt to get around the snail car failed. It came to a stop at the mouth of the aisle where Emma stood, and I skidded into it, the nose of my car tapping a dent in the fender. I jumped out and ran.

My stunt had caught the attention of Dee, Anna, and the attorney, but Emma remained fixated on her phone.

"Gun!" I yelled as I charged toward Emma. I pointed toward Lilith but no one turned to look at her, everyone still trying to make sense of my chaotic arrival.

Lilith quickened her pace, pulling the gun from her purse.

Again I yelled, "Gun! Get down!"

In my periphery I saw Anna take off at a dead run, charging away from the shooter—away from Emma. Her attorney dived behind Dee's SUV, but Dee stayed put, turning desperately to search for Emma.

Emma had lifted her head from her phone. She looked right at me, still unaware of the danger just thirty feet away. She stood in the open, a row of unoccupied handicapped spots to her right and a few empty spaces to her left. She had nowhere to go for cover.

Lilith stopped walking and raised the gun, one hand on the grip, the other beneath it to steady her aim. She settled one foot slightly forward, her knees bent, the muzzle aimed at Emma's chest.

Somehow, I got to Emma first. I grabbed her by the arm and pulled her behind me, locking my hands around her elbows to keep her from moving. I saw Lilith smile as a flash exploded from her muzzle.

It felt like someone had driven a sledgehammer into my chest. It knocked me back and everything went dark. I had no breath in my lungs. My body refused to inhale, and my jaw hurt for some reason, but when I opened my eyes, I was still on my feet—and I was angry!

Lilith was trying to kill my daughter. Rage settled into my joints, rusting them, stiffening my body. I would take every bullet I could. I would protect Emma until I could no longer stand. I closed my eyes to await the next.

A shot rang out followed by two more in quick succession—but I felt no pain.

I opened my eyes to see Lilith tilting to her side, one of her legs bent, the other struggling to keep her upright. Her right hand dangled limp at her side, gun hanging from her fingers.

"Drop the gun!" came a loud yell from my right. "I said drop the gun! Now!"

A deputy, his gun drawn and pointed at Lilith, moved toward her in bold steps. Another deputy followed closely behind. Lilith started to lift her gun again, but it fell from her fingers. Then she crumpled to the ground.

In that same moment, my legs buckled and I sank to the pavement. I could see blood on my shirt, but it wasn't spreading in a plume as I had expected. They were droplets in a line falling left of center. The pattern confused me.

"No!" Emma held my head as I eased myself to the ground, the pain in my chest nearly unbearable. A second later, Dee was at my side. She tore open my shirt, her face awash in confusion.

A deputy took a knee to my left, his face also a tale of puzzlement. "Jesus Christ," he whispered. Then he reached down and lifted the necklace off my chest, raising it high enough for me to see the dent in the middle of the steel plate where the bullet had hit. "You have got to be the luckiest son of a bitch on the planet."

A second deputy whispered, "It's a goddamned miracle."

CHAPTER 59

I rode to the hospital in the second of two ambulances, the first one taking Lilith Cain. I had given thought to declining the ride, but when I tried to speak, the pain in my chest caused my body to stiffen. Dee noticed my wince and put her hand on my cheek. Emma stood behind Dee, looking stunned and frightened. I tried to tell her it was okay, but again the pain stopped me from speaking.

A deputy rode with me in the ambulance, and as we neared the hospital, the pain in my chest had eased enough that I tried to explain what had happened—who I was and why Lilith had shot me. This time it was the pain in my jaw that stopped me. I would learn later that Lilith's bullet splintered when it hit the necklace, a shard ricocheting up to bruise my mandible. I gave up trying to explain my predicament and mumbled that the deputy should call Detective Griffin MacDonald; he could bring them up to speed.

A nurse took me to a small examination room, where they cleaned the wound in my chin and inspected the bruise on my chest. After I explained what had happened, they sent me to get x-rays of both injuries. Satisfied that there were no bone fragments floating around, the doctor purled a stitch along my jawline, wrote a prescription, and called it a day.

I left the examination room, walking instead of riding in the wheelchair they offered, and opened the doors to the waiting area to find Dee and Emma. They had been holding vigil, waiting for me to come out.

Emma sat with her legs together, her shoulders a bit slumped, her nervous fingers picking at the hem of her shirt. Her dark hair covered one eye, but with the other she peeked up at me as I walked into the waiting area.

Dee stood and crossed the room to meet me, wrapping her arms around my waist and gently leaning her cheek into my chest.

"You nearly stopped my heart out there," she said in a soft voice.

"I nearly stopped my own," I muttered.

She took a step back and examined the bandage on my chin. "Are you okay?"

"I'm good."

She placed her hand over my heart, carefully touching the place where the bullet should have entered. "I'll get the car."

I nodded.

Emma remained sitting, but looked up at me as I walked over and sat in the chair beside her. An old man across the room stared at the clock on the wall, worried and attentive, as if each click of the second hand lessened his hope. A woman in a brown hijab cried quietly into a tissue as a toddler looked up at her in confusion. At the door to the examination room, a doctor spoke to a middle-aged couple, their faces a picture of relief.

Beside me, Emma still picked at the tail of her blouse, her head tipped down.

"I'm sorry," I said. "All those years...living in the same house...I wasn't there for you. I thought..."

I was a man of words, but at that moment, finding the right ones seemed impossible. "You should've never had to worry about feeling loved, feeling like you had a home. I should have shown you, but I didn't. I've been struggling to make sense of what your father did, but...that doesn't change what I know now. You're my daughter and you always will be. I love you. Until the end of time, that will never change…no matter what happens."

I put my arms around her and held her. She seemed so frail curled up against me, her face tucked into my chest. I tipped my chin down and kissed the top of her head. "Just tell me that you can forgive me for being an old fool."

"Of course I forgive you," she said through sniffles. "You're my Poppy."

Poppy. So much music in such a small word. I wanted her to say it again and again.

It was then that I noticed Dee standing at the exit, her arms folded across her chest, one hand raised to her lips.

I held Emma a few precious seconds longer before tapping her head and pointing to Dee. Emma wiped tears from her cheek, and when we stood, she reached her hand to mine. I held her hand and gave her fingers a squeeze as we made our way out of the hospital.

CHAPTER 60

I was released from the emergency room in less than two hours. Lilith did not fare so well. Three bullets had perforated her torso, causing significant damage; the loss of blood sent her into a coma. It took three weeks for her to find her way back to consciousness. Now, two months later, she's almost well enough to be transported to a prison hospital to continue her recovery and await her trial for the murder of Christina Gideon.

It turned out that back when Ed Cain was stealing from his clients, he and Lilith had invested in some hunting land up north, fifty acres with a small cabin. In the months after Ed's arrest and before the feds auctioned the land to pay restitution to Ed's victims, Lilith had been living at that cabin with Christina. I know this because Detective MacDonald, along with agents from the Minnesota Bureau of Criminal Apprehension, took cadaver dogs up there and found Christina buried in a grove of birch trees, a bullet hole in the back of her skull.

MacDonald also managed to track down a retired doctor who remembered making a house call to that cabin eighteen years ago. He identified by photo the two women present: a pregnant Christina and Lilith Cain. Christina had been bleeding and was only in her twenty-eighth week. The visit stood out to him because Lilith had paid him twice his normal fee—in cash.

With that witness and the remains of Christina Gideon, MacDonald believes he can prove his case to a jury beyond a reasonable doubt.

Lilith had isolated Christina at that cabin and offered to pay for the birth of the baby. Ray Gideon pointed out that Christina must have wanted to keep the baby. If Christina had planned to give the baby up for adoption, Lilith wouldn't have needed to kill her.

Jessica also awaits trial for murder, although in juvenile court. Ray Gideon has been stopping by the jail once a week to visit her, but she refuses to see him. In her confession, Jessica admitted to telling Lilith about killing Jalen Bale. She showed Lilith the DNA results on Bale's laptop. Lilith then destroyed the evidence. Jessica swears that she never put it together—that Lilith had killed her birth mother. To this day, she refuses to call Lilith anything other than Mom.

As for Elijah, I've been meaning to go see him, or at least call Dr. Cohen to find out how he's doing, but it's taken time for my jaw to heal enough that it doesn't hurt to talk. And we've been busy moving to the new house.

I like my new office. Fewer shelves, but it has more space to walk around, as well as a large window that looks out over the backyard. I threw away most of my old law books in the move. Since the advent of the internet, they were more for show anyway. Now I fill the shelves with novels and our two Bibles: Dee's fancy one, and my beat-up wreck, still taped shut. The rest of the shelves are filled with pictures of Dee, Emma, me, and Rufus.

On the corner of my desk, sealed in a glass case the size of my mom's old recipe box, is the steel necklace that Elijah gave me, the quote about dog bones smudged by the bullet's dent.

I turn in my chair to look out over my backyard, where my wife is doing her best to throw a baseball to Emma. I am, as the deputy put it, the luckiest son of a bitch on the planet.

The guardianship hearing went forward, even though Anna's case completely fell apart. Emma wrote a new affidavit, telling the court that her Aunt Anna had promised to let her get her inheritance early if she chose her over us. To sweeten the deal, she'd promised to take Emma on a first-class trip to Japan. Her new affidavit spoke of the love Emma has for Dee and me. It told of a bond that went beyond the roles of guardian and ward. As far as she was concerned, we were her parents.

If that hadn't been enough to sink Anna's case, there were the surveillance tapes. Cameras outside the Law Enforcement Center caught the entire gunfight: Lilith shooting me in the chest as I shielded Emma, Dee standing firm, and Anna running as far away from the danger as she could. She never even looked back. We had DeChamp's taped admission again, which was found with my briefcase in Lilith's home office. It was a slam dunk, but Anna pushed forward anyway. The judge ruled in our favor from the bench.

I give thought to going outside to take over for Dee, whose arm seems to be wearing out, but I get distracted by a shard of sunlight reflecting off the necklace. It pulls my attention away from the window as though to point out that I have been putting off my call to Dr. Cohen for too long.

I pick up my phone and dial.

"It's good to hear from you," she says. "I read about what happened. Amazing."

"It was quite the afternoon," I say. "I was just calling to see how Elijah's doing? I assume he's been transitioned out of the Security Hospital."

"He's living with his sister in Duluth, under the care of social services. He's doing quite well."

"That's great to hear."

"He wanted me to tell you thank you."

It surprises me to hear that. Not that Elijah had ever been impolite, but to thank me seems an implicit admission that I got him out of that hospital and not some benevolent, invisible force. "I was just doing my job," I say with forced modesty. "I'm sorry he didn't get to finish his mission there."

"His mission?"

"He told me that he wasn't ready to leave the hospital because he had one more person to help."

"Yes, he told me that same thing."

"Catching Bale's killer kind of threw a wrench into that."

"What do you mean?"

"I took care of things a little faster than he expected."

"Mr. Sanden, did Elijah tell you who that one person was…the last one he needed to help?"

"It was that guy—John—the one who tried to blind himself."

"No, Mr. Sanden, it wasn't. He didn't tell you?"

"Tell me what?"

"The last person he needed to help…was you."

"What do you mean?"

"He said he couldn't leave until he helped you."

"Help me? How?"

"I don't know."

I hear Emma squeal with delight outside, and I turn to see that Rufus has stolen their ball. From out of nowhere I think about that Bible quote from the Book of Malachi: *I will send you the prophet Elijah. He will bring fathers and children together.*

"Listen, Doc," I say. "I…gotta go."

I stand at my window, trying to understand why Elijah would say that to Dr. Cohen. I didn't need Elijah's help and he had given me none—in fact, he had been a major pain in my ass. Besides, everything that happened could be explained. Correlation does not equal causation. Coincidences happen; I'm simply overthinking this. If I want to see a naked woman in the ice cube of the whiskey advertisement, I'll see her whether she's there or not.

I dismiss my confusion and go outside to play with my family, stopping at a closet to dig out my old baseball glove. I spend the next hour playing catch with Emma. Dee sits in the Adirondack chair on the back patio with Rufus at her feet.

When night falls, we talk about taking a trip out west before Emma starts school in the fall, maybe to Yellowstone. We talk about where Dee wants to plant flowers in the spring. We talk about Emma wanting to try out for volleyball. We have those normal conversations that a family has, yet in the back of my mind I can't shake Dr. Cohen's words: Elijah had stayed to help me.

As a teacher of criminal law, I am a student of memory. Some truths can hide in the folds of the brain, standing firm against the passage of time. Yet there are other slices of memory that wither to dust despite our desperate efforts to hold them tight. Most memories fall into a middle ground, not forgotten but becoming skewed by time and distance. Like a grain of sand inside an oyster, they change and grow. Sure, a pearl emerges to give us comfort, but it is a far cry from the speck of grit that begat it.

When I am on my deathbed, straddling that agnostic divide of what comes next, will I remember those ten days as they actually happened, or will time wrap that memory in a shiny new husk? Will I reject everything as coincidence, or hold it up as proof of something divine?

And so, now that Emma has gone to bed, I sit back in my study with a legal pad, determined to capture a faithful accounting of what happened, get it down in writing before time massages away the rough edges.

I write:

I hold no faith in distant memories.

ACKNOWLEDGMENTS

I wish to extend my heartfelt gratitude to the people who have helped create *Saving Emma*. As always, I must start with my wife and first reader, Joely, whose help and guidance has been, as always, unwavering. I want to thank my agent, Amy Cloughley, who has had my back from the beginning, my editor, Helen O'Hare, and the rest of my team at Little Brown/Mulholland: Michael Noon, Allison Kerr Miller, Bryan Christian, Gabrielle Leporati, Josh Kendall, Liv Ryan, and Gregg Kulick.

I also want to thank Gordy Larson, Tami Peterson, Julia Jonas, and Beth Zabel, who provided the technical insight and knowledge to let me fill in the details of this story. And finally, I would like to thank my proofreaders, Joely, Nancy Rosin, and Terry Kolander, for spotting what I couldn't see.

If you, as a reader, have enjoyed this novel, you have the people above to thank for it—at least I do.

ABOUT THE AUTHOR

ALLEN ESKENS is the *USA Today* bestselling author of *The Life We Bury*, which has been published in twenty-six languages, and seven other novels, most recently *Forsaken Country*, *The Stolen Hours*, *The Shadows We Hide*, and *Nothing More Dangerous*. His books have won the Barry Award, the Rosebud Award, the Silver Falchion Award, and the Minnesota Book Award. Eskens is a former criminal defense attorney and lives with his wife, Joely, in greater Minnesota.